Ben's BOSS

Maine Men Book Two

K.C. WELLS

This is a work of fiction. Names, characters, places, and incidents either are the product of the author's imagination or are used fictitiously, and any resemblance to actual persons, living or dead, business establishments, events, or locales is entirely coincidental.

Cover Art by Meredith Russell
Edited by Sue Laybourn

Cover content is being used for illustrative purposes only and any person depicted on the cover is a model.

The trademarked products mentioned in this book are the property of their respective owners and are recognized as such.

Maine Men

Levi, Noah, Aaron, Ben, Dylan, Finn, Seb, and Shaun.

Eight friends who grew up in Wells, Maine.

Different backgrounds, different paths, but one thing remains solid, even eight years after they graduated – their friendship. Holidays, weddings, funerals, birthdays, parties – any chance they get to meet up, they take it. It's an opportunity to share what's going on in their lives, especially their love lives.

Back in high school, they knew four of them were gay or bi, so maybe it was more than coincidence that they gravitated to one another. Along the way, there were revelations and realizations, some more of a surprise than others.

And what none of the others knew was that Levi was in love with one of them…

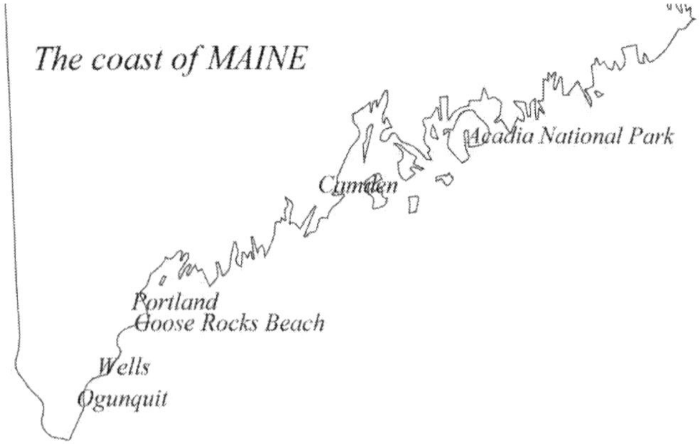

Prologue

From Finn's Fantasy:

"Guys, I almost forgot." Ben's eyes sparkled. "I've got a job interview next week."

Joel loved the hoots and whoops of obvious delight that filled the night air.

"That's great," Levi exclaimed. "What's the job?"

"Working in a gift store—and it's right on my doorstep, in Camden. Apparently, this place has been owned by the same family for eighty years. Not that I've ever been in there. What do I want with a gift store for tourists? It's owned by the Pearsons." He grimaced. "That's a popular Maine name, right?"

Noah widened his eyes. "Oh God, I hope so."

Joel frowned. "Am I missing something?"

Finn scowled. "There was an asshole in high school—Wade Pearson—who made Ben's life hell, all because he got it into his fat head that Ben was gay."

When Joel gave Finn a puzzled glance, Ben burst out laughing. "Okay, so I am gay—now—but back then I was still figuring stuff out. Fucking homophobic asshole." His eyes gleamed. "Pity he was such a good-looking homophobic asshole, because in another life, I would've been all over that guy like a rash. And I'm not even gonna entertain the possibility that these Pearsons are remotely related to him. God wouldn't be that cruel."

Noah shook his head. "Which God are we talking about

here?"

Seb held up his hands. "Nope. We are not gonna talk religion."

"Not even to say a quick prayer?" Ben asked. "Because I need this job, guys."

Seb raised his eyes heavenward. "Hey, God? Make sure Ben gets this job. And while You're at it, don't let whoever's gonna interview Ben be in any way connected to that asshole Wade Pearson. You got that?" He gave Ben a smug smile. "That oughta do it."

Ben rolled his eyes. "Yeah, thanks for that, Seb."

Finn laughed. "If Grammy heard you, Seb, she'd take her broom to your ass."

Seb looked quickly toward the window behind them. "She sleeps on the other side of the house, right?" Everyone laughed. He peered at Aaron. "Must be getting into your busy season right about now."

Aaron snorted. "Don't I know it. What is it about the summer that brings out all the idiots?"

"Aaron's a ranger at Acadia National Park," Finn told Joel. He grinned. "I think he's lost count of how many times visitors makes jokes about Thunder Hole."

Joel blinked. "Seriously? That's a place?" He'd heard the name before. When the kids were growing up vacations were a visit to Boise to stay with his parents. They hadn't explored much of the northern part of Maine, much to his regret.

Aaron nodded. "It's a giant cave that belches seawater up in the air, sometimes as high as thirty or forty feet." He snickered. "Sort of like a college frat party." He shook his head. "All those forests and miles of rugged coastline, and that's all people talk about?"

Noah got to his feet. "I'm going to get another beer." He touched Levi lightly on the arm. "You want something?"

"I'm good, thanks," Levi told him with a smile.

"You gonna ask us too?" Seb grinned. "'Cause I sure could down another cold one." He tapped the label on his bottle. "Specifically, this one. Somebody actually brought some decent brew to this shindig."

Joel bit back a smile. "Oh, I don't know. Some folks are happy with a Bud."

Seb snorted. "Training beer, I call that. Tastes like—"

"Don't!" Shaun interjected. "We all know what you think."

"And why do we know?" Finn grinned. "Because you've only told us about a million times. And I happen to like Bud, so shut the fuck up." That raised more chuckles.

"Hey, Seb. School's out for summer, right?" Aaron asked.

"You know it. I spent the last week there, getting all my stuff ready for the next semester. So now it's time to kick back and party all summer long."

"Well, you can't party on your own. Hey, Joel?" Dylan laced his hands behind his head, and Joel steeled himself. "Know anyone else your age who might be interested in Seb?" His eyes gleamed. "Because we all know Seb wants a Daddy."

Both Finn and Seb glared at him, but Joel laughed. "Okay, I'm no Daddy, and I wouldn't dream of assuming to know what kind of guy Seb likes." He gave Seb a sideways glance. "Although after seeing him in action, I do have an idea."

"Okay, we're done here." Finn got to his feet. "Time we were going to the hotel."

Ben cackled. "Which translates as… Finn has an itch, and he wants Joel to scratch it." Everyone laughed, including Finn and Joel.

"It was good to meet you all," Joel said as he stood. "Finn talks about you a lot."

"Whereas we didn't have a clue you existed until today," Shaun said with a smile.

"Speak for yourself." Seb's smile was still smug. He

looked at Finn. "Are you guys coming to my place for lunch tomorrow? There'll be plenty of food. And then we can talk some more."

Finn glanced at Joel, and he nodded. "We'd love to." Now he'd dipped his toes in the water the idea of going deeper caused no trepidation. He grinned. "But now we'll leave you to talk about us behind our backs."

There was a moment of silence which was broken by Finn's laughter, and the others joined in.

"Okay, he'll do," Aaron said with an emphatic nod to Finn, who rolled his eyes.

"Gee, thanks. Not that I need your approval, but hey, don't let that stop you." Finn grabbed Joel's hand. "See you tomorrow."

"Enjoy the hotel," Ben called out to them as they walked toward the house.

"We will," Finn murmured.

Chapter One

June

Ben White had lost count of how many beers he'd drunk, but he didn't care. Grammy wasn't going to give him grief about it—she'd gone to bed—and it wasn't as if he was shitfaced, right? He'd gone to Grammy's birthday bash with the goal of getting mellow with the guys, but at some point, the booze had worn off.

He could pinpoint the moment too.

Jesus, eight years since I last laid eyes on the asshole, and he still *haunts me.*

Except haunt was an exaggeration, and he knew it. He did his best *not* to think about that dickhead.

Ben leaned forward, his elbows on his knees, the neck of his half-empty beer bottle held loosely between thumb and forefinger. The fire pit was still going strong, and its warmth combated the chill in the night air. Finn had been the first to leave, but no one appeared surprised by that. If Ben had brought a gorgeous guy to the party, and had the prospect of a sexy night between hotel sheets, *he'd* have left early too. Joel seemed like a nice guy, and it was obvious—to Ben, at least—they were a good fit.

If he can survive a grilling by this lot, he's a keeper.

"Where'd everyone disappear to?" Dylan sat in the chair next to Ben's, a bottle in his hand. "I only went to take a leak."

Ben leaned back, the bottle between his thighs. "Shaun had to go."

Dylan sighed. "Poor guy. I was surprised to see him, to be honest."

"I hadn't seen him since Teresa's wedding. Had you?"

Dylan shook his head. "I don't think he gets much time to himself, what with all the hours he works, and looking after his dad. It's no life, taking care of someone. My mom used to say that. When my grandmother got sick, she moved in with us. I was just a kid. Mom gave up her job to look after her. All I can remember about that period is her looking tired all the time." He drank from his bottle. "Okay, we know where Finn is." He chuckled. "Did you know about Joel?"

"Not a word. Talk about a dark horse."

"So what do you think? Is he hot?"

Ben snorted. "You got eyes, don't ya? What do *you* think?"

"How would I know if he's hot?" Dylan retorted. "I'm not gay."

"So what? I think Jessica Biel is hot, and I'm not straight." Ben grinned. "Okay, yeah, he's hot, in an older man kinda way." Then he laughed out loud. "*Seb* liked him."

Dylan frowned. "Did he leave too?"

"Nah, he's in the house. He got a call. Levi and Noah are in the kitchen, clearing up."

"Ah. I didn't look in there. And I don't know where Seb went to take his call, because *I* didn't see him." Dylan glanced at the now empty yard. "What about Aaron?"

Ben cackled. "He got a better offer." When Dylan

gave him a puzzled glance, he leaned in. "You know Grammy's neighbors? The old couple who are always doing something to their front yard? Well, they were at the party—and they brought along their granddaughter, who's staying with them."

Dylan grinned. "Seriously? So where's he gone?" His eyes widened. "If he's taken her to the guest room, Grammy will pitch a fit. What was her number one saying when Levi was a teenager?"

Together they intoned, "Not under my roof, boy!"

Dylan chuckled. "I hope she's not still saying that. Levi'll never get laid." Then he stilled. "Hey, you don't suppose… I mean, he can't still be… you know, a virgin."

Ben gaped at him. "Excuse me? So what if he is? It's none of our beeswax." Not that he hadn't thought about it too. "And no, Aaron *hasn't* taken her to a bedroom. He's being a gentleman and walking her home." He bit back a smile. "All the way to next door." They laughed.

Dylan glanced toward the house. "I just don't ever remember Levi going on any dates, that's all."

"Christ, will you stop that? Just because we don't know the ins and outs of his sex life—"

Dylan snorted. "'Ins and outs'."

Ben rolled his eyes. "Jesus, it's like talking to a twelve-year-old. What I'm *saying* is, Levi's not Seb. He's not Finn. He doesn't broadcast his feelings, his conquests—although, that's more in Seb's line than Finn's. Levi is—" He struggled to come up with a word that would encapsulate one of his dearest friends, and fell at the first hurdle. There was no label for Levi. They all knew he was gay, but the word didn't define him.

"Levi is the best." Dylan raised his beer. "So here's to him."

Ben copied him, and the glass bottles clinked. After Ben had taken a swig, he gazed with interest at Dylan. "Levi's not the only one around here who's secretive."

Dylan blinked. "Meaning?"

He grinned. "You keep your cards pretty close to your chest too."

"Hey, we can't all be Seb, right?" Dylan sighed. "Nothing to tell, to be honest. Can't remember the last time I got some action."

Ben clinked bottles again. "I hear ya, dude. I'm in the same boat."

Dylan took a long drink. "Bet Finn's having a great night."

The remark stopped Ben dead in his tracks. "You know, for a straight guy, you sure do a lot of thinking about what goes on in gay guys' bedrooms." But that was Dylan, even when they'd been in their teens. He asked *so many* goddamn questions.

"Just curious, that's all." Dylan lowered his gaze. He cleared his throat. "Why did you take so long to come out? I mean, Levi, Seb, Finn, they knew pretty much from the start."

He laughed. "I was twenty-one. And just because some guys like to bring it all out into the open, doesn't mean everyone goes down the same path. When I was fifteen I knew I liked girls. So that made me straight, right? Not that I was *interested* in any of 'em, but hey…" He swallowed. "Then everything changed." He drained the rest of his beer, and peered at the bucket on the other side of Dylan's chair. "Any of these left?"

Dylan took a look. "One. I think it's got your name on it." He lifted it from the melted ice that had filled the bucket, and handed it over. "Here." He picked up the bottle opener and gave it to Ben.

Ben popped the cap and took a long, cool drink. "When I was in junior high, there was always some asshole or other who wanted to redecorate my face with his fists. I thought things would get better in high school, but they didn't."

"That's because the whole concept of high school is totally fucked up. I remember something Levi said, right before we graduated. It was something along the lines that high school was a microcosm, some kind of science experiment, where they stuck a whole bunch of people together to see who would migrate to whom, and why. And that once they were out in the real world, none of what happened back then was actually relevant."

Ben huffed. "He nailed it, all right." Another swallow of beer. "Except some of the things that happened back then don't go away. They linger. At least, the memory of them does."

"I guess you're speaking from experience."

He nodded. "That asshole I was talking about earlier. Wade fucking Pearson. Except he didn't hurt me with his fists. He did just fine with only his words." *And his looks. Don't forget those.*

As if he could.

"Which you don't need to repeat. I remember them."

So did Ben. They were burned into his memory.

"You know what? I think maybe I *did* have a tiny inkling back then that I might like boys. Some quiet little voice in the dim recesses of my mind. So quiet that I thought it was insignificant. And then when Wade started on me…" Ben drank some more.

"You don't have to talk about this if it makes you feel bad," Dylan murmured.

Ben snorted. "We're past that. Talking about that interview tonight brought it all back. The thing is, Wade made me feel I was broken. That liking boys was wrong. That being gay was the worst thing on earth. That I had to push down deep on such feelings." He shuddered out a breath. "Then I got around Levi and the others, and I learned that being gay *wasn't* wrong. Because how could my best friends be wrong?" Ben sighed. "You wanna know what's *really* fucked up? When I was seventeen, I had my first crush. My first real clue that I wasn't straight."

Dylan frowned. "I don't get it. What's fucked up about that?"

Ben stared into the flames. "The problem was *who* I was crushing on. Because being attracted to a guy who obviously thought I was dog-shit to be scraped off his boots went *way beyond* fucked up. Talk about being a masochist."

Dylan widened his eyes. "Christ. Wade?"

He nodded. "It didn't make any sense, for God's sake. I mean, he was good-looking, sure. And big." Wade had carried a *lot* of weight, most of it muscle. "But he was an *asshole*. Who hated gays. Why would my screwed-up brain decide *he* was attractive?" Maybe it had been the muscles. The *solidness* of him.

And there he goes again, creeping into my thoughts.

Ben cleared his throat. "Anyhow, that was it. I was done. I took whatever I was feeling, and I fucking *buried* it."

"Only to dig it up when you got into your twenties?"

Ben chuckled. "That was when I thought, 'Fuck it.' My mom was always asking when I was gonna bring a girl home, and I'd reached the point where I could be honest with myself, and know it was never gonna happen. And that meant being honest with everyone. So…" He took a drink. "You do *not* repeat this, okay?"

"You got my word."

Ben glanced toward the house, but there was still no sign of Seb. "One weekend, I called Seb up, and asked him if I could go with him to that bar in Ogunquit—MaineStreet. Within ten minutes of walking out onto the patio, I'd hooked up with a guy, and a half hour after *that*, I wasn't a virgin anymore."

"Oh my God. That was fast work."

"I know, right?" Ben chuckled. "Even *Seb* said that. He also said I had to be a contortionist to fuck in one of the restroom stalls." He grinned. "What can I say? I'm flexible. Not to mention an exhibitionist. And just to prove I was *still* a fucked-up little puppy, that first guy looked a lot like Wade. A lot leaner, but he had these amber eyes, and muscles…"

For fuck's sake. Telling them about his interview had opened up a kind of Pandora's Box, and *everything* was spilling out of it.

"Okay, you've sold me." Dylan raised his bottle. "Here's to you, the most fucked-up guy I know."

Ben laughed as they clinked. "A therapist would have a field day with me. Is there a complex for crushing on the guy who bullies you?" He grinned. "Hey, maybe I'm the first one to have it. I'm Patient Zero."

"At least you can joke about it now." Dylan stared. "You don't suppose he *is* connected to the Pearson family that owns that gift store?" His eyes became huge. "What if you walk in there for your interview, and it's him?"

"It's not."

"How do you know?"

"Because for one thing, I peered through the window last week, and there was only an old guy at the cash register. And for another, like I said before, God would *not* be that cruel."

"But why do you want to work there? You have a job, right?"

"Sure. I work in a supermarket. And I'm *sick* of stacking shelves with cans of soup and shit like that. *This* is a cute little gift store, filled with really quirky stuff. I took a peek in the window one day as I was passing, and what can I say? I liked the look of the place. Then I saw they were hiring, so I put in an application. The lady in the store said they'd had a lot of interest, so I'm stoked to get an interview. This is a new year-round full-time job, and that's *way* better than what I've got going for me at Hannaford."

They fell silent, the only sounds the crackle of the fire pit and the hooting of night birds. Then the silence was broken as Seb burst through the doors.

"Christ on a cracker, I do not fucking *believe* this!"

"Seb. You'll wake Grammy," Ben said. "Get over here. What's wrong?"

Seb strode over to where they were sitting, his hands clenched, his hair unruly. "That was my mom on the phone." His chest rose and fell rapidly.

"Breathe, dude." Ben had never seen Seb in such a state. "Now calmly… what happened?"

Seb made an obvious effort to comply. "My uncle Gary went and broke his goddamn *pelvis*, that's what happened." He scraped his fingers through his hair, not for the first time, Ben suspected.

Ben frowned. "Are you and he close? Is that why you're so upset?" Except Seb wasn't upset—he looked *pissed*, to the point where he was visibly vibrating with rage.

"No, we're not close. Wait—we *were*, when I was a kid, but I haven't seen much of him. We kinda drifted apart. And what's *happened* is that my mom told my uncle I'd help him out. Because I'm the only one who can, apparently."

"You're not making any sense," Ben told him.

Seb sat on the nearest chair and leaned forward, his head in his hands. "I had *plans*, goddamn it. I was gonna chill out, get laid, get laid some more…" He took a deep breath. "Uncle Gary has his own fishing business, down in this tiny little place along the coast. Cape Porpoise. Cute name, huh? It's exactly how it sounds. Cute, quaint, idyllic—and quiet. Like, deathly quiet, because there's nothing going on. And Mom told Uncle Gary I'd go stay with him for the rest of my summer vacation, and take over for him."

Ben bit his lip. "*You're* gonna fish?" He shouldn't laugh. He really shouldn't.

Fuck, it was hilarious.

Seb jerked his head up, his eyes wild. "It's not funny, dude."

"It is from where I'm sitting. I remember when you were younger, that summer you went and helped out. That's what all the family did, wasn't it? You took turns being a deckhand for the summer." Ben grinned. "And *you* bitched and complained, then said that was the last time anyone would ever get *you* on a fishing boat."

Seb gaped. "What makes it worse? I'm gonna be doing it for *free*. You should've heard my mom. 'You're a teacher, you're already getting paid. You don't need the money.' Like fuck I don't. 'Take over for him,' she says. Yeah, right. Can you *really* see me getting up at the crack of whenever, to go out in some boat and be a glorified deckhand? Because that's all I'd be." He straightened in his chair. "You know what? I'm not even gonna think about it. Because that would be like talking it into existence, and it ain't happening. Gary can find some other schmuck." He got up. "Sorry, guys. I'm outta here. That call has given me a sour taste in my mouth. I'll call ya, soon." And with that, he strode back into the house.

A moment later, both Ben and Dylan burst into laughter.

"We shouldn't," Dylan said, wiping his eyes.

"No, we shouldn't," Ben agreed, his sides aching. Then he stilled. "Hey. We're supposed to be staying at Seb's tonight. He was gonna give us a ride."

"And we were all going over there for lunch tomorrow too."

"You never know. He might've calmed down by then."

Levi walked out onto the patio. "Guys? You wanna stay here tonight? I just told Seb."

"Really?"

Levi smiled. "I don't think he would be much company right now, do you? I'll make up the bed in the guest room. You'll have to share it though."

Ben laughed. "As if we haven't done that before. Thanks, Levi. If you're sure we're not putting you out.

What about Aaron? He was staying at Seb's too."

"I can make up the camp bed for him and put him in with you guys—*if* he comes back." Levi's eyes twinkled. "He's been a while saying goodnight to Angie." He peered at the dead bottles standing around the fire pit. "I'll clear these up in the morning. Put out the fire, Dylan, would ya? Then we'll call it a night." He gazed at them. "You two been chewing the fat?"

"Raking over stuff best forgotten, actually." Ben smiled. "So I'm gonna forget I ever mentioned a certain asshole."

As if he *could* forget.

Chapter Two

Ben took one last glimpse at his reflection in the bookstore window to check his appearance. *God, my hair.* It was longish and straggly, and he'd brushed it furiously in an attempt to get it to behave. No way was he getting it cut though. *And if someone says, 'Hey, if you wanna work here, get a haircut'? What then, dipshit?*

He'd deal with *that* situation if it arose. At least his suit was presentable. It was the one he'd bought for Teresa's wedding. Maybe a suit was going overboard for a job working in a tourist gift shop, but he wanted to make a favorable impression.

He stood for a moment and took in Main Street with its striped awnings and cedar shakes-covered storefronts, not to mention the white railing where tourists could gaze down into the Megunticook River before it went under the street. Camden was a pretty town, there was no denying it. Ben had first fallen in love with the place several years ago when he'd accompanied his friends on a camping trip to Acadia National Park. They'd stopped in Camden as it was the halfway point between Wells and Bar Harbor.

One look was all it had taken. The quaintness of the place had captivated Ben from the start. He'd kept an eye out on Monster.com for any jobs in the area, and when one had turned up at long last, he'd sent in his résumé the same day. That had been three or four jobs ago. The latest was in a supermarket on the street where he lived, so getting to work was easy.

And speaking of work…

He crossed the street and stood in the wide-open doorway of *Mainely Treasures*. A chalkboard sign provided a colorful invitation to browse the store, and he stepped into the interior, catching the scent of lavender and balsam fir from the candle display.

This store has everything.

There was the usual stuff for the tourists: hats, belts, tote bags, jewelry, collectibles, and even sleepwear, covered in mini lobsters, of course. Blankets and throws with images of Maine on them were folded neatly, and bags hung from the ceiling. A set of building blocks that produced a mini lighthouse made him smile, as did the cute seal plushy perched on top of a pile of children's books. He gazed at the wall of T-shirts, chuckling at the one with the three cartoon lobsters rolling across it, and the words *Lobster Roll Maine*. There were boxer shorts too, and he laughed out loud when he saw one particular design.

"Oh, I *gotta* get me one of these," he murmured.

"Which one?"

Ben almost jumped out of his skin, and the middle-aged lady next to him widened her eyes. "Oh my. I startled you. I'm so sorry." Her warm brown eyes sparkled, and the skin around them crinkled into laughter lines. "Apparently I make a habit of it. My son says I'm part ninja."

He smiled. "Your son nailed it, ma'am." He recognized her instantly as the lady from his previous visit.

"I'm Mrs. Pearson, and judging by that elegant suit, you're here for an interview."

Ben held out his hand. "Ben White." *And yay, she*

likes the suit. He was off to a good start.

She shook it, then pointed to the boxers. "So, which one caught your eye?"

He bit his lip. "That one." He pointed to a pair of black shorts with a comical duck on each cheek, and the words *Butt Quack* in the center.

Mrs. Pearson laughed. "Ah. That's a popular line with the younger people who come in here."

His gaze drifted to the rack of coasters, and he scanned the cute, sweet, or just plain funny wording on them. *My exercise routine consists of doing nothing but diddly squats* made him smile, but he burst into laughter when he saw the last one on its row. "That's it. I *gotta* buy that one." He picked it up. On it was written *My boss hates it when I shorten his name to Dick, especially since his name is Steve.*

Mrs. Pearson laughed too. "Then I'll put it aside for you. I'll even give you ten percent discount."

"You don't have to do that," Ben protested as she took it from him and placed it next to the cash register.

"Nonsense. You obviously love it. I can see that by the look in your eyes. The laughter was a bit of a giveaway too." She tilted her head to one side. "I remember you. I was here when you brought in your résumé and application form." That sparkle was back. "I remember that smile."

Ben gestured to the shop. "It's hard not to smile when you're surrounded by all this." He meant it. The shop was a treasure trove of adorable trinkets and quirky, cute souvenirs.

She studied him for a moment. "You like this store, don't you?"

"Yes, ma'am—I mean, Mrs. Pearson—I do. It's

such a different atmosphere to where I work now."
He wondered when the interview would begin, and where. He couldn't see it taking place on the shop floor.

"Have you seen our back porch?" When Ben shook his head, her smile widened. "Then let me show you." He followed her through the store, through the rear door, and onto a porch that ran the length of the building.

"Oh wow." Before him were the Megunticook Falls, where the river tumbled and cascaded over rocks, bubbling its way into Camden Harbor. To the left was a place he recognized as Harbor Park, an expanse of green space overlooking the river and the harbor. Moored boats of all shapes and sizes were everywhere.

He noticed the troughs fastened to the porch's wooden railings, brimming over with flowers in vibrant colors. To one side of the porch stood a small table, covered on one side by a hot plate on which sat a kettle, and on the other by polystyrene cups, plus several Maine mugs containing stirrers, tea bags and packets of coffee, powdered creamer, sugar, and sweetener.

"We provide free tea and coffee for anyone who wants to sit out here and enjoy the view."

Ben filled his lungs with the flowers' sweet-smelling perfume. "I imagine a lot of your customers do that. It's a beautiful view." He was sorry when she turned to go back into the store. He'd almost forgotten he had an interview. Mrs. Pearson had put him at his ease, and that had to be a good sign.

When they got back inside, a family was browsing the mugs display. Mrs. Pearson patted Ben on the arm.

"If you wait here, my son will be out in a moment to take you into the office."

He frowned. "Your son? But aren't you…?"

"Me? Oh no, dear, *I'm* not interviewing you. My son is the general manager. He'll be conducting it." Another pat on the arm. "I wouldn't worry. I told Wade I got a good feeling about you when you came by with your résumé."

Wade. *Oh… shit.* The warmth of Mrs. Pearson's smile was not enough to counteract the flood of ice that filled Ben's veins.

He pasted on a smile. "Oh, I see. I thought *you* ran the store. Or maybe an older gentleman I saw here once." *Please, tell me I'm right. Please.*

"That would be my father-in-law, Wade's grandfather. We both help out here, and we have seasonal staff too, but we need someone full-time." She gazed at him, her brow furrowed. "You'll be fine," she said in a soothing tone. "Wade's a sweetheart. You two will get along just great."

If you only knew…

Then a door opened behind him, and he froze.

Mrs. Pearson beamed over his shoulder. "Here's Wade now."

Ben couldn't turn, couldn't even twitch, weighed down by the heavy feeling in the pit of his stomach.

"Mr. White?"

Oh dear Lord, that voice.

He had to do something, if only to keep up the illusion of normality for Wade's mom. Ben took a deep breath, steeled himself, and turned to—

Holy fuck.

Wade Pearson had grown into a vision of hotness.

He'd lost weight since the last time Ben had laid

eyes on him, morphing into a lean, muscled, walking wet dream. *No fucking lie. If sex had legs, he would be it.* Every single part of him was ticking every button Ben possessed, from his artfully mussed coiffed hair to his broad shoulders and equally broad chest, his open, crisp pressed shirt revealing a glimpse of hair. But what stilled Ben's heart was not the dark beard that hugged Wade's jawline, or that full pink lower lip.

It was his eyes.

All he had to do back then was look at me, and I'd shiver. Well, fuck, Ben was shivering now, but for an entirely different reason.

Somewhere, God was laughing His ass off.

For a moment Ben was stunned into silence, incapable of a response. Not that he would've had a clue what to say. Nothing his brain came up with was even *close* to appropriate in the circumstances.

Hello, asshole. Long time no see.

You're looking good.

You're hot AF.

Hey, Wade. Made anyone's life hell recently?

Do you even remember *how you treated me?*

What came to mind last was that there was *no fucking way* Ben was going to get this job.

He cleared his throat, searching for words, *any* words. "Good morning."

Wade strolled over to him, his hand extended. Ben had no choice but to shake it. Wade's grip was firm. He still towered over Ben, but so did most people: Ben had been five-feet-six since he was sixteen.

Wade gestured to the office. "Would you follow me please, Mr. White?" Wade's voice cracked on his surname, and he gave a short cough.

Sure. Not that this is going anywhere and we both know that, right?

Ben nodded, the only response he could manage, and Wade headed for the office he'd just exited, Ben behind him. Ben's legs shook, and his stomach was a roiling mass. Wade pushed the door open and stood aside, waiting for him to enter.

This is a mistake.

Why don't I just turn around, and leave now?

Except Ben knew he wasn't going to give Wade the satisfaction.

He edged past Wade into the small office, and stood by the desk, awaiting further instructions, his chin held high.

Wade closed the door. "Please, take a seat." After a moment's hesitation, he added, "Ben."

He'd thought *Mr. White* had sounded awkward as fuck, but Wade using his first name had it beat, and he had no clue why. He sat in the plastic chair facing the desk. "It's been a while."

Wade blinked. "I wasn't sure if you'd remember me." He went to the only other chair and sat, his hands clasped on the desk.

Big hands. Long fingers.

Why the fuck am I fixating on his hands?

Then Wade's words registered. *Are you fucking* kidding? Ben swallowed. "Trust me. I couldn't forget you." This was a farce. Wade wasn't going to give him the job, so why were they prolonging the inevitable?

Then he got it.

He's waiting for me to throw in the towel. Well, fuck all over that.

"You're looking well," Wade commented.

Ben wanted to say *You too*, but he was afraid how

much those two words would give away. Instead, he ignored the compliment and headed for safer ground. "Your mom says you're the general manager." *I can do this.*

For once in his life, Ben was going to *adult.* So what if he'd lost the job? He was going to prove to Wade he wasn't that scared, mixed-up kid anymore.

Wade nodded. "We've got four shops now. My job is to oversee them all." Ben gave a polite nod, and Wade peered at the sheet in front of him.

Ben guessed the small talk was over.

"I see you've had a lot of experience in retail. Why did you apply for this job? You're working at Hannaford. You don't like the job?"

Duh. Why else would I be trying to get the hell out of there?

Ben remembered the golden rule—never diss an employer. It looked bad. "It's okay. The clientele is a little different here, and that might be a big motivation."

"What do you mean?"

"People shopping for groceries are usually in a hurry. They get stressed out if they find you've moved the aisles around, and they can't find their favorite brand of jelly. Or they get annoyed if you run out of something they specifically came into the store for." He pointed to the door. "Out there is a shop where people come to buy memories. They're on vacation. They're relaxed. And working here would be more than stacking shelves and being yelled at."

Wade stroked his bearded chin. "So what do you think your most important role would be—*if* you got the position?"

And I think we both know that's a pretty humungous if.

"Well, it's obviously more than ringing up purchases. You want customers to feel welcome, to feel like they can come back any time. I'll bet you have customers who come back here, year after year."

Wade smiled. "We do."

Ben nodded. "And you have no time for employees who stand around looking useless. You want staff who will talk to the customers, maybe tell them about places they might not have visited. I can do that. I'm a people person."

Wade chuckled. "You certainly charmed my mom. She doesn't remember everyone who came in here for a job, but she remembers you."

Ben shrugged. "What can I say? I'm memorable." He couldn't resist. "Hey, *you* remembered me, right?"

Wade erupted into a cough, and Ben smiled inwardly. *Score one for me.*

"I assume you read the job description, and I don't think there'd be anything you haven't already experienced, given your past positions. Do you have any questions?"

So many, Ben had lost count, but none of them were to do with the current situation.

"You said you manage four shops. How often would you be working here?" Not that he harbored any illusions. No *way* was Wade going to take him on. Ben was past caring about that. He was on a mission to show Wade he was made of stronger stuff than the kid Wade had taunted and teased and—

Enough.

"I pop in and out all the time," Wade told him. "My mom works here part-time, and my grandfather can't keep away from the place. But I guess that's understandable when a shop has been in the family for so long. Mom is the one who trains our staff."

"Mrs. Pearson said you have seasonal staff too?"

Wade nodded. "We have a number of staff who work with us every summer, so it would be very unlikely you'd find yourself alone in the store." A hint of a smile lurked around his lips. "You know, in case there was something you didn't know how to do, or if the shop got too busy."

Ben had the impression he'd just been insulted. "I'm sure I'd cope just fine once I've been trained."

Wade gave Ben's application form another glance. "I have all your contact details. Thank you for attending today. I'll be in touch."

And that was apparently the end of the interview. Ben had never been so relieved.

He got to his feet, his hand extended. "Thank you." *Yay me. Ben the grownup.*

Wade rose too, and they shook. Wade came around the desk and opened the door for him. Ben strode out, his head held high, smiling at Mrs. Pearson as he passed her. "Goodbye," he said.

She returned his smile. "I hope to see you again." Then she went back to talking with her customers.

I doubt it. Which was a pity. Ben really liked her.

He walked out of the store, crossed the street, and removed his phone from his pants pocket, going through a list in his head of who would be around to take a call. He stopped by the bookstore and composed a short text to Dylan.

You on a break?

Seconds later, his phone rang. "What are you, psychic? Isn't it interview day? Did you get the job?"

"No, I'm not, yes, it is, I have no idea, and Jesus, I hope not."

"Ben? You okay? You sound kinda rattled."

He snorted. "I'll give you three guesses who interviewed me."

There was a moment of silence, and then he caught Dylan's sharp intake of breath. "No fucking *way*."

"Yes way. And you know what? It's official. Wade Pearson sold his fucking soul to the Devil."

Dylan cackled. "Okay, I'll bite. What makes you say that?"

"Because the asshole grew into one Holy-Shit-Fuck-Hot-Dude, that's what."

Another pause. "I have to ask. Was it difficult to concentrate on answering his questions when all the blood rushed from your head to your dick?"

"Don't even fucking *go* there. And as if it matters what I said in there. He's not gonna give me the job."

"So now what?"

"Now? I go home and have a drink, because after that, I need one."

"Dude? It's ten-thirty. Don't you have work today?"

Shit. Ben had only taken the morning off. *How the fuck could I forget that?*

Easy. One interview with Wade Pearson would've addled anyone's brain.

He sighed heavily. "I'm glad *one* of us is thinking straight."

Dylan laughed his ass off. "That would be me—*you're* the one who likes dick."

There were moments when Ben wasn't so sure about that.

"Okay. I'll go home, play a game on my phone, and try to calm the fuck down."

"Sounds like a plan." Ben caught a muffled voice in the background. "Dude, I gotta go. You sure you're okay?"

"I'm fine. Get off the phone. We'll talk soon, all right?" He disconnected and put his phone back into his pocket. Ben glanced across the street at Mainely Treasures—and froze for the second time that morning.

Wade was standing in the doorway, looking right at him.

Ben resisted the urge to yell across the street, *'See? Still standing here.'* He sucked in a lungful of air, and pulled himself together. Without another glance in Wade's direction, he headed for Elm Street, picking up speed as his heart pounded.

Back to the drawing board. There'd be other jobs. At least he was currently employed.

Yeah. Look at the bright side. It was way better than thinking about Wade.

Chapter Three

Wade watched Ben walk down the street and out of sight, his heart racing.

Dear God, if that was what the interview *was like, how in the hell am I going to cope when he's working here?* Just the sight of Ben in his suit had been enough to set Wade's stomach clenching. *How can he possibly be more gorgeous than he was in high school?* Those clear green eyes still made Wade feel as if Ben could read every thought, a supposition that had frequently resulted in tendrils of panic coiling around Wade's heart back in high school. How many times had the words *He knows! He'll tell everyone* echoed inside Wade's head?

Except Ben couldn't have known. Because if he had…

Coming out of the office to be confronted by Ben had almost stalled Wade in his tracks. Ben's hair was that same shade of—what exactly? Wade had never been able to decide whether it was light brown or strawberry blond. It curled on the back of Ben's neck like it always had, falling in soft waves that framed his face.

Fuck. The urge to stroke Ben's nape had consumed him at age seventeen. It hadn't lessened one jot in the intervening eight years since Wade had last laid eyes on him.

Ben certainly hadn't grown any taller, and that was bad, very bad. Wade didn't want to remember the longing Ben's slight frame had engendered in him, the way he'd wanted to—

"Thank you." The customers who'd been talking to Mom were leaving.

He forced a smile, aware of his racing heart. "Come back any time."

"Oh, we will," the man said with a grin. "The kids want to spend more money in here before we head back home."

"I *love* your shop," the woman said, her eyes shining. "You have so many cute things. I could spend hours in here." They walked past him, the boy and girl swinging their dark green paper bags bearing the shop's logo, and continued along Main Street.

Wade took a deep breath. *Get a grip.*

"Are you okay?"

He gave a start. "I swear, I'm going to buy you a necklace for your birthday, with a bell on it. That way, at least I'll have some warning when you're around."

Mom laughed. "Your grandfather says the same thing on a daily basis. And you haven't answered my question."

"I'm fine," he assured her. Not that he was, in the slightest, but Wade wasn't about to share.

She tut-tutted. "He forgot his coaster."

Wade had to smile, despite his clenched stomach. "You'd think by now I'd be used to your squirrel mind. I don't have a clue what you're talking about."

She chuckled. "You know what they say. If you want to know how you'll turn out, look at your parents. So if I were you, I wouldn't mock that squirrel brain of mine. One day, yours will go the same way."

I can't very well look at my dad, now can I?

Wade stomped down hard on the thought. Mom

pointed down the street in the direction Ben had taken. "I was talking about the young man—Ben, wasn't it? He was looking at the coasters, and one of them really tickled him. I put it aside for him, but I guess his nerves got the better of him, and he forgot all about it."

Wade wasn't fooled for a second by her uncertainty. She knew his name, all right. She probably had his entire résumé memorized. Then he frowned. "You thought he was nervous?" Ben had seemed a lot quieter than he remembered. That *could* have been nerves.

"A little. Not at first, maybe."

He folded his arms. "Let's have it. What's your judgment?" She was going to tell him anyway, not that she hadn't already shared her impressions of Ben, based solely on his first visit to the store.

That must've been one hell of a first impression. But then, that was Ben, even when he was sixteen. He lingered in the mind.

Wade had never been able to shake off those memories, for different reasons.

Mom cocked her head to one side. "I think he's very personable." Then her eyes gleamed. "I remember now why he stuck in my mind. I read his résumé. He went to Wells High School too. In fact, he would have been there the same time as you."

Wade didn't trust himself to speak, those same tendrils of panic sprouting and coiling inside him. *Leave it, Mom. Don't go there.*

"Did you know him back then?"

"Yes, I knew him. Only, he was a junior when I was a senior." Panic fluttered in his chest. "Okay, back to your impressions of him."

"I think he has lovely manners, and he's clearly interested in the shop. But when I mentioned the interview, yes, I saw a flicker of nerves." She smiled. "But that was okay. I'd rather have nerves then someone who walks in here full of arrogance, like that young man you interviewed last week." Her brow furrowed. "I didn't like him. He had a … swagger when he walked in here, as though he'd already got the job."

Wade bit his lip. He'd had the same thought.

"And then there was the young lady before him. *She* couldn't crack a smile. We can't take on someone who doesn't smile."

"She could have been nervous too," Wade observed.

Mom's eyes glinted. "My gut says differently."

And that was what it all boiled down to. Wade trusted his mom's gut. She really *saw* people, a skill honed by years of dealing with the public.

"Never mind about the coaster. You can give it to him when he starts working here. You can even make it a welcome-to-the-store present."

She gazed at him with widened eyes. "You've already made up your mind?"

He chuckled. "You mean you hadn't?" Ben had been the final candidate for the job. Not that it mattered *when* Wade had seen him—the outcome would have been the same. "Besides, your opinion carries a lot of weight. I mean, *you'll* probably be spending more time with him than I will." Which was no bad thing.

"He obviously has the experience."

Wade nodded. "And you're right. He *is* personable." But then again, he always was.

"Does he know he's got the job?"

"Not yet. I'll wait till this evening to call him." By then Wade might have got his own nerves under control.

Mom studied him. "I think it will be good to have someone working here that you know."

And he was done. There was no way he could continue the conversation. "Okay, I'm going to the office to do some paperwork. I'll sort out the forms to email to Ben. I don't suppose he'll be able to start right away—he's working at Hannaford—so we'll have to see how much notice they want. It'll be at least a couple of weeks."

Then he realized he was making an awful assumption.

What if he doesn't want the job anymore, now he knows who he'd be working for? Not that Wade would blame him for that. The cold hand of remorse tightened around his heart.

"Great. We'll have him just in time. You know how busy we get in the summer. We've already got Cameron back for the summer, and Abi too. And next week Madison is with us again, and that new boy, Zach." She patted Wade's arm. "Go on, I'll take care of the store." Her eyes twinkled. "After all, I've been doing it for a good many years."

"Which is why you're handing a lot of it over to me. It's time you and Gramps enjoyed the fruits of your labor. You need to rest. So when Ben starts and you train him up, you can begin to ease back on the number of hours you work in this place. And if I need to spend more time here so you can do that, so be it." The lie fell easily from his lips, and he hated himself for it. "This *is* why you sent me to that community college after all. So that I could be ready to take on the responsibility."

Mom walked back into the shop with him. "There's more to life than work, you know." She stroked his back. "I remember when you were in college. I asked you why you didn't have a girlfriend, and you told me there would be time for that later, that your studies were more important." She sighed. "I hate to tell you this, but once you throw yourself into a job, there's no time then either."

"But I'm okay with that," he told her in a firm voice. "I want to make the stores the best they can be."

"And I'm grateful for that. You have *no* idea how grateful, especially because David shows no such inclination."

"He was never going to stay in Maine, and we all knew it." Wade's older brother, David, had moved to New York as soon as the ink had dried on his diploma. He wasn't interested in the stores.

"Your grandfather is *so* proud of you."

Warmth radiated through him. He and Gramps had always been close. Wade could remember standing with him behind the cash register, when he could barely see over the display case on which it sat. Helping Gramps had been his favorite way to spend weekends and school vacations throughout his childhood. Mom and Dad would set off early from Wells every Saturday to make the two-ish hour trip to Camden. Dad would help out in the store and Mom would spend time with Wade's grandmother.

Wade would be with Gramps.

"Don't worry, he'll probably want a hand in training Ben too." She inclined her head toward the office. "Now go on. Get some work done."

Wade chuckled. "Slave driver." He went into the office and closed the door. Wade leaned against it, his eyes closed, thankful for the lack of window.

If you only knew, Mom. I was going to offer Ben the job before he'd even crossed the threshold.

On paper he was perfect, and in the flesh, even more so. Wade had felt a twinge of guilt about that, but hey, what was one more twinge, when he was already dealing with a deluge of the stuff? Mom had nailed it. The previous candidates hadn't been suitable, whereas Ben…

Seeing him up close after all these years had been… shocking? Earth-shattering? Did *one word* exist that would encapsulate his tumultuous emotions?

Wade doubted it.

When Mom had brought him Ben's résumé and application form, he'd had to fight to maintain his calm, shaken to the core by his visceral reaction at seeing Ben's name after all these years. He hadn't finished reading it before he'd decided he had to see Ben. By the time he'd gotten to the end of the résumé, Wade had formed a plan. Ben would get the job. He'd told Mom to call Ben and arrange the interview—there was no way Wade could talk to him.

I need to do this.

Christ, he'd been one messed-up kid back then. He'd hated himself for every drip of poison that had fallen from his lips, every scornful gaze he'd aimed at Ben, and others like him. He knew *why* he'd done it, sure, but that didn't lessen the impact of his actions. Everything had been executed with the all-powerful goal of *fitting in.*

How did I ever start on this path? Wade could

pinpoint that moment with startling accuracy. It was the day he'd looked at Ben White, and the one thought in his head had been *He's cute.* It didn't matter that everything he'd done after that was the exact same thing others had done to him. He'd learned nothing. From that day on, Wade had made sure he fell into the right clique, got in with the right kids, and made himself believe that treating Ben like shit *validated* Wade somehow.

Ben is never going to know how I felt about him back in high school.

He glanced at Ben's résumé on his desk. *Can I do this?* That stab of remorse was only going to get worse the more time Wade spent around him, but so what? *Fuck it.* This was penance.

Wade had one goal—to make it up to Ben—and he was going to accomplish it, no matter how painful the process.

He had an idea this was going to be painful as hell.

Wade picked up his phone, his hand trembling. *Do it. Do it now.* He peered at the résumé and keyed in Ben's phone number, his heart pounding. After four or five rings, Ben answered.

"Hello?"

"Hi, Ben, this is Wade Pearson." He swallowed, his mouth suddenly dry.

There was silence for a moment. Ben cleared his throat. "I didn't think I'd hear back so fast. I literally just got through the door."

"I won't keep you." Wade had a good idea what was going through Ben's head right then. *He doesn't think he's got the job.* Wade supposed he'd feel the same way, given their history, and a wave of shame swamped him for a second. "Thank you for attending the interview today. If you're still interested, the job's yours." Silence fell once more. "Ben?"

Wade couldn't miss Ben's exhalation. "I see. Yes, I'm still interested."

"Great. I'll mail you the confirmation. Let me know what notice Hannaford require. If you have any questions, please feel free to call. And… welcome aboard."

"Thank you. I… Thank you."

"We're glad to have you working with us. And now I'll let you get on with your day." He disconnected. Wade dropped into his chair, his pulse rapid.

Please don't let me fuck this up.

Then he reconsidered.

Please don't let me fuck this up even more than I already have.

Chapter Four

The last two weeks had sorely tested Ben's patience, but at last he was on his way to his new job. He'd said goodbye to the few co-workers he'd gotten to know during his six months at the supermarket, had gotten a firm handshake and best wishes for his future employment from the manager, and that was it, he was out of there.

Only thing was, Ben wasn't sure what he was walking into.

Am I making a huge mistake here? Because there were moments when he felt as though he was about to enter the lions' den. He told himself Wade couldn't be any more of a dick than he had been in high school. *He won't wanna look like an asshole in front of his mom, right?* Except there might be times when she wouldn't be there, and it would be just the two of them.

He didn't want to think too deeply about that.

I was right. Eight years on, and he's still in my head. So why the fuck was he even *thinking* of working there? Maybe it was just last-minute jitters. It was Sunday night, and he was due to start there the following morning. *That's all it is. Nerves.*

Ben grabbed his phone and composed a short text. *You there?*

Seconds later it rang, and Dylan laughed. "Your mind-reading skills are awesome. I literally just finished taking a leak."

"Ew. Hope you washed your hands. Do you know your phone is one of the worst places for—"

"Dude." Dylan's voice was gentle. "What's wrong?"

Ben took a deep breath. "Am I doing the right thing?"

"Hang on. Lemme sit." A moment's pause. "Okay, I figure we're talking about the job."

"Duh." He shivered. "I keep thinking about that interview. So what if Wade wasn't a dick? Maybe that was the exception, and he's gonna revert to the asshole we all knew and loathed the minute I start working there. Why would I even contemplate putting myself through that?"

Dylan's soft sigh filled his ears. "You're nervous. That's understandable. But there are a couple of things you need to consider here. One—you want this job. Like, *really* want it. Two—you turn it down, and Wade wins. Now, *you* might feel so what? Fuck him, but me? I wouldn't want to give him the satisfaction. And three—can I just point out something obvious here? Wade wouldn't *dare* be a jerk. Shit like that in a small town? It gets around." Another pause. "But here's my final point. It's *your* decision. You have to decide how much you want this—and if you're prepared to let Wade take it from you."

Ben shuddered out a breath. "I knew there was a reason why you and me are friends. You talk a lot of sense."

"Did any of it help?"

"Yeah, a lot." Ben was calmer, for one thing. "I think I need an early night. Got a big day tomorrow."

"Knock him dead." Dylan chuckled. "Just… not literally, okay?"

He laughed. "Thank you."

"Before you go? Levi's been talking about some of us coming up to your neck of the woods one weekend. So far, it's him, me, Finn… and Finn's new man, of course. How does that sound?"

Ben thought it sounded wonderful. "Gimme a couple weeks to settle into the job?"

"No problem. Get some sleep. You've gotta dazzle a certain asshole tomorrow."

"If he's there." Ben wasn't sure about that part. Then he snorted. "You know, I came up with the perfect idea to get my revenge on that son of a bitch."

"What was that?"

"I was gonna make gay porn under the name Wade Pearson. That way, if people Googled him, they'd think he was a gay porn star."

Dylan sounded as if he was choking. "Dude… tell me you didn't…"

"Fuck no." Ben grinned. "But isn't it a great idea?" He said goodnight and disconnected. The next day would bring new challenges.

I can do this.

One glance at the time on his phone screen told him it wasn't going to be such an early night. He thanked God for friends who answered calls, whatever the hour.

And speaking of God…

"Let me have a good night's sleep, please." Ben wanted to be on the ball the next day.

I'm gonna dazzle Wade so much, he'll need shades.

The following morning, Ben dressed in the clothes he'd picked out and ironed Sunday night. In his email, Wade had suggested business-casual, so Ben had gone for a pair of dark blue pants, a button-down shirt, and a tie. He'd glanced at his red-and-black plaid shirt hanging in the closet, and chuckled. *Nope. Not going there.* His hair was… presentable. No mention had been made of *that*, thank God. He'd even polished his shoes. If they were too formal, he assumed someone would say something. And if they did, then it was time to go shopping. Ben might've gotten away with worn sneakers on the sales floor of Hannaford—*not* in Mainely Treasures.

The shop opened at nine o'clock, but Wade had requested Ben to be there by eight. The shop was less than ten minutes away on foot from Ben's apartment, and as he closed the main front door of his building behind him, his phone vibrated in his pants pocket. Ben peered at the screen and smiled.

Aw guys. There were messages from all his friends, wishing him good luck. The fact that they'd all arrived within seconds of each other told him this had been a synchronized event, and warmth filled him. *I have the best friends.* Dylan's text made his heart beat faster.

You are better than him. Remember that.

Ben sucked in a deep breath. *Yeah. I am.* He had

no idea if Wade would be there that morning—there'd been no mention of it in the email. He only knew his morning would be spent learning all about the shop. Hopefully the systems wouldn't be all that hard to pick up.

Please, let him not be there. Ben didn't think he could deal with that on his first day. As he turned the corner and crossed Main Street, he heaved a sigh of relief. Mrs. Pearson was opening the door to the shop, and Wade was nowhere in sight.

Thank you, God. As an afterthought, Ben glanced skyward. *You did kinda drop a bombshell though.* Of all the Pearsons in the entire state of Maine, why did it have to be Wade's family who owned the store?

She smiled as he approached. "Good morning. You look nice."

He grinned. "Just following instructions, Mrs. P—Mrs. Pearson."

Her brow furrowed. "Okay. First lesson for the day. If we're going to be working together, I'm Mary, okay?" Her eyes sparkled. "Definitely *not* Mrs. P."

"Got it." He peered into the shop. "Just us this morning?"

She nodded. "And we've got a lot to cover before the shop opens, so let's get to it." He gave her a salute, and she laughed. "I think you and I are going to get along just fine." She bit her lip. "But I wouldn't try saluting when my father-in-law is here. He doesn't have the same sense of humor."

"Got that too. Thanks for the head's up." Ben was glad his first impressions of her had been accurate. *I think we'll get along too.*

Mary made coffee, and then she showed him the rooms above the shop where the stock was kept. They went over the basics: keeping an eye on stock levels, making sure there were no gaps in a display, using the cash register… They'd covered everything in the space of an hour, at which point it was time to open the doors.

"Any questions before I let in the hordes?" she asked with a smile.

"I don't think so. Your POS system is very easy to use." Then he had a thought. "One question." Ben pointed to his shoes. "Too much?"

She peered at them. "You might want to get yourself a pair of nice boat shoes. They'd be more comfortable. After all, you'll spend a lot of time on your feet." She smiled. "Which is why I don't come to work in heels." She looked elegant in pale slacks, a cream blouse, and flat white shoes, a string of pearls around her neck. She tilted her head to one side. "Ready for the morning rush?"

He laughed. "This is Camden. It's the *afternoon* rush you need to watch out for here." That was usually when buses pulled into the town's parking lots and disgorged their load of summer visitors. Not that it ever got *too* busy.

The wide doors fastened back, Mary stood on the threshold and gazed into the street. "I love the mornings," she said with a happy sigh. "When the town is just starting to wake up and come alive." She glanced at Ben. "You know what would be perfect right now?"

"Another cup of coffee?" he guessed with a smile.

She laughed. "Clever boy. You know where the coffee pot is."

He chuckled and headed for the office.

As the morning progressed, Ben watched Mary as

she interacted with everyone who came through those doors. He liked her manner with customers. *I guess she's been doing this a while.* He'd soon worked out that the best way to get on the right side of people was to simply be himself. And when his first customer left with a smile and a wave, Mary gave him a nod.

I can do this. It was a different pace to his previous job, and he relished the opportunity. By lunchtime, there had been no sign of Wade. What disturbed Ben was the fact that he didn't know if he was relieved or disappointed.

When lunchtime arrived, Mary told him to eat in the office, while she remained on the floor. Once he'd finished, it was back to work.

After a small flurry of customers, Ben did a quick check on the shop, tidying here and replenishing stock there. Then he realized he was being watched. Mary stood by the cash register, holding her purse, her pale yellow scarf around her neck.

He gave her a hopefully confident smile. "How am I doing?"

She chuckled. "I was just thinking how quickly you've picked up how things work around here. Anyone seeing you in here would never know it was your first day."

He grinned. "Must be something to do with the excellent training I got." There was nothing complicated about their POS system, and he'd soon worked out where to go for stock when a gap emerged. He gestured to her purse and scarf. "Going somewhere?"

"Well, I did have some shopping to do. I don't have to go. I could do it later."

Ben saw through to the root of her indecisiveness.

"I'll be fine. How long are we talking here?"

"An hour?"

He smiled. "Then go do your shopping. And don't hurry back on my account. I know what I'm doing."

Her eyes twinkled. "Yes, you do give that impression. If you're sure?"

Ben waved his hand toward the door. "Shopping. I can handle this."

"Okay then. You've got my number if you need me." And with that she left.

Within ten minutes of her leaving, it was as if someone had flicked a switch, or a bus had dropped off a load of tourists in the center of Camden, and all of them had made their way to the gift shop. For the next hour, Ben had his hands full. If there was something he didn't know, he was honest, and told them to check the website. No one got annoyed at that. His morning spent familiarizing himself with the stock was put to good use when a little girl asked for a puzzle, and Ben was able to find exactly what she was after. He dealt with families, couples, singles, teenagers… The number of customers gradually tapered off, and by two-thirty the shop had emptied.

Is it like this every day? Ben didn't mind in the least. He'd never had so much fun in a job. It didn't matter that he had a shitload of tidying to do before Mary returned. Towels and throws needed folding, mugs straightening, the floor needed sweeping…

And then Wade walked in.

Christ on a cracker. Sometimes, God didn't play fair. *Does Wade have to look so goddamn edible?* He wore a different suit, but the effect was still the same—sex on legs. *Long* legs.

"Good afternoon," Ben said with trepidation.

Wade gave him a nod. "So how has your first day been so far? He glanced around the shop. "Wow. This place looks like a bomb hit it."

"For 'bomb' read a busload of tourists. And I was just about to make the place look presentable again." He went over to the table and started refolding the throws, his heart pounding.

Fuck, he makes me nervous.

"Where's my mom?"

"She's gone shopping. She won't be long now though." *Please come back, Mary. Like,* now*?*

"I didn't come to see her. I came to see how *you* are doing."

Ben turned to face him, making an effort to present a calm front. "I'm doing great. Mary talked me through the stock this morning, and told me about the deliveries on Thursdays." When Wade arched his eyebrows, Ben added, "Hey, she told me to call her that."

"Then you're obviously doing well. And about the deliveries… I was going to mention that." Wade looked him up and down. "There will be times when you'll have to put out the stock, and lift boxes. They can be heavy."

Ben squared his shoulders. "I can do that. Hey, I might not be big, but I'm strong. I started working out when I was fourteen."

Wade smiled. "Let me guess. You wanted to be a bodybuilder."

Ben returned his smile, his pulse quickening. "No, I wanted to survive high school." He felt a stab of guilt when Wade flushed, but pushed it aside. *The* fuck *will I feel guilty for making you feel bad about high school. Not after what* you *did.*

Wade went over to the cash register and ran a report. "Wow. How did you manage to do all this on your own? That's a lot of sales."

Ben gave a shrug. "I just kept a smile on my face, did my best, and everyone was very understanding."

"You can leave at four," Wade said after a moment. "It's been a long first day, and Cameron will take over from you. But I take it you'll be okay working till nine p.m. once you've been here a while?"

Ben frowned. "Why would that be a problem?" The opening hours had been in his contract for God's sake. "When I worked at the supermarket, they were open till late every day. I'm used to that."

"I just wondered if you had someone who might be unhappy about you working late hours," Wade said with a nonchalant air.

You didn't wonder that at all. You're angling for information.

Ben knew it was reckless, but he wasn't about to hide. He looked Wade in the eye. "No, I don't have a boyfriend right now. I'm young, free, and single."

There was no missing Wade's reaction. His eyes widened, his lips parted, and his expression grew dazed.

Ben smiled. "There. Now you know. I'm gay. Looks as if you were right about me all along."

Wade blinked. "I see." Whatever else he'd been about to say was lost as Mary walked back into the store. Wade coughed. "I'd better leave you two to get on with your day." He greeted his mom, gave her a kiss on the cheek, went into the office, and closed the door.

Ben frowned. *What the fuck just happened?*

He knew one thing for certain. He'd just flustered the fuck out of Wade.

"I'm sorry," Mary said to him. "I meant to be back here by two o'clock, and it's almost three. I ran into someone I know and lost all track of time." Mary's eyes widened as she took in the state of the shop. "You've been busy too."

"Look at the report. 'Busy' is an understatement." Ben inclined his head toward the office. "Wade says I can go at four."

She nodded. "I think you've done enough today. I'll make us some coffee, while you finish clearing up." She smiled. "Well done."

He chuckled. "It did cross my mind you might've stayed away longer on purpose. You know, to throw me in at the deep end." He grinned.

Mary laughed. "I've done that before. But no, not with you. And you've earned that coffee." She patted his cheek, taking him by surprise. "You're a good boy, Ben." Then she headed for the office.

Ben stared after her. *If Wade had been more like you, how much better high school would have been.* He went back to his task, now and again casting glances toward the office door.

He was calling me gay before I *knew for certain that I was. So why the hell did he seem poleaxed by learning that I am?*

July

Chapter Five

Ben supposed it was a sign things were going well if he'd been there two weeks and it felt like forever, but in a good way. The place kept him busy, and that was also a good thing. It stopped him thinking about Wade. Not that Wade had spent much time in store. And when he *was* there, Ben couldn't help but notice the tension that filled the air, and the feeling of low-lying awkwardness. It had been like that since his revelation.

Whatever. It's Wade's problem, not mine. Ben had been honest with him, right?

He and Mary got along like a house on fire. She wasn't there all the time, and that was great, because she obviously trusted him to run the store without her. Not that he was on his own. The regulars were a pretty good bunch, although he hadn't had much chance to get to know them. Cameron had worked three summers at the shop, and nothing seemed to faze him. Madison was still in high school, but she'd worked there the previous summer, as had Abi. Zach was a newbie like him. Now and again, Gramps helped out.

Ben had liked Gramps from the start.

The first time they met, Gramps had introduced himself and insisted there would be *"none of that Mr. Pearson crap."* He was Gramps, and that was that. He reminded Ben so much of Levi's Grammy, and that was definitely a good thing. Gramps had come into the office armed with a photo album when Ben was taking his lunch. He'd sat beside him and talked while Ben ate. There were black-and-white photos of the shop from the 1940s, taken when Gramps was just a kid. When Wade's great-grandfather had started the shop, Gramps was just three years old. Ben had loved looking at this slice of the past. The storefront had changed very little, but the interior had moved with the times. He learned it had been Gramps's idea to provide tea and coffee for the visitors.

After that, Gramps popped into the shop every day for a couple of hours, when it was usually just the two of them. Ben loved watching him putter around the store, chatting with the customers, straightening things, or giving Ben sales pointers. He was a tall man with a dusting of white hair, and dark eyes set into a sea of wrinkles. He didn't move so fast, or so Ben had thought at first. On the few occasions Wade turned up, it was obvious watching them together that he adored his grandfather.

Then came the day a group of kids ventured into the store, and Gramps was on the alert the moment they crossed the threshold. He watched them like a hawk, and eventually they left.

Ben laughed. "Who needs a cop when you're around?"

Gramps snorted. "Kids. I catch 'em now and then, tryin' to steal stuff. They usually do it when we're right out straight. I guess they think I won't notice with all the people around." He hooted. "Ya think they'd know me by now."

"You move pretty fast when you want to, don't ya?" As soon as he'd spotted the kids, Gramps had been out of the office like a bat out of hell.

Gramps laughed. "Two things I never could stand comin' into the shop—kids and critters."

Ben laughed. He knew the latter referred to the cat belonging to the lady who owned the clothing shop along Main Street. It was forever wandering in and out of the stores. "Tux is a sweet cat. He doesn't do any harm. Did you ever think that him strolling in here is what keeps the mice at bay?"

"T'aint likely. Mary puts down so many traps, a mouse wouldn't dare *fart* in here, for fear of settin' one off." Gramps scowled at the kids who peered in through the windows. "I know I'm happier when summer ends and they go back to school." He gave another snort. "Though I'm sure the kids don't feel that way about it. Your schooldays are supposed to be your happiest. That's a crock." He peered at Ben. "Were *you* happy at school?"

Now *there* was a question.

"Yes and no. I made some great friends there, people I'm still close to, who I wouldn't be without. But yeah, there was other stuff going on too that was *not* so good." His gut felt as if it was in a twist. Then it rumbled, and he gave Gramps a sheepish glance. "Sorry. I skipped breakfast this morning." He'd had a night of restless sleep, and had woken up later than usual.

Gramps' eyes twinkled. "You got snacks in that pack of yours in the office? The ones you're always eatin'?"

Ben chuckled. "Don't act like you don't know. You think I haven't noticed you sneaking a few Cheez-its out of my bag when you think I'm not looking?"

"And I thought I was bein' subtle." Gramps ruffled his hair. "Cunnin' boy."

"Except maybe this is where I should add, I left them out for everyone to share, so you didn't need to be subtle."

"In that case…" Gramps pointed to the office. "Go get 'em. I won't tell Mary if you eat 'em out here. Course, there's a price for my silence."

Ben rolled his eyes. "Gee. I wonder what that could be." He went into the office and returned with his backpack. "This way, if she comes in suddenly, I can hide the evidence." He reached into it and pulled out the clear plastic bag filled with the snack. He held it out to Gramps. "Go on. I won't tell on you." He knew Mary kept an eye on Gramps's diet.

Gramps cackled. "You're the finest kind." He grabbed a handful, and Ben followed suit. It was only eleven o'clock, way too early for lunch. Mary was due in the shop at noon.

Gramps stared at his backpack. He leaned in to peer at the rainbow flag enamel badge Ben had pinned to the strap, then tapped it with one long, bony finger.

Ben's heartbeat quickened. He wasn't sure why he should be nervous, but he wasn't sure what to expect.

"Lots more rainbows about nowadays. More than when *I* was a kid," Gramps observed.

Ben swallowed his mouthful of Cheez-its. "Yeah?"

Gramps cackled. "I ain't numb. I know what it means. But you know what I say? Live and let live."

Ben stifled a gasp. Gramps was *awesome.*

Gramps stuck out his thumb, pointing toward the left. "You know the bookstore?" Ben nodded, and Gramps grabbed the stool behind the cash register and sat on it. "Back in the fifties, the fella who owned it? There was talk. Not that folks aren't always yakkin' about something, right? But I liked Pete. He didn't do no one no harm. He kept to himself. I never did see what was so wrong with it. I mean, what's wrong with lovin' someone? Plenty of folks out there say they *love* Jesus—and then what comes outta their mouths is pure hate. Some people out there are *wicked* ignorant." Ben gaped at him, and Gramps cackled. "Had ya worried for a second there, didn't I? Bet you were wonderin' what was comin'."

He laughed, mostly from sheer relief. "Was it that obvious?"

Gramps patted his hand. "You don't need to worry around me, boy." He cocked his head to one side and gazed thoughtfully at Ben. "You steppin' out with anyone?"

Okay, I didn't expect that. Ben smiled. "No. There's no one."

"Are you lookin'?"

He laughed. "I figure if it's meant to be, love'll find *me*." He had to admit, seeing Finn all loved up had stirred something inside him, and then he'd pushed down hard on the feeling. *I don't need love, I just need to get laid.*

It had been *way* too long.

Gramps nodded. "Ayuh. I wasn't lookin' for my Judy, but she found me anyway." He winced, and his shoulders drooped. "Lord, I miss her."

Ben's throat tightened to hear the grief in Gramps's voice. "When did she die?"

"Ten years ago. Too damn soon. I wasn't ready to lose her." He brought a handkerchief from his pocket, wiped his eyes, and blew his nose. Gramps gave Ben an inquiring glance. "Mary says you and Wade went to the same school." Ben nodded. That was as much as he could manage. Gramps didn't say anything for a moment, but studied him in that thoughtful way of his. "Yeah," he said at last. "His school days weren't the happiest either."

It was all Ben could do to keep from bursting out, "Yeah? I think Wade's time in high school was a walk in the park compared to mine."

Gramps cleared his throat. "I think I'm gonna head home. I'm done for the day."

Now that he mentioned it, he did look tired. "Good idea." Ben gave him a reassuring smile. "I'll hold the fort." He patted Gramps on the arm.

Gramps patted his cheek. "You're awful cunnin'." He got off the stool and headed for the office where he'd left his hat. Ben loved the dark brown wool Fedora Gramps always wore. *He's not doing so bad for eighty-three.* Then he smiled. He now knew three generations of Pearsons, and two of them were good people.

Two outta three ain't bad. It seemed as though one particular apple not only fell far from the tree, the wind must have caught it before it had gotten anywhere near the ground, and flung it several feet away.

Then he reconsidered. No matter what Wade had been like in high school, he showed no signs of continuing to be an asshole. *I just can't see past that.* Which was understandable in the circumstances.

Madison arrived not long after Gramps had left, and she took over on the cash register while Ben did a quick check on the stock. At noon, Mary arrived, and as soon as she walked into the store, Ben knew something was up. Her eyes sparkled, her cheeks were pink, and her smile appeared to be stuck on her face.

"*Someone's* had a good morning," he teased.

She laughed, then called out to Madison. "Could you pour me some coffee, please? And then could you go along the street to Walgreens? I need some aspirin."

"Sure, Mary." Madison disappeared into the office.

Mary put her purse down on the stool and let out a happy sigh. "I'm a grandmother again."

He beamed. "Wow. That's great. Congratulations. Boy or girl?" She'd told him her eldest son David and his wife Debra were expecting their second child any day now.

"Girl. Seven pounds two ounces. Debra's doing fine."

Something about her behavior the last couple days finally registered, and he gave her an inquiring glance. "But you were worried about her."

Mary cupped his cheek briefly. "Can't hide much from you, can I? It's been a difficult pregnancy, that's all. I was just praying the birth would be simple, but no, that grandchild wasn't going to make things easy."

"The baby's okay?"

Mary nodded. "Want to see a picture?"

Ben laughed. "Of course. That's what being a grandmother is all about, right? Showing off the latest member of the family." He waited as she got her phone from her purse and scrolled. When she handed it to him, Ben smiled. "I never know what I'm supposed to say when I look at baby pictures. I mean, she's a little pink blob right now."

"Blob?" Mary gave him a mock glare. "She's

precious, that's what she is."

"They already have a little boy, don't they?" He'd seen a framed photo in the office, a cute little boy with a fishing rod.

"Liam. He's almost eight. For a time there, we all thought he was going to be an only child." She chuckled. "Just like his dad. David was six when I discovered I was expecting Wade." She bit her lip. "He was a surprise." Mary gazed at the photo, expanding the image of her granddaughter's face. "Too soon to tell who she's going to take after."

"Are David and Wade alike?" David would have been *way* before Ben's time at Wells.

Mary's face tightened, and Ben wondered what on earth he'd said. "My mom always said David looks like me, and Wade looks like his father." Then she glanced toward the door. "And we've got customers." Seconds later she was with them, greeting them warmly. Madison returned from the drugstore and joined her. Ben was soon engaged in a hunt for a specific souvenir the customer had seen in the window.

At four o'clock there was finally a lull, and Ben made coffee. He brought Mary a mug, and she gave him a grateful smile. Madison's shift finished, and she left.

Ben took advantage of the quiet. "I'm sorry if I said something to upset you earlier."

She patted his shoulder. "You didn't, sweetheart. I was just thinking about my husband." She shook her head. "We lost him seven years ago. Still feels as if it was yesterday." Mary sighed. "Not that his cause of death was a surprise—anyone could've told you it was on the cards—but fifty-three was *way* too young."

"What do you mean about the cause of death?"

Then he stilled. "Forget I asked. This is none of my beeswax."

She smiled. "Wade says that a lot too. And it's okay. He died from heart disease. Stubborn fool never did heed his doctors' warnings. High blood pressure, high blood cholesterol, overweight, smoked like a chimney… When you add all that up, it's not really a surprise he went when he did."

Ben blinked. "He didn't take after Gramps, did he?" Gramps was as lean as they come.

"No, he inherited *his* genes from his mother. And she passed not long before he did. Three years before."

"I know," Ben murmured. When she blinked, he shrugged. "Gramps and I talked a lot today."

There was her hand on his cheek again, warm and gentle. "You're getting to be one of the family, aren't you?"

He laughed. "Gramps says I'm 'cunnin''. It's a word I heard a lot when I was growing up. One of my best friends, Levi… his grandmother comes out with the weirdest things." Being around Gramps was like going home.

"Gramps has really taken to you." Mary returned her gaze to her phone. "And now I want to visit."

"Well, why don't ya? There's me, Gramps, Wade… We can look after the shop. What's to stop you going there for a weekend? New York isn't exactly far away, right?" When Mary bit her lip, Ben's heart went out to her. "At least think about it. I mean, I wouldn't go right this minute, but in a couple of weeks, why not?"

"I'll think about it," she assured him. Then she grinned. "You're not working this Sunday. Got any plans? It's going to be glorious weather."

"Some of my friends are coming up to see me."

Her face glowed. "That's good. Make the most of your day." Then she cleared her throat. "We have incoming. I'll let you deal with them while I drink my coffee and look at baby pictures."

He laughed. "You do that." He loved it when it was just the two of them.

Be honest. You just love it when there's no Wade.

Wasn't *that* the truth?

Chapter Six

Ben walked to the edge of the rocky outcrop and came to a stop, drinking in the view before him. "Worth the climb?" The bay curved below them, the blue water dotted with boats of all shapes and sizes. A canopy of trees spread out from where they stood toward the water's edge. Camden looked so small from up there, nestled in all that lush green.

Beside him, Joel gazed at the panorama, open-mouthed.

"I think that's a yes," Finn said with a chuckle. He laced his fingers through Joel's. "Happy, babe?"

"Oh my God. This is incredible." Joel's contented sigh echoed his words. "Ben, you live in such a beautiful place."

Levi grinned. "Now I know why you said to wear shoes we could walk in."

"Hey," Ben protested. "The forecast said it was gonna be a glorious day. Too nice to stay indoors and shoot the breeze. Not when you've got all this to look at." He drew in a deep breath, filling his lungs with the delicious air.

"Just one thing." Joel's eyes twinkled. "I would argue with whoever described the trail as easy. It was anything but. And I can see why some people drive up here rather than climb."

It was an hour's hike up to the summit of Mount Battie, but Ben was used to it. "I always feel as if I'm on the edge of the world up here," Ben told them. "Sometimes I pack a lunch and come up here, just to sit and look out at all this."

"If I had this view on my doorstep, I'd do the same," Joel assured him. Finn stood next to Joel, their arms around each other's waists as they gazed at the view.

Damn, they're a good fit. Ben didn't think he'd ever seen Finn so happy and relaxed.

Dylan nudged him. "They don't need a view," he murmured. "They've got each other to look at."

"And that is *so* cool."

Dylan smiled. "It sure is."

"Can we stay here a while?" Joel asked. "I don't want to go back right away."

Ben smiled. "We can stay up here as long as we like." He stared at the vast sweep of sky, pale blue where it met the horizon, its hue deepening the higher he looked. The nearby islands were dark blue smudges, and the sails of boats were tiny flashes of white against the aquamarine waters of Penobscot Bay.

Ben sat on the outcrop, hugging his knees, and Levi joined him. "This was a great idea," Levi admitted. "Sometimes I forget what a beautiful part of the country we live in. It's good to leave the everyday world behind, and drink all of this in."

"I thought Seb might've come too," Ben remarked.

Levi sighed. "Not likely. Seb's time isn't his own right now. He gets one day a week to himself."

"He's helping his uncle, right? With his fishing business?"

"Yeah. And he is *not* a happy bunny."

"I know how he feels," Ben murmured. He

frowned. "Is there anything we can do for him?"

Levi shook his head. "We talk now and then. I think that helps. I just let him vent. I guess it's mostly getting used to a new schedule." His lips twitched. "And the quietness of the place. He complains that all he does is work and sleep."

Ben sighed. "So what he *needs* is a hunky fisherman who keeps the same hours he does, and wants to fuck like bunnies when they're not working."

Levi chuckled. "You don't want to *know* what Seb thinks of the guys who fish out of that place. His final text last night summed up the way his summer is going."

"What did it say?"

Levi leaned in close and whispered, "Thank God for porn."

Ben snorted. "Yeah, that sounds like Seb."

Levi studied Ben for a moment. "Want to tell me why none of us have heard from you since you started this job? We were getting worried. Are they making you work all the hours God sends?"

"No, nothing like that."

Levi stilled. "But there *is* something."

Ben swallowed. "I'll tell you later, when we all go back to my place." He shivered. "Let me enjoy this, okay?" Then he breathed a little easier when Levi put his arm around Ben's shoulders and squeezed.

"We've got your back."

Ben flashed him a grateful smile, then focused on the view, breathing in calm, and expelling every thought of Wade-fucking-Pearson that clouded his head.

Ben closed the main door to the building, and pointed to the stairs. “Up there, guys. Keep going till you reach the top. You’ll know if you’ve gone too far because you’ll be on the roof. My apartment’s on the right.” Then he cringed as the door on the left opened, and Mrs. Smith poked her head around it, frowning when she saw the five men.

“We’re not having a party up there, are we?”

Ben pasted on a polite smile. “No ma’am, *we’re* not.” He followed his friends up the staircase to the two attic apartments, opened the door to his, and ushered them inside. Once he’d closed it behind them, he rolled his eyes.

“And *that* was my landlady. She gets all her girlfriends over, and they watch chick flicks, and eat pizza like it’s going out of fashion, and there are always enough bottles the next day to put a bar to shame, but *I* can’t have a party.”

“This is okay.” Finn glanced at the studio apartment. “I mean, you don’t need a whole lotta space, right?” He grinned.

Ben narrowed his eyes. “I’m gonna ignore that dig at my slim, compact body, knowing as I do it was born out of sheer jealousy.” Finn snorted. Ben surveyed the small accommodation. “It’s not a home but it’ll do.” The apartment on Elm Street had been the cause of much ribbing and teasing. *Why the hell did I have to live at number sixty-nine?* "Sit where you want, guys."

Finn glanced at Joel. "And your sister says *our* place is tiny." He tugged Joel over to the bed, and they sat at the foot of it. Dylan and Levi took the small couch under the window.

Ben blinked. "'*Our* place'?"

"Oops." Finn bit his lip. "Yeah. About that…"

Joel chuckled. "We had to do some quick thinking. His landlord had a couple of tenants looking for a place, and nowhere to put them. And seeing as Finn was renting a summer place from him, I suggested he move in with me."

Ben gave them a smile that he knew was pure smugness. "See? So me asking who was moving in with who wasn't such a far-fetched idea after all." He couldn't resist a little dig of his own. "Nice cover story, guys."

Joel gaped. "But it's true."

Finn leaned into him. "He's yanking our chain, babe."

Ben laughed as he went to the fridge. "I got sodas if anyone's interested."

"After that hike? You'd better have *something*," Dylan quipped.

Ben brought over bottles of water and cans of soda, handed them out, then went back for bags of chips and snacks. He grinned at Finn and Joel. "Just give us plenty of notice, okay?"

Finn frowned. "Notice for what?"

"The wedding, doof. We wouldn't wanna miss *that*."

Joel burst into laughter, and Finn gazed at him with such love that Ben's heart ached to see it. It was funny to think that back in April, Finn had complained about there being no one on the horizon. *Now look at him. Head over heels in love.*

Levi cleared his throat. "Okay, we're here. Now tell us what's going on."

"You took the words right out of my mouth." Dylan stared at Ben. "Start talking. And don't say nothing's going on, because we *know* you."

Ben sat cross-legged on the worn rug, a bottle of water in his hands. He wasn't sure where to begin. "Let's get one thing straight. I *love* the job. Hell, I even worked the Fourth and didn't bitch once about it. That's gotta tell you something, right?"

"What about the staff? What are they like?" Levi asked.

"I work mostly with Mary—that's Wade's mom—and Gramps—that's his grandfather. They're good people. Then there's four seasonal workers, and *they're* okay. The shop gets wicked busy at times, but I like that. There's always something to do. I'm never just standing around twiddling my thumbs." He smiled. "Unless Mary and I are having a coffee and putting the world to rights."

"Sounds like you get along with her," Joel commented.

Ben nodded. "She's sweet." He couldn't help himself. "Nothing like her son."

Finn gave him a knowing glance. "And *now* we're getting down to it. I figure Wade is the fly in the ointment."

"You got that right."

"Has he said something to upset you?" Dylan asked.

"No, but that's kind of the problem. He doesn't

say anything. We don't talk. Especially since I told him I was gay." *So much for honesty.*

Dylan blinked. "O-*kayy.*"

"Oh, he was fishing, so I threw him a bite. I told him I was young, free, and single. I also told him 'Hey, guess what? You were right all those years ago. I *am* gay.'"

"How did he react to that?" Levi asked.

"He was kinda speechless, as though he'd been half-expecting me to come out with something like that, but it still took him by surprise. Up until that point, we were talking okay. I mean, we weren't bosom buddies, but we were civil, and there was conversation. *After* that..." Ben's stomach clenched. "I am so freaking *tired* of feeling awkward the whole time. I'm tired of the tension. I still don't know why he hired me."

"Because you were right for the job?" Finn suggested.

"Fine, but there had to have been *lots* of applicants who were just as good. Why did he hire *me*?" Ben twisted the cap on his water bottle on and off. "You know, I thought he'd say something. *Anything* about what went on in high school."

"Were you expecting an apology?" Joel asked.

Ben stared at him. "I don't know. I sure was expecting *something.* But this radio silence is killing me."

"Then do something about it," Dylan suggested.

"Like what?"

"Oh, I don't know." He stared pointedly at Ben. "*Talk* to him, maybe?"

"And say what? 'Hey Wade? Wanna tell me why you were such a dickhead in high school? Wanna tell me why you thought it was okay to call me gay boy, faggot, ass bandit, fudge packer, and anything else your tiny little mind could come up with?'" He snorted. "You know, Gramps said Wade had a bad time in school. I wanted to laugh my ass off. Yeah right."

"But you don't know, do you?" Joel's voice was gentle.

"What do you mean?"

"You have no idea what his experience of high school was like. You only know it from *your* perspective. He could have been going through shit, and you would never have known."

That gave him pause, but only for a second or two. "I found out a few days ago that when Wade was twenty, he lost his dad. Heart disease. Sounds like he was an accident waiting to happen, to be honest. And he must've lost his grandmother when he was still at Wells. So yeah, there was probably some shit going on in his life, but that was no excuse for what he did."

"Then maybe you *do* need to talk to him." Joel's eyes were kind. "I wouldn't suggest doing it while you're both working. And definitely not when anyone else is around. Pick your moment. But have it out with him. Because until you do, this is going to drive you crazy."

Ben sighed. "I'm sure you're right. It's just not a conversation I'm looking forward to."

"Put it this way. If things continue in this vein, is it going to poison the way you feel about the job? What if a few weeks or months down the line, you and Wade are spending *more* time working together?" Joel cocked his head to one side. "How does it make you feel when he walks through the door?"

"Like someone's got my guts in a twist. It's like my stomach is tight the whole time."

Joel nodded. "And that will only get worse. I know what it's like. Hiding the way you feel is *not good.* I did it for *way* too long. Thank God that time is over." He clasped Finn's hand, brought it to his lips and kissed Finn's fingers.

The sight made Ben's throat tighten. *Maybe Gramps had the right idea after all. Maybe I need somebody to love.*

"I'll think about it," he told them. Ben expelled a breath. "Thanks, guys, for coming all this way."

Levi grinned. "Yeah, we drove for *hours.*"

He laughed. "I mean it. Thank you. A dose of you guys was just what I needed."

"If you need to talk more about this, please feel free to call me," Joel said.

Ben gave him a grateful smile. "Thank you. And now can we change the subject?"

Levi peered at the solitary bookcase in the corner of the apartment. "Hey, you've got Monopoly."

Ben groaned. "No. No."

Finn batted his lashes. "Aw, please? We haven't played that in such a long time."

"You wanna know why that is?" Ben glared at him. "One, we grew up, and two, it brings out the worst in *some* of us."

"I feel as though I'm missing something," Joel commented, his eyes bright.

Finn snorted. "Trust me. We start playing, and you'll soon know who loves to win." He grinned. "Right, Dylan?"

Dylan gaped. "Me? Why, I—" He folded his arms, his jaw set in a firm line.

Ben fell about laughing. This was *exactly* what he'd needed.

Don't think about Wade. Don't give him head space.

Except Ben knew he'd have to talk to him, sooner or later.

Later seemed like a pretty good plan.

Chapter Seven

Wade sat at the dining table, going over the figures. So far July had been a great month, and there was still a week to go. The foot traffic for all four stores had been incredible.

The house was quiet. Gramps had long since gone to bed, and the only sound was the steady, rhythmic *tick* of the clock that stood in the hallway. That was Gramps's pride and joy. He and Wade's grandmother had bought it not long after they'd married, and no one was allowed to touch it. That lesson had been drummed into Wade as soon as he'd been old enough to understand.

"Do you have a minute?" Mom stood in the doorway to the dining room, a glass of whiskey in her hand.

"Sure." Wade put down his pen. He glanced at the glass. "You okay?" Mom wasn't a big drinker.

"I'm fine. I've also been thinking." She walked into the room, pulled out the chair facing him and sat, leaning back.

"Should I be worried? I mean, if you needed a drink to broach whatever it is you want to discuss with me…" he teased.

She rolled her eyes, then took a sip. "I think it's time you found a place of your own."

He blinked. "That was subtle."

Mom chuckled. "Not exactly my best opener.

What I *meant* to say was, I know why you stayed here, and I do appreciate it, really."

"I'm sure I don't know what you mean." *Am I* that *transparent?*

Mom regarded him with warm eyes. "I've coped without your dad these past seven years. I know I was a mess when he died, but I'm stronger now. You don't need to keep an eye on me anymore. And at twenty-seven, you really shouldn't be living with your mom and grandfather. You need to think about the future. Because what happens when you get yourself a… partner—I believe that's the modern term—and you're ready to start a new life with them? You can't live under this roof. Not if you want your relationship to survive."

For a moment, his heart fluttered at that one word—partner. *Why didn't she say girlfriend?* Then he quelled his panic. *She doesn't know. If she did, she'd have said something more.* "Who says I'm looking for a relationship?" That was the last thing Wade wanted to think about.

She sighed. "I don't want you to be alone. We all need someone to come home to. We all need something that isn't work. You're doing a great job, but there has to be more to your life than this." She speared him with a look. "I'm not throwing you out, okay?"

Wade gave his brow an exaggerated wipe. "I'm glad to hear it."

She laughed. "What I'm *saying* is, think about it. Start looking. Maybe get an idea of *where* you'd like to live. Let's find you a home for the future. And before you say anything, yes, I *know* house prices are pretty steep at the moment, but you don't need to worry about that." Mom reached across the table for his hand, and squeezed it. "Your dad made sure we were all taken care of before he died. Your brother couldn't have afforded that house in upstate New York without the money your dad left him. And your share is sitting in the bank, waiting for you." She took another sip. "I guess what I'm saying is, don't go looking at houses for *one*. You can look bigger than that."

"I'll start looking." He wasn't going to need much space, not when it was just him. *And it looks like it'll* be *just me for the foreseeable future.*

Maybe things could have been different if he'd—

Nope. Not going there. Wade had burned those bridges eight years ago.

"And speaking of your brother…"

It took him a second or two to reconnect. Wade grinned. "Wow. That took longer than I expected."

She gave him an inquiring glance. "Excuse me?"

"I expected you to book a train ticket to New York the day after you heard about the baby. It's taken you a full two weeks. I'm impressed. I didn't know you were capable of such restraint."

She laughed. "David called me. He asked if I'd like to go there this coming weekend. I said yes. You don't need me at the shop, not with you, and Gramps, and Ben, and all the rest. So I was thinking of taking the train Thursday, and coming back Monday."

"Good idea. You might want to book your seat quickly though. The Downeaster gets busy on the weekend."

Her eyes twinkled. "Already booked it. *And* my connections from Boston."

Wade chuckled. "A weekend of holding your new grandchild. Just what you need. You don't have to worry about the shop. We know what we're doing." He smiled. "Especially Gramps."

"So you'll be at the Camden store that weekend?"

He nodded. "Anything to stop you worrying."

"Me? Worry?" She grinned. "What do *I* have to worry about?" She got up from her chair and walked around the table to where he sat. Mom stroked his hair. "Apart from *you*, that is…"

"Why would you worry about me?" Wade had spent hardly any time at the Camden store. It was safer that way. *Maybe I made a mistake hiring Ben.* Because on those few occasions when Wade had to be there, being around Ben left him in a mess. Guilt, remorse, regret, shame… *Why did I ever think I could do this?*

Seeing Ben was a reminder of just how badly Wade had fucked things up.

"I'd love to know what's been on your mind lately." Mom's voice was soft.

"What do you mean?" *And just how much do you see?*

Mom widened her eyes. "I'm not blind. I'm not stupid either. I don't know what's going on, but I know *something* is. So I'm asking right now, is it anything I need to know about?"

"No, Mom."

There was nothing she could do to help. This was Wade's mess. And somehow he would have to fix it.

She focused on his face, then sighed. "When you were a little boy, I always knew when you were hiding something. And now you're a man?" She leaned in and kissed his cheek. "Nothing's changed," she whispered. Then she straightened. "Don't stay up too late." Mom walked out of the dining room, leaving the door open.

Wade rested his elbows on the table, and put his head in his hands.

You'd think I'd have learned, right? You'd think being on the receiving end of all that crap would've taught me something. But no. I ended up being as bad as those assholes who made my life a misery.

And Ben was the one who'd suffered.

Except that wasn't quite true.

Wade had suffered too. He hadn't been able to forget those years, and bringing Ben back into his life had only made it worse.

Ben handed Gramps his first cup of coffee, then called out to Zach. "Coffee in the office for ya." Madison was already in there on a break.

"Thanks, Ben. Be right there."

Gramps chuckled. "He means he'll come get it when he gets off his phone."

Ben stared at him. "How do you know he's on his phone? Unless you can see around corners."

Gramps snorted. "Don't need to, not when there's *that*." He pointed to the mirror that was angled to give a view of the rear of the shop. He cackled. "Number of kids I've caught tryin' to slip something into their pockets, an' they just *gape* at me. 'How did you know?'"

A customer came into the shop, and before Ben could put down his cup, Zach was there, smiling as usual.

Mary trained us all well.

"Did Mary get to Brunswick on time?" She'd been in the shop Thursday morning, and Ben had had visions of her missing the train.

Gramps chuckled. "Ayuh. That woman worries too much. Told her we'd be fine." He grinned. "You'd better keep an eye on me though." His eyes twinkled with good humor. "I'm so old, I'm liable to set fire to the shop and burn it to the ground."

Ben laughed. "I won't let you out of my sight," he joked.

Then Wade walked into the store, and that was the end of Ben's good mood.

He strolled over to them. "Hey, Gramps. Thought I'd better show up, seeing as Mom's not around."

Gramps laughed. "You ain't foolin' no one. She called, didn't she? Told you to get your ass over here an' make sure everything was shipshape."

Wade coughed. "Well, not in so many words, but…"

Ben waited for some acknowledgment of his presence, but Wade avoided his gaze. *You asshole.* It had been at least a week since Ben had seen him. It was almost as though he was avoiding the shop. He'd asked Mary about Wade's absence, but she said he was busy with the other stores. *Yeah, right…*

Wade went over to the cash register and ran a report, and Ben gaped at him in disbelief.

So I don't even rate a hello? Some indication he even sees *me?*

Madison came out of the office. "We're running low on throws. I found three in a box in there, so I'll fold them and put them out."

"No, don't do that. Mary put them in there to be sent back when the delivery van comes next week. They have imperfections."

"Oh. Okay. I'll carry on with the collectibles then." She waved at Wade. "Hey there." When he returned her wave, Ben was pissed.

You know what? I am so *gonna make you notice me.* His heartbeat sped up a little. He knew he was being reckless, but didn't give a flying fuck. Y*ou wanna ignore me and make me feel uncomfortable? Well, let's see how* you *like it.*

"Hey, Madison," Ben called out. "Which high school do you go to?"

"Watershed School."

He blinked. "Wow. That's pretty cool. Not many kids go there, right?" He knew it was a private school not far from where he lived.

"That's right. There are only thirty of us."

"Do you like it?"

She laughed. "I love it. You can be yourself, and no one will judge you for it."

That sent a pang through him. "That sounds awesome." Ben snuck a glance at Wade before continuing in a slightly raised voice. "When you see the stuff that goes on at most high schools? It's no wonder some kids find it tough." When Wade stiffened, Ben knew he'd hit his mark.

"That's why I love it," Madison continued. "There's no place for a bully to hide. The teachers work hard to make it a good place. I'm *so* lucky to go there."

Wade went into the office, and Ben was torn. He'd gotten a reaction, hadn't he? That was what he'd been aiming for.

Then why do I feel like shit?

"Who's doing the lunch run today?" Gramps asked. "Best to go now before we get too busy."

"I'll do it," Ben offered. They took it in turns to collect food from the deli down the street. "Madison? You want your usual sub?" She nodded. He peered toward the rear of the shop where Zach was back putting out the new children's books. "Zach? What about you?"

"I'll have a green salad, and a skinny latte, heavy on the foam, with two sweeteners." When Ben stared at him with arched eyebrows, Zach chuckled. "Nah. Just yanking your chain. I'll have my usual meatball sub and cherry coke."

Ben laughed. Zach was a fun guy. It hadn't taken him long to settle in.

"What about you, Gramps? Want me to bring you back some soup?" Gramps nodded, and Ben headed for the office. "I'll just grab my wallet." As he pushed open the door, Wade came through it, and for a second Ben got a whiff of Wade's cologne. *Not playing fair, God. Why does he have to smell so good?*

"Excuse me." Wade squeezed past him. Ben stood in the doorway, his chest tight.

I shouldn't have made that pointed comment about bullying. It felt… underhanded. There had to be other ways of getting Wade's attention. Being mean in front of others was beneath him.

Gramps patted Ben's shoulder. "You forgot someone." He inclined his head toward Wade who stood behind him, reading the report intently.

Ben forced a smile. "Wade was so quiet I forgot he was here." He cleared his throat. "Wade? You want something for lunch?"

"I'm good, thanks. If I want something later, I'll go out for it. You just see to everyone else." Then Wade went back to his task.

Obviously not in the mood to talk today.

Then Zach sauntered over to Wade, and the two talked in quiet voices. Ben's stomach felt hard as iron.

Well, not in the mood to talk to me. Not that Ben blamed him after his remarks.

I'm not sure how much longer I can put up with this.

Chapter Eight

When Mary walked into the store on Monday at three o'clock, still carrying her bag, Ben laughed out loud. "You must have been on the first train out of New York to get here at this time." He grinned. "You missed us."

Mary chuckled. "I can't tell you the last time I was away from this place for more than a day." Cameron and Abi gave her cheerful waves, then went back to dealing with their customers.

Mary went to the cash register to run a report, and Ben left her to it. He went into the office to pour her some coffee. Gramps was in there, taking a break in the big chair. From the look of it, he'd dozed off, his chin almost resting on his chest, his breathing even. Ben gave his arm a gentle nudge. "Gramps," he said in a low voice. "Mary's here."

Gramps jerked his head up, blinking sleepily. "Hmm?" Then his expression brightened as Mary came into the office. "Hey. You're back. How was New York? How's my new great-granddaughter?"

"It was New York. Enough said. And Lucy is adorable." She went over to Gramps and kissed his cheek. "I'll show you the photos this evening." She straightened. "So how did it go this weekend?"

"Shop's still standin', ain't it?"

Ben poured her a cup of coffee. "Madison got on with it like she always does. Zach was great. When he wasn't dealing with customers, he was filling the gaps in the stock. We had a bit of a rush on Saturday afternoon, but we coped. Yesterday got crazy busy at one point, but me and Cameron handled it just fine. Which reminds me. We need to order more tote bags. Seems like everyone wanted one. If we order them today, they can be here with Thursday's delivery."

Mary frowned. "Wade worked this weekend too, didn't he?

Ben's stomach clenched. "Oh yeah. He was here."

Gramps chuckled. "No clue what the hell was goin' on with these two. You could've cut the tension in here with a knife."

Mary glanced at Ben, her eyes narrowed. "Problems?"

"No problems," Ben assured her. *At least, none you can do anything about.* He gave Gramps a hard stare. "Gramps was seeing things."

Gramps rolled his eyes. "Sure. Let's go with that. And now *you're* here," he said to Mary with a smile, "I'm goin' home." He got to his feet, picked up his Fedora, and patted Ben on the back. "I'll see you tomorrow."

"You don't have to come in," Mary told him. "Take a couple of days off. You've earned it."

"Maybe." Gramps kissed her cheek. "If I wake up in the mornin', and I'm still breathin', I might as well come in. Got nothin' *else* to do with my day. I'll see you later." He put on his hat and strolled out of the office, calling out to Cameron and Abi as he exited the shop.

Ben studied Mary. "Are you okay?" He couldn't put his finger on it, but there was a distracted air about her.

"I'm fine," Mary assured him. "You were right, of course. I was up very early this morning."

Ben wasn't convinced, but he let it ride. "Then drink your coffee, and I'll get back to work."

She patted his cheek. "You did good, Ben."

He smiled. "I had help. Drink your coffee." Then he went out of the office, just in time to greet seven or eight tourists who were *ooh*-ing and *ah*-ing over the tea towels.

At four o'clock, Cameron and Abi finished for the day, and it was just him and Mary.

An obviously distracted Mary.

Ben waited until the shop was empty, then seized the moment. "Are you okay?"

She regarded him with arched eyebrows. "I said I'm fine."

Ben wasn't buying it. "Well, considering you just got back from spending a weekend with your brand-new granddaughter, you don't *look* fine. Was everything okay there?"

Mary sighed. "Nothing I want to talk about. I'd much rather know what's going on with you and Wade."

"*Nothing* is going on with me and Wade." *How the hell can there be anything going on when he doesn't even talk to me?*

She said nothing for a moment. "I *had* hoped you and Wade would get along, seeing as you knew each other at school."

Ben stilled. "How did you know that? Did Wade tell you?" *And what* exactly *did he say?*

"He said he knew you. That was all." Mary bit her lip. "I'll be honest. When I read your résumé and realized there was a chance Wade had known you back then, I knew I wanted you to work here."

"But why?"

Mary said nothing for a moment. Then she sighed, a heavy sound that tugged at Ben's heart. "You can't repeat any of this, you hear? And you *especially* can't let Wade know we've been talking about him behind his back."

That shocked him into stillness. "I won't say a word."

She gazed at him so intently that his skin prickled. "He works so hard. He always has. But… he has no friends. None. And that's not right. So I *hoped…*"

Oh dear God. "You hoped Wade and me… we'd be *friends*?"

She frowned. "Is there anything wrong with that?"

If only you knew…

"Is that what's on your mind? Wade's lack of friends?"

She shook her head. "I'm sorry, Ben. I can't talk about that now. Maybe another day when I've had chance to think about solutions." Her face softened. "You know us moms. We're always trying to come up with those." Then a family came into the shop, and all conversation ceased.

Ben wished he could help her. He didn't have the heart to tell Mary her wish for him to befriend Wade was not about to come true any day soon.

You can't solve this one, Mary. The roots ran too deep.

Ben muted the sound on his TV when his phone rang. Not that he was really watching. It was just background noise. When he saw Finn's name, he smiled. "Your timing is great."

Finn chuckled. "That's not what Joel said last weekend."

Ben grinned. "What did you do now?"

He laughed. "I decided to surprise him. He's been working a lot recently, so I thought I'd do something to put a smile on his face."

"Oh God. What did you do?"

"He was sitting at the table, working on his laptop, so I decided to get under the table, and… erm…" Finn laughed again. "How was *I* to know he was expecting a zoom call? Like, right that second?"

"Tell me you didn't try to suck him off while he was talking to clients."

"What do you take me for?" He chuckled. "I waited till he'd finished. Then *I* finished what I'd started."

Ben laughed. "I'm just trying to picture Joel doing his best to keep a straight face."

"So tell me, why is my timing so great? I was just calling because I haven't heard from you since our hike, and Joel was worried about you."

"Seriously?" Not that Ben was surprised. Joel

seemed like a sweet guy.

"Yeah. Well, we both were, but I guess what you said that day really got to him. He's talked a lot about you since then. So I thought I'd give you a call, and see if anything has happened since we last spoke. Are things any better?"

"Nope. They're worse." *And that's my fault.*

"Really?"

Maybe it was time Ben faced the truth. "I'm not sure how much longer I can put up with this."

"You're not thinking about quitting, are you?"

His heart quaked. "I'd be a liar if I said no." Not that he wanted to. Mary, Gramps, Cameron, Madison… They were like a family, and working with them was a joy.

It was only Wade's occasional presence that fucked everything up.

Finn said nothing for a moment. "Have you said anything to Wade?"

Ben snorted. "That would imply we spend any time in the same room long enough to have a conversation. I walk into the office, he walks out. I walk out of the office, he goes in. I try to talk to him, so he talks to someone else. It's like dealing with a fucking *child.* And if this is how it's gonna be from now on? Fuck. That."

"Then Joel was right. You can't let this go on. You need to say something."

Ben knew he was right. "Maybe I should say something *before* we get to the point where I just blast him with the first thing that comes to mind."

"Yeah, I wouldn't recommend that. Say something when you've thought about it, you're in control, and you know what you want to say."

Ben shivered. "That's the tricky part. I don't know what to say to him."

"Nah, that's the easy part."

"Ya think? How do you make that out?"

"He's not an idiot, is he?"

Ben snorted again. "No, as assholes go, he's highly intelligent."

"Then all you have to do is look him in the eye and say *why*? He'll know what that means. Just pick your time. And if you need me, call. If you need me to come over there, call. Because I will drop *everything* to be there for you."

Ben's throat tightened. "I've said it before and I'll say it again. A guy never had better friends."

"We were there for you in high school. Stands to reason we're gonna be there for you now. We just didn't expect the same guy to be causing you problems." Another pause. "Don't put up with any more shit. Talk to him." Ben caught a muffled voice in the background. "Joel says do it for the sake of your mental health."

Ben laughed weakly. "Yeah, my mental health ain't that good right now."

"Exactly. We'll be thinking of you."

Despite the roiling in his stomach, Ben smiled. "That 'we' sounds damn good."

"It does, doesn't it?" Ben could hear the smile in Finn's voice. "Oops. Gotta go. Got a man to kiss." Finn disconnected the call.

For the first time, Ben envied his friend.

I want that. Someone to kiss. Someone to come home to.

Someone to love.

Mary put the phone down, her forehead creased in a frown. "That was the delivery guy. They've had a few issues today, and they're running late. They say they'll be here before we close."

"That's good of them," Wade commented dryly. "We could have done with that delivery this afternoon, if we want to be ready for the weekend." He took in Mary's furrowed brow. "Look, if they can't make it here by nine-thirty, they'll just bring it tomorrow. I know we'd prefer to go at Friday with a fully stocked shop, but hey… we'll do what we can."

"If it does get here before closing, I'll stay," she said. "I can have everything put out before tomorrow."

"No, *you* won't," Wade said in a firm voice. He could see she wasn't going to budge on this. "You've been here since eight this morning. You took a half hour for lunch. So *you're* going to go home, and *I'll* stay. First of all, I'll check the tracking site to make sure the order will definitely arrive. And if it is, I'll make a start as soon as it gets here. Whatever is left will get put out once the shop is closed."

Mary glanced at Ben. "Can you stay too? It'll get it done faster if there are two of you."

Ben shrugged. "I can do that. No problem."

Wade's stomach clenched. "Don't put yourself

out. I can do this on my own."

Ben arched his eyebrows. "Of course you can, but what Mary is saying is, you can do it faster if I help. Many hands and all that."

Wade knew there was no way around this. "Fine." He turned to Mary. "Now go home. We've got this."

Great. After hours with Ben.

It sounded like torture.

Wade locked the front door and switched the sign to *Closed.* By the time he turned around, Ben had already opened the boxes and was busy taking out the stock. He glanced up, as if he was aware of Wade's scrutiny. "The faster we start this, the sooner we can go."

Wade had no problem with that.

Ben reached into the box of coasters and began filling the cupboard beneath the display. "Good thing these arrived. We were really running low."

Wade said nothing, but opened a box of tea towels covered with images of Maine.

"So…are we gonna do this in silence?"

That would've been Wade's first choice. "I figure it's like you said. The less time we spend talking, the quicker we'll get this done."

"I agree, but unfortunately, we need to talk. While

it's just us."

Wade's heart pounded. It wasn't as if he hadn't known this was coming. He knew he couldn't put it off any longer. "I guess I owe you an apology."

Ben blinked. Blinked again. "You *guess*?"

"I know what I did was wrong, but… you have to understand, I was a whole other person back then." His hands trembled as he reached into a box of *I Heart Maine* sweatshirts.

Then he realized how silent the shop had become.

Wade jerked his head up to find Ben staring at him.

"That's it? That's all I get?"

That's all I can give you. Wade swallowed. "I don't think there's anything else I can tell you."

Ben snorted. "Really? Well, I think there's *plenty* more you could say." He dropped his hands to his sides. "You shocked the hell out of me when you hired me."

"Why? You were right for the job."

Ben got up from his crouch and walked over to him. "Let's leave my qualifications and experience out of this. I was shocked because you hired *me*. And I've been asking myself why ever since." His eyes glinted. "I have a couple of theories. Wanna hear 'em?"

Wade's stomach was like iron. "Do I have a choice?"

Ben's face hardened. "No, not anymore. Because job or no job, I can't go on like this. So… is hiring me a way to forgive yourself for being such a dick in high school?"

His remark was so close to the truth, Wade winced.

Ben folded his arms. "I see you're not *denying* you

were a dick. Except *dick* is pretty mild, considering all the shit you put me through. So I guess what it all boils down to is… Why? *Why* did you treat me the way you did? And given our history, why the fuck did you hire me? Because my first thought was that you'd done it to continue where you left off, except then I saw you weren't the same guy anymore."

Wade seized on that last part. "No, you're right, I'm *not* the same guy." *Didn't I just say that?*

Ben's eyes blazed. "But I'm not talking about *now*. I'm talking about *then*. I want to know what you have to say for yourself." When Wade stared at him, Ben gaped. "'I was a whole other person back then'? That's it? *That's* your excuse? I mean, what made you pick on me?"

There was no way Wade could answer that.

Ben studied him. "You wanna know something? I didn't know I was gay back then. Not for sure. And yet somehow, you found that weak spot and you homed in on it, like it was a fucking *beacon*."

What the hell could he say?

I knew it was wrong of me.

I knew why I was doing it.

I couldn't let you see the real me.

I couldn't let you see what I really thought of you.

I had to hide.

Who was he kidding? He was *still* hiding. Because there was no way he was going to say *any* of this.

Ben's gaze was cool. "You still have nothing to say for yourself? Fine. I guess I know where I stand. I've said all I've got to say. You drove me to that. You've done nothing but avoid me since day one. Well, if that's how you wanna play it, fine. I'm not gonna stick around here to be avoided and ignored.

I've had it with tiptoeing around you."

"What are you saying?"

Ben stared at him. "Want me to spell it out? If you're not gonna get your shit together and cut out all this crap, then you can find yourself another employee."

Fuck. Wade was wedged between a rock and a hard place, so tight they were cutting into his flesh. Ben leaving would solve everything, but…

I don't want him to go. Not yet. Not when Wade hadn't achieved his goal.

Say something. Make him stay.

Wade shuddered out a breath. "You're right. I *have* been avoiding you. Maybe that was because I knew this conversation had to come. But it's out now. We *have* talked about it."

Ben gaped at him. "And I'm no better off. I *still* don't have a fucking clue why I was the one who ended up in your sights all those years ago." He narrowed his eyes. "And you're not gonna tell me, are ya?"

"I *can't*, okay?" The words came out so fucking loud in the quiet of the shop. "All I can do, is assure you I'll try to do better. No more avoidance. No more awkward silences. Just… promise me you won't quit." When Ben arched his eyebrows, Wade plunged ahead. "You work well here. Mom and Gramps, they've come to rely on you."

"So I'd be staying for *them*."

And for me. Because maybe if I'd acted differently in high school, perhaps you and I…

Yeah, no. Wade was under no illusions. That bridge was well and truly burned.

"If you stay, it would need to be for *you*, not

them. I'll be the first to admit how great you are with the customers. We *all* need you here." He swallowed. "I've said I'll do better. You just have to give me a chance to prove that." Wade's stomach churned, and his chest was so goddamn constricted he could hardly breathe.

"If you mean all that… if things *do* get better… then yeah, I'll stay."

The weight rolled off Wade's chest, and he dragged air into his lungs. "Thank you."

"But not for you, you got that? I'll stay for your mom and Gramps." Ben coughed. "It's getting late. Let's get all this out so we can go home." His eyes met Wade's. "Tomorrow is another day, right?"

Wade nodded. "And it'll be a better day, I promise."

For a moment, Ben said nothing, his gaze unwavering. Finally, he shrugged. "We'll have to see, won't we?"

It was a truce—for the moment. And right then, Wade would take it.

Chapter Nine

By the time Ben got home, he was still shaking. He'd thought the walk would have gotten rid of the tension, but *nooo*, he was wound up tighter than Grammy's old clock. He'd grabbed a bite before the shop had closed, but right then he wasn't hungry.

He also needed to talk to someone.

He flopped onto his small couch and got his phone out. It was way too late to call Levi. He wasn't a night owl. Dylan would probably be in bed, with an early shift to look forward to the following day. That hotel sure kept him busy. No *way* was Ben about to call Finn—heaven knew what shenanigans he'd interrupt.

Ben glanced at his rumpled bed. It seemed so… empty.

I could get on the bike on Sunday and go to Ogunquit. Portland. Anyplace where there's the chance of meeting some hot guy who wants to burn up the sheets with me. Then he snorted. *Who am I kidding? Right now I don't need* hot—*I need a warm body to snuggle against, arms to hold me, lips to kiss mine till they're swollen…*

He *worked* with hot—it was overrated.

And there he was, back to Wade again.

Maybe that was what stung the most about this whole mess.

Why the fuck does he have to be so… so….? There was a time back in high school when Wade would've stared at him, and Ben would've shivered, because he knew, sure as shit, that *something* was coming at him. Some jibe, some snarky comment, a word flung at him, a slur… Whoever had said names didn't hurt was so full of shit they probably squeaked when they walked.

Except everything had changed.

Now when Wade gazed at him, Ben's shivers were for entirely different reasons. Hell, he'd been shivering like that since day one at the store.

What words come out of those soft-looking lips when you're holding some girl in your arms? When you're touching her? When you're inside her? Ben closed his eyes and his mind did the rest, like he'd known it would. *How would it feel to be lying on my back, Wade pinning me to the bed, nothing to do but surrender to hours and hours of kissing and touching?* He could almost feel it, the *weight* of him, the solidness, the *heat* of him…

But he doesn't have a girl. He doesn't even have friends. Mary said so. And this kind of thinking was getting him hard as a rock.

Ben raised his eyes to the ceiling. *You see this, God? He can't even apologize properly, he's been avoiding me like the plague… and despite all that, I want him.* That was all the proof Ben needed that God had a sick sense of humor. *Look at me. Hung up on a straight guy. Talk about a lost cause. You don't think you could maybe send a* gay *guy my way, God?*

Getting laid on the weekend would scratch his itch, sure, but that wasn't what Ben needed, not really. What he craved was something to feed his *soul*, to take away the sour taste of Wade's excuse for an apology.

Ben needed to *breathe,* and he knew the perfect spot to do just that.

His thumbs flew over the screen as he composed a text. The likelihood was that Aaron wouldn't see it till the morning, but at least—

His phone rang, the shrill sound making him jump.

"You're up late," he told Aaron as the call connected.

Aaron laughed. "Didn't stop you from texting though, did it? Are you okay?"

Ben put two and two together. "You've been talking to some of the guys."

"Duh. Figured I'd get a call sooner or later. Sorry I couldn't make it to Camden with the others. My schedule was pretty much set in stone for that weekend."

"Don't suppose it's any less rigid *this* weekend." Ben crossed his fingers. Okay, so it was short notice, but even if Aaron could only spare him his lunchtime, they could meet up.

"Well, that depends. What are you doing Sunday?"

He stilled. "You're not working then?"

Aaron chuckled. "I do get time off for good behavior, you know. I take it you're free too?"

"Free, and in need of a hike."

Aaron laughed. "Take your pick. We've got lots. Now, if you need to get the blood pumping, there's always—"

"Nope. Nope. Not doing Precipice Trail." Aaron had been trying to get Ben to do that since he'd first become a park ranger. *Maybe one day.*

Another deep rumble of laughter. "Okay. Then how about ocean breezes, trees, glimpses of sandy beaches, the sound of the waves on the rocks…"

"Oh, man, you've just sold me." That sounded exactly what Ben needed.

"Okay. I don't have to remind you it gets wicked busy here in the summer, do I?"

He snorted. "I'm not gonna wait till September when it quiets down."

"Fine. Then get up early Sunday, get on the bike, and I'll meet you in the parking lot near the Beehive Lagoon. That's the starting point for the Ocean Path trail. Bring food and water. We can make a day of it, or however much time you need out there."

Warmth tingled through him. "Thanks, Aaron."

Aaron's voice softened. "What are friends for? Get some sleep, and I'll see you Sunday." He disconnected.

Ben breathed deeply. Two more days of work. He could get through that. Two more days, and then he could shrug off this whole Wade mess for a day.

Lord, let him take a couple days off. You can do that much, right?

Ben could always hope.

Ben gazed at the soft golden sand. "I should've brought my swim wear," he joked. Sand Beach was right by the parking lot, and was already filling up, despite the early hour. "It's only eight-thirty." He'd gotten up at dawn, knowing it was a two-hour ride to Bar Harbor, and the roads would be busy as fuck. *Christ. Route 1* anywhere *north of Wiscasset in the summer is torture.* The first part of his route had hugged the coast, until it headed inland to go through Orland and Ellsworth before dropping down to Trenton when he crossed the Mt Desert narrows and Thompson Island to follow Bar Harbor Road all the way to the beach.

Aaron looked cool in his dark green shorts and matching tee. "You're not here to swim," he reminded Ben. The straps of his backpack lay snug over his shoulders and under his pits.

Ben rubbed his own smooth chin. "The face fuzz is looking good, by the way." It was a little fuller than it had been in June. "So how is our one and only ginger?"

Aaron cackled. "*You* can talk."

Ben tossed back his wavy hair. "I'm no ginger. But seriously, how are you?" They left the beach and followed the path as it looped through trees, the crash of the waves accompanying them as they strolled. "Did anything happen with that girl from Grammy's party? What was her name? Angie?"

"What was likely to happen? She was only visiting her grandparents for the weekend, then she went back to school."

"So no one new on the horizon?"

Aaron chuckled. "Yeah, right. Who has time for romance?"

"How many hours a week do you work?"

"Forty."

Ben came to a dead stop and stared at him, his arms folded. "That leaves an *awful lot* of hours for romance."

Aaron arched his eyebrows. "So who are *you* seeing?" When Ben blinked, Aaron gave him a smug glance. "As I thought. How did that saying go? *Physician, heal thyself*?"

Ben snorted. "And who says that?" Then he laughed when they stared at each other and said "Grammy" in unison.

Aaron pointed to a gap in the trees. "Cut through there." Ben did as instructed, and gasped when they emerged onto a rocky bluff of warm, beige-and-gold stone, the ocean pounding the shore below them. Here and there, trees sprang up from between the clefts in the rock, their bases surrounded by dense green mosses and heathers. Shrubs dotted the landscape, their pale yellow, red, and green leaves so bright against the bluff.

"This is beautiful." Ben moved over to the edge and peered down. The waves crashed over the rocks, and he could see inlets where the water had eroded the stone, creating pools and small tors. He sat on a ledge that had been warmed by the sun, and stared at the aquamarine waters in the bay to their left. "I could sit here all day and look at this view," he murmured.

Aaron joined him and leaned back on his hands. "It's not like we're running to a schedule, right? We can sit here as long as we like."

That sounded pretty damn perfect.

Ben removed his backpack, took out his bottle of water, and drank half of it.

"Dylan told me, by the way."

Ben jerked his head toward Aaron. "Told you what?"

"Who your boss turned out to be. Have to say, that sucks."

"Oh. Him." Ben drank some more. "He's the reason why I had to come here. I needed space to think." Thankfully Wade hadn't been around the last two days.

What do you know? Sometimes God does *answer prayers.*

"Is he giving you a hard time?" There was a hint of steel in Aaron's deep voice. "I don't care how big he was back then—that doesn't mean I won't flatten him if he makes your life miserable. He got to do that in high school—well, not anymore."

Ben's chest swelled. "You don't have to do that. I think I've got this, but thanks for the thought."

Aaron grinned. "Anytime. Just call if you change your mind, and you want me to pulverize him." He tilted his head to one side. "So… how did he turn out? Because if there's any justice, he got fat and ugly."

Ben snorted. "Oh, come *on*. Wade was *never* gonna be ugly." Aaron arched his eyebrows, and Ben cleared his throat. "What I mean is… well, he was always…"

Aaron bit back a smile. "I see. Well, aren't *you* full of surprises?" Then his face straightened. "Tell me he's not the same asshole he used to be."

Ben had to be honest. "No, he's not. He even attempted an apology a few days ago."

Aaron widened his eyes. "No foolin'. Wow. Wade *does* have a conscience." He studied Ben's face. "So… he's no longer an asshole, he's hot—"

"Did I *say* he was hot? Hmm?"

Aaron chuckled. "You didn't have to." That appraising look was back. "Is that what's bothering you? That you're attracted to him?"

"Yes! How sick is that? How the fuck can I be attracted to him, when he treated me like shit?"

"But he's not the same guy, you said."

"Doesn't matter. I was also attracted to him back then. The only thing that's changed? He got even *hotter*. I mean, where's the freakin' justice in *that*?" His pulse sped up and his breathing quickened.

"Maybe it's like that syndrome they're always talking about."

He frowned. "What syndrome?"

"*You* know… Stockholm Syndrome."

Ben bit his lip. "Pretty certain Wade Pearson didn't kidnap me or any shit like that. And I'm *also* pretty certain I'm not in love with him." *Infatuated? Sure. Obsessed? Getting that way. And did I forget the part where he's fucking* straight*?*

Aaron reached into his backpack for his own bottle of water. "You know what? You need a boyfriend."

"Say what?" Ben gaped at him.

Aaron nodded. "Someone who'll treat you right. Better than how *he* treats you, at any rate."

Ben struggled to get his head around Aaron's logic. "But that sounds as if you're saying I need an alternative to Wade. It doesn't matter *how* Wade treats me—he's never gonna be boyfriend material because *I've* got the wrong equipment. He might not have a girlfriend right now, but I haven't forgotten the whole part about him not liking guys. He made that pretty clear in high school."

"People change," Aaron said in a matter-of-fact tone.

Ben snorted. "You think Wade Pearson switched *lanes*?"

"Hey, these things happen. You read about guys coming out in their forties or fifties or even older.

Look at Finn's guy, Joel."

"Not Wade," Ben declared resolutely.

"I still say you need a boyfriend. Hell, we *all* need someone."

The tightness in Ben's chest eased off. "Even you, Mr. Park Ranger?"

Aaron smiled. "I guess I'm getting picky in my old age."

He let out a loud snort. "Dude, you're twenty-six. That ain't old."

"Twenty-seven next month, and then it's a hop, skip, and a jump to thirty. Look at me." Aaron's expression grew sober. "When I was seventeen, eighteen, and dating anything in a skirt, I assumed I'd settle down at some point. But then the right girl didn't materialize, and…" He sighed. "I just didn't find that… connection I was looking for, and I kinda stopped looking."

"Isn't that the point of dating? To meet people and increase your chances of *finding* that connection?" Ben grinned. "You said it yourself at Grammy's party. If *Finn* can find someone, there's hope for the rest of us. And just because you haven't found that connection yet, doesn't mean you give up."

Aaron's eyes glittered. "Maybe using Finn as an example wasn't quite right. Now, if it had been *Seb*…" Ben gave an exaggerated shiver, and Aaron peered at him. "You cold?"

Ben grinned. "Nope. That was me imagining Hell freezin' over." They both laughed at that.

"We *can* talk and walk, y'know," Aaron said with a chuckle as he got to his feet. "And there's a whole lotta trail left."

Ben hooted. "Dude, it's two miles to Otter Point.

That's about two to three hours of strolling, not including the time we'll spend at your favorite spot." When Aaron frowned, he grinned. "Thunder Hole."

Aaron rolled his eyes. "Two miles there, *and* two miles back. And while we walk, you can tell me all about your job. *Especially* the parts where you get to work with Wade." He chuckled. "He didn't get fat, did he?"

"No," Ben groaned. "He got leaner." *And why the fuck am I even giving him head space?*

Aaron was right. He needed a guy of his own, if only so he could walk into that store on someone's arm, and watch Wade's face. Ben was never going to get a satisfactory answer as to why Wade chose to make *his* life a misery.

Revenge would sweeten that.

Chapter Ten

August

"Lord, it's wicked hot out there," Gramps said as he came back into the shop. He took off his hat and wiped his brow with a handkerchief. "It's at times like this I wish we had the air conditionin'."

Ben chuckled. It wasn't the first time that summer that Gramps had brought the subject up. "It *is* August. I've got the rear doors open." Not that August was usually *this* hot. He glanced at Wade, who was checking the sales figures. There were *some* benefits to the heat—Wade had taken off his jacket and tie, and wore his shirt open at the neck.

What is it about the sight of a man in a crisp white shirt that makes me go weak at the knees? Ben averted his gaze.

It didn't help. He could *smell* Wade, a heady mix of cologne, soap and musky sweat.

Playing dirty again, Lord?

Why the fuck was he doing this to himself? Had he sunk this low that a *straight* guy pushed all his buttons?

"Can you boys manage without me if I go sit in the office?" Gramps asked.

Ben looked closer at him. "Are you okay?"

Gramps's face was drawn. "I'm just tired, is all." Gramps brought his hand to his chest. "And that soup I had for lunch is giving me heartburn somethin' awful. So I'm gonna sit in the chair and switch the fan on full blast."

"You do that," Wade said from behind the cash register. "Stay as cool as you can." He peered around the shop. "Look, we're not that busy, we've got Cameron, and Mom will be here at three. If you want to go home, then go. We can manage."

"It's just the heat. I'll be fine once I've cooled off a bit." Gramps went into the office and closed the door. Seconds later the fan whirred into life beyond it.

Ben caught Wade's gaze. "I don't care what he says. He doesn't look okay to me."

"We'll keep an eye on him. We'll pop into the office as often as we dare, just to check on him."

Ben bit his lip. "Yeah, because if we do it too often, he *will* notice."

"You know what?" Wade's eyes gleamed. "I think it's time for a coffee break."

Ben grinned. "Now *there's* a good excuse for going in there. Yes please." He called out to Cameron. "You want coffee?"

"Please," Cameron called back. "And some water too?" He was clearing up on the back porch, and replenishing the supplies of tea, coffee, creamer and sweeteners.

Wade went into the office, and Ben smiled to himself. The ceasefire appeared to be holding, and that had been the first flash of humor Wade had exhibited since Ben had started working at the store.

Maybe this armistice will last. There had been no evidence Wade was avoiding him, although the odd moment of awkward silence still prevailed now and then. It was *way* better than the stomach-churning, gut-wrenching silences that had gone before.

A small win, but one Ben was happy to accept.

He went to stand in the doorway, gazing out at Main Street. It seemed the sudden spike in temperature was too much even for the summer visitors. Foot traffic had been low so far that day, not that he was complaining. Just then, a gentle breeze wafted down the street, and Ben loved its cooling effect on his warm skin.

"Ben!"

He jumped. "Has the shop caught fire or something?" He spun around to find Wade dashing toward him, his face ashen. *Oh fuck.* "What's wrong?"

Wade's dark eyes were huge. "It's Gramps. I think he's having a heart attack."

God, no. Ben was in the office in a heartbeat, his pulse racing. Gramps was slumped in the chair, his breathing labored, but still conscious.

Ben crouched beside him. "Okay, Gramps? Tell me what you're feeling." Wade hovered behind him.

Gramps swallowed with obvious difficulty. "Feels like there's a heavy rock or something pushin' on my chest. Can't breathe." His voice was strained.

"You got any pain or discomfort in your arms?" Ben tried to recall all the symptoms of a heart attack he'd learned while he was working at Hannaford.

Gramps managed a nod. "Both of 'em. Feel sick." His forehead glistened with sweat, but he shivered. "Suddenly feel cold."

"He's not going to die, is he?"

Ben jerked his head toward Wade to tell him to hush that shit right there and then, but the words died in his throat when he saw Wade's face. He was so freaking *pale.*

Okay, I need to step up here.

Ben grabbed the phone from the desk and dialed.

"911, what's your emergency?"

"I need paramedics. An elderly man, eighty-three, having what looks like a heart attack."

The woman at the other end asked him questions, and Ben did his best to remain calm and give as much information as she could. When she asked if Gramps was taking any meds for a heart condition, Ben relayed the question, praying Wade was on the ball enough to recall. Wade shook his head. When she had all the details, she told him the paramedics were already on their way from the Camden Fire Department, and that they'd be taking Gramps to the Pen Bay Medical Center in Rockport. Ben thanked her, then disconnected.

He glanced at Wade, who knelt beside Gramps's chair, holding his hand, a dazed look in his eyes, his breathing as labored as Gramps's. "Hey," Ben said softly. "Paramedics are on the way. He's gonna be okay."

Wade shuddered. "Can't lose him."

"We're not gonna lose him, all right? Just keep doing what you're doing. Talk to him."

Wade nodded, then returned his attention to Gramps.

Ben speed-dialed Mary's number. Before he could get a word in, she chuckled.

"I'll be there in an hour or so. Can't it wait?"

"Gramps is having a heart attack. The paramedics are on the way."

"Oh, good Lord." She sounded as panicked as Wade.

He snuck a peek at Wade. "When they get here, I'll drive Wade to the hospital in his car." Ben's motorcycle was at home, not that he could envisage

Wade riding behind him on his Kawasaki. Besides, Wade was in no state to drive.

"Are you sure?"

"Absolutely. Cameron can take care of the store until I get back. The hospital is only about ten minutes away, if that, and all I'm gonna do is get Wade there, find out where they've taken Gramps, and make sure they know who Wade is, and to expect you. Then I'll come back here."

"Maybe you should close the shop."

"There's no need to do that. Just call me when you get to the hospital, and let me know how he's doing. I'll be there as fast as I can once the shop is closed tonight."

Mary's sigh filled his ears. "Thank you. I'm glad *someone* is keeping their head. I'll leave now." She disconnected, and Ben replaced the phone in its stand. Wade had loosened Gramps's tie and unbuttoned his shirt.

Ben took his hand and felt for his pulse. It was thready but there. "Hey, Gramps, you still with us?"

Gramps pointed a long finger to his chest. "Hurts up here."

Ben nodded. "The paramedics are on their way. You're gonna be fine. They're gonna take care of you." He spoke with as much confidence as he could muster.

Within a few minutes, the paramedics arrived, and Ben was relieved to let them take over. He took Wade's arm and led him out of the office after grabbing Wade's jacket from the back of the chair. Once they were standing in the store, Ben handed it to him. "Car keys."

Wade looked at him as if he'd grown a second

head.

"Your car keys," Ben repeated. "Where are they? We can follow them in your car. I'll drive."

Wade nodded. "Okay." Then he stiffened as the paramedics wheeled Gramps out on a gurney. There was an oxygen mask on his face, clouding with every breath. He was already hooked up to a monitor that almost seemed to be in sync with the drip, drip, drip of the IV fluid flowing into his arm.

"Oh, God, Ben. *Look* at him."

Ben put his hand to Wade's back. Despite his size, Wade seemed to have… *shrunk*, as though the weight of all that anxiety and distress was pressing in on him.

"Hey. He's still with us, right? And they're gonna take good care of him."

Cameron crossed his arms, watching as they loaded Gramps into the ambulance. Ben went over to him. "Okay, you've got the place till I come back. I'll be less than half an hour." Cameron blinked, and Ben patted his arm. "You know what you're doing."

His confident tone got through, and Cameron took a deep breath. "You can rely on me."

Ben gave him a warm smile. "I know." Then he tugged on Wade's shirt sleeve. "Come on. Time to go."

Wade had regained a little more control. "My car is parked in the lot at the end of the street."

"Then let's go get it." Ben couldn't begin to understand what Wade was going through. *But then I haven't lost as many members of my family as he has*. Both sets of grandparents were still living, even though Ben didn't get to see them all that often.

All that mattered right then was helping Wade.

Night had almost fallen by the time Ben returned to the hospital. He left Wade's car in the parking lot and hurried into the building, following the signs. Mary had texted him to tell him they were in the Cardiac Care Unit. As Ben approached, he spotted Mary and Wade on chairs in the hallway. Wade's eyes were closed, his head against the wall.

Mary stood and walked over to Ben. She inclined her head toward Wade. "He's worn himself out. I'm not surprised. I know exactly how he feels. We're not ready to lose Gramps yet." She appeared so tired.

Ben was tired too. Working till closing time had been tough. His thoughts kept going back to how Gramps had looked and Wade's obvious distress, and focusing on customers had been a real chore. When nine o'clock arrived, he'd sent Cameron home, locked up, and headed back to Wade's car.

"How is he?"

"Still with us. The doctors are running all kinds of tests. They say he doesn't need surgery, he's responding to treatment, and he's not in any pain."

Ben shuddered out a sigh of relief. "Thank God for that." Then he frowned. "Why aren't you in there with him?"

"The doctor's in there now, and then they say they'll leave him to get some rest. Besides, visiting time finished over an hour ago."

"How is he?" Wade blinked and rubbed his eyes. "Why'd you let me sleep?"

Mary went over to him. "Because you obviously needed it. And now you're going home and you're going to bed."

"No," he protested. "I want to stay."

Mary cupped the back of his head. "Sweetheart, there's nothing you can do here. He's getting the best care. And if he thought you were out here worrying…"

Wade bit his lip. "Yeah. I can imagine how he'd react to that."

Ben held out Wade's car keys. "If you think you're awake enough. If not, I'll drive you."

Wade took them. "I think I can manage to stay awake long enough to get home." Then he covered Ben's hand with his. "Thank you. I don't know what I would have done without you today. You kept your cool when I lost mine."

Ben couldn't miss the sincerity in Wade's voice. "Not all that surprising, really. He's *your* grandfather, not mine. Don't get me wrong, he's a wonderful guy, but I can *never* have the connection with him that you do." He squeezed Wade's hand. "He's gonna be okay. Now go get some sleep."

"Are you staying?" Wade asked him.

"Just for a little while. I'd like to see him before I go. If they'll let me."

"But how will you get home?"

"I'll take Ben back to his place," Mary assured him. She kissed his cheek. "You can come back in the morning, okay?"

He nodded. "You're right. I do need to sleep." He

grabbed his jacket. "I'll see you tomorrow," he said to Ben.

"No, you *won't*," Ben said in a firm voice. When Wade stared at him in confusion, Ben squeezed his arm. "Because while *I* will be at the store, *you* will be here, spending time with Gramps. You got that? I don't wanna see you all day tomorrow. We can take care of the store. You don't have to even think about that."

Wade's breathing hitched. "Thank you really doesn't cut it, but right now, it's all I've got." With one last nod to Mary, he trudged slowly toward the exit, his shoulders hunched.

Mary gave Ben a grateful smile. "You were wonderful today. Thank you so much." She leaned in and kissed his cheek. "I'm glad I was right about you."

Ben was intrigued. "And what did you get right? That I can keep my head in a crisis?"

She shook her head. "I knew you were a kind person who would be a great addition to the team."

"Want to know something?" Ben squeezed her hand. "I don't see it as a team… more of… a family."

Her face glowed. "I'm glad about that too."

The door to CCU opened, and the doctor emerged. She gave Mary a kind smile. "We'll keep a close eye on him for the next twenty-four hours, then we'll reassess. You can go in for a moment, but that's all. He needs his rest."

"How long will he be in here?" Mary asked.

"If he's stable after twenty-four hours, we'll move him to another floor where the cardiac care team will look after him. He might be able to go home in two to four days' time." She gave Ben a nod, then walked away.

A nurse opened the door once more. "You want to come see him for a few minutes?" She led them into the unit, and over to the nearest room.

Gramps's bed was surrounded by monitors and blinking lights. An oxygen mask sat on his face, and he appeared to be asleep. Mary went over to him and took his hand. Ben stood beside her, gazing at Gramps.

"He looks so much older," he whispered.

Mary's free hand curled around his, and he held it tightly.

"I'll be right outside the door." The nurse checked Gramps's pulse and oxygen levels, then left them beside the bed.

Mary leaned over and kissed Gramps's forehead. "Love you," she murmured. Ben's throat tightened. Then she moved away, and he drew closer.

"You hurry up and get better," Ben whispered. "Who's gonna scare all the kids if you're here?" He caught Mary's muffled chuckle.

The nurse came back in. "I'm sorry, but it's time to go."

Mary thanked her, and they exited CCU. As they drew nearer to a coffee vending machine, Mary came to a halt. "How about a little hot chocolate? I could sure use some sugar right now."

Ben reached into his pocket and pulled out a handful of quarters. "I got this." He fed them into the machine, and a minute or two later, they had two paper cups of steaming hot chocolate. They headed for the exit and out into the night.

"Let's sit in my car," she suggested. "I'm not ready to go just yet."

Neither was Ben.

They got into Mary's car, and she put her cup in its holder. "Lord, I'm tired."

"Want me to drive?"

She patted his knee. "I'll feel better after I've drunk the hot chocolate." Then she leaned back and closed her eyes. "Why is it you never get only one bad thing at a time? They always have to travel in pairs, or even worse, in threes."

Ben studied her. "Okay, it's just us, so why don't you tell me what's been going on?"

She sighed. "I've had a lot on my plate, that's all."

"Uh-uh. You've been like this ever since you got back from New York." His stomach clenched. "Is there something wrong with the baby?"

Her eyes widened. "No, nothing like that. Lucy is fine."

"Then what's wrong? Is it your son? Your daughter-in-law?"

She expelled a breath. "No, they're okay. It's… it's my grandson, Liam."

Aw fuck. "Is he sick?"

"No, he's just having a few problems at school."

Ben frowned. "How old is he? Seven, almost eight, I think you said?" Mary nodded. "So what kind of problems are we talking about?"

Silence fell, and the skin prickled on the back of Ben's neck.

"He's being bullied. And I don't think David's attitude is helping."

A wave of nausea crawled over Ben. "Is he being bullied for a particular reason?"

Mary swallowed. "Liam takes after his mom, not his dad. He's a delicate little thing, not into football or sports. He loves music. He's learning to play the piano. And if a kid is going to be *that* different, he's going to attract bullies."

"Ain't that the truth?" Ben murmured.

Mary stared through the windshield at the lit windows of the hospital, so bright against the night sky. "You think you get better at dealing with things. You think you have all the answers once you get to my age. But you don't. And it's just as upsetting second time around."

Ben gazed at her, perplexed. "Excuse me? I don't understand."

She looked him in the eye. "This is one of those you-do-not-repeat-this conversations, do you hear me? Wade *cannot* know we were discussing this."

He nodded in silence, his mind racing. *What the hell?*

"Okay then. The thing is… I've been through this already when Wade was a kid."

His heart hammered. *Oh my God, she knows*. "Oh?" It was all he could manage. *He told her?*

She nodded. "I wanted to take every kid involved, and hang them by their balls, for how they made him feel. Kids can be vicious little bastards. You have *no* idea how much pain they caused him."

Ben froze. *Wait*—Wade *was bullied?*

Chapter Eleven

Ben's head was spinning. "But… I was at high school with him. No one bullied Wade." *No one would have dared.*

"This was before high school."

He stared at her. "Really?" It did *not* compute. *But…* he *was the bully.*

"He was always chunky as a kid. In fact, he was *so* like his dad." Mary sighed. "I think my husband burned every childhood photo he possessed. Wade was the same. At school he was teased for his weight, and they made his life miserable. Imagine a kid his height—he was always tall—carrying a lot of weight. They might as well have painted a target on his back."

What flashed through Ben's mind was all those statistics of how kids who were bullied grew up to be the bully. "What happened?"

"When he got to seventh grade, he told me he wanted to exercise. He couldn't go to a gym—he was too young—and he didn't want to do it at school, because that would have resulted in more teasing. So he asked me to buy him some weights." Mary turned her head to gaze at him, her chin trembling. "How could I say no to that?"

Ben couldn't speak. His throat seized up, and a rush of heat threatened to overwhelm him. His mind raced, trying to come to terms with the concept of Wade suffering as he'd made Ben suffer.

"By the time he reached high school, he'd turned an awful lot of that weight into muscle. I kept telling him, he didn't *need* to be a big hulking brute, but I guess his experiences had left him feeling insecure. He was obsessed about body image." She peered at Ben. "How do *you* remember him from that time?"

Aw fuck, how am I supposed to answer that?

"We might have been at the same school, but we had a different circle of friends." Ben struggled to keep his voice even. "He was a big guy, I remember that. Not overweight, but… built." The kind of guy Ben was subconsciously drawn to, not that he'd realized that back then. It was only later he'd worked it out—he had a type. Forget guys who looked like him—Ben wanted a man who would envelop him, surround him, protect him.

The irony was crushing.

"As Wade got older, and went through college, he developed the shape he has now. He has to work hard to maintain that shape, mind you. Not with excessive exercise, always living in a gym—we're talking about diet. Because after what happened to his dad, he swore he wouldn't go down that same road. He didn't want to be another heart disease statistic."

"I had no idea."

"He doesn't talk about his dad," Mary said quietly. "Losing him just about broke Wade." She picked up her cup and drank a little. "But back when all this was going on? All that hateful bullying? He was *so* unhappy." She swallowed hard. "There was a time when I was really scared he'd do something stupid. I know that sounds dramatic—he was just a little kid after all—but he felt it so deeply. I suppose if you've never been bullied, you have no idea how it feels."

Ben laughed bitterly. "Believe me, I know *exactly* how it feels."

Mary caught her breath. "Oh, Ben. You were bullied too." It wasn't a question.

Ben came to a quick decision. "Okay. I'm gonna invoke the you-do-not-repeat-this rule. You tell *nobody* about this. Not even Gramps." *And please, for the love of God, don't mention it to Wade.*

"You have my word."

He took a drink of hot chocolate. *Christ, this is hard.* Ben took a deep breath. "When I was at high school, I was bullied, because somebody thought I was gay. Apparently they didn't like that—maybe they took it as some kind of affront to their own insecure masculinity, who knows?—so they made my life a misery. The really ironic thing? Back then, I was still sorting my shit out. I didn't know *what* I was." He paused. "Except… that's not quite true. Earlier this summer, I was telling one of my friends that maybe deep down, I knew I was gay back then. What hurt was the way this… bully made me *feel* about being gay. And if it hadn't been for my friends, I think it would have broken me too."

"Then I'm so glad you had them." She coughed. "I can't say I had no idea—sometimes you just get a *sense* for these things, don't you?—so it's not really a shock. I also get the feeling it's just part of who you are. It doesn't define you."

Ben shrugged. "I don't shout about it, but I don't hide it either. There's a rainbow pin on my backpack, if anyone cares to look." He glanced toward the hospital. "Gramps saw it. He knew what it meant too."

Mary chuckled. "That doesn't surprise me. The

man misses nothing. He was okay with it, wasn't he?"

Ben nodded. "That was when I knew I was in the right place." Well, apart from Wade's continual avoidance, but they'd moved past that.

He hoped.

"I can't get over how much you and Wade have in common. The experiences you both went through… I know I said I'd hoped he'd take you on, because I wanted the two of you to become friends. Now? I think you were meant to join us. He needs someone who understands what he went through."

Ben's heart ached. There was no way he could tell her the truth. Because that would sound crazy.

I could fall for Wade in a heartbeat, if it weren't for the fact that he was the guy who made my life a misery. Oh, and he's straight. Let's not forget that *part. So unless he's really changed, I don't see how someone like that could ever be friends with someone like me.*

He figured that would break her heart.

"I think it's time I took you home." She gazed at him intently. "If I give you the shop keys, would you be okay opening up tomorrow morning? I'd like to be here."

Ben squared his shoulders. "Sure, I can do that. I'll text the others to see who can come in too. All hands to the pump, right?" He covered her hand with his. "You just concentrate on Gramps. He's what matters right now."

Mary swallowed. "Yes, you were meant to join us." She wiped her eyes. "Let's get out of here."

As she backed out of the parking space, Ben's mind was not on the following day, but on Gramps—and Wade.

Mary had just thrown him a curve ball of epic

proportions, and he wasn't sure how he felt about it.

Two in the morning, and Ben was still awake. At this rate he'd be exhausted by the time he got up to go to work. He couldn't switch his damn brain off.

I thought I knew where I was. I thought I had a handle on all this. But now?

His head had been awash with thoughts of Gramps in the midst of all those machines and monitors, and visions of a much younger, chunkier Wade being taunted by other kids. It was so unlike every other picture of Wade that had ever flashed through his mind, and Ben couldn't deal with it.

He reached over to the nightstand and grabbed his phone, its bright screen illuminating the ceiling as he switched it on with his fingerprint. He composed a text, not a coherent one, but more an outpouring of his jumbled thoughts.

Can we talk when you have time? So confused right now. You're not gonna believe this. Yeah, it's about Wade. No surprise there right? Dude, this is messing with my head.

He sent it to Dylan, and put his phone back on the nightstand. Seconds later it burst into life. Ben grabbed it and clicked Answer. "What the fuck are you doing awake at this hour?"

Dylan chuckled. "It's called the night shift. You

know, when you stay in a hotel and it's the middle of the night, and you call down to reception for whatever it is that's just occurred to you that you can't possibly do without, or if you go to the bathroom and the toilet collapses under you, or you flush and suddenly everywhere is flooded… *Someone* has to man the desk. Well, that's me tonight."

"What time does your shift finish?"

"Seven a.m., and I've been on since eleven. Another quiet chuckle. "Man, it is *dead* here."

"So what do you do all night?" Sitting around like that? It would've driven Ben nuts.

"Uh-uh. Not telling you. Let's just say, if anyone caught me. I'd be in deep shit."

Despite his restless state and churning mind, Ben laughed. "*Now* I know why you answered the phone so fast. You were on it, weren't you? But what exactly were you *doing* on your phone?" As if he didn't have a really good idea.

"I refuse to answer that question on the grounds I might incriminate myself. Besides, that can wait. What's confusing you about Wade? We already know he's an asshole."

"You are *not* gonna believe this."

"Yeah, you said that in the text. So what am I not gonna believe?"

Ben hesitated for a moment. "Okay, I promised not to talk about this, but I think that was more a case of me not letting *Wade* know that *I* know, if that makes any sense."

"Right now you're making no sense at all."

"It was something Wade's mom told me. I'm breaking a confidence to tell you, but it's not like you're ever gonna see him. I have to tell *someone*, if only to get my head straight."

"And there you go again. Do I have to remind you? *Me* straight, *you* gay."

"Hush." He quickly relayed the bare bones of the conversation with Mary. When he was done, Dylan hadn't said a word. "You still there?"

"Still here. Confused as fuck, but still here."

"You and me both."

"So why exactly is it messing with your head?"

Ben tried to put his tangled emotions into words. "I thought I had it all sorted. All the roles were clearly defined. *I* was the victim. *He* was the bully."

"And now you find he was a victim too. Does that change anything?"

"It shouldn't," Ben replied forcefully. "Because there is no excuse for bullying."

"But now you're seeing him differently, aren't you?"

Shit.

"Yeah. I can't help it. I think what really got to me was when Mary said she'd been afraid he'd do something drastic. I mean, even in my worst moments, I didn't feel *that* bad. But then again, I had you guys. He had no one, by the sound of it. So how bad must it have gotten for her to think that?"

But it wasn't just that. He'd seen another Wade that night. A Wade who was scared of losing someone dear to him. A Wade overwhelmed by panic.

Nothing like the Wade Ben knew.

"Is it going to change how you are with him?" Dylan asked.

"How can I answer that?" He wouldn't know that until he and Wade met again. "Tonight he was vulnerable. I've never seen him like that."

"Seems to me you saw him for the first time as a human being."

Ben caught his breath. "Maybe." Christ, he was tired. "Listen, thanks for calling. I really needed to hear a friendly voice."

"Anytime. Get some sleep. You never know, everything might be much clearer in the morning." Dylan chuckled. "Well, later this morning. I guess when I finish here, you'll be getting up for work. Do me a favor? Don't call me?"

Ben laughed. "I won't. Now go back to your porn." He disconnected on Dylan's gasp. He put the phone back on the nightstand, and curled up in a ball on his side, hugging his pillow.

It was one thing to want someone big and strong to hold him—it was another to have that someone show him a glimpse of what lay beneath the surface.

Vulnerable Wade was someone Ben could fall *so* hard for.

Chapter Twelve

Wade stopped at the door to CCU, peering through the glass, his phone to his ear. "What should I tell Gramps if he asks where you are?"

Mom chuckled. "Tell him I'll be there in an hour or so. Besides, I thought you might like some time for just the two of you."

"Thank you. See you later." He disconnected, then pushed the buzzer on the wall. Inside, the nurse caught sight of him, and pressed the button to give him access. She came over to him, smiling.

"Good morning."

"Morning. How is my grandfather?"

"He had a comfortable night. I'm not sure if he's awake at the moment, but go on in. There's a chair you can pull up. I'll be checking on him every twenty minutes or so." Her eyes twinkled. "He's making a very good recovery. He's quite a character."

Wade bit his lip. "Is this where I need to apologize for him?"

She laughed. "Tell you what. I'll give you a couple of minutes, then I'll be in there to put him in his chair."

"He can get out of bed?"

She smiled. "Sweetie, he can probably go home day after tomorrow. I'm doing bloods every eight hours, and if nothing unexpected shows up seventy-two hours after admission, we can discharge him." She patted his arm. "Go on in."

He thanked her and went into Gramps's room. Sure enough, Gramps appeared to be sleeping. He'd gained a little color since the previous night, and the oxygen mask had been replaced by a clear tube under his nose. An IV stand next to the bed carried one clear bag, releasing its contents drip by drip into the tubing that ran down to Gramps's forearm. On one side of his bed was a reclining chair, and on the other was a mobile stand with a computer sitting on it.

Wade spotted another chair under the window. He picked it up as quietly as he could, and brought it a little closer to the bed. He sat, his gaze focused on the whirring machinery and the steady *beep* of the monitor. It was scary as shit.

"You look right spleeny. Stop that."

Wade flinched. "For God's sake, Gramps. I swear, you're taking lessons off of Mom on how to make me jump out of my skin."

Gramps cackled. "Hey now. I think I taught *her* a thing or two."

Wade could believe that. "And of course I look anxious. I saw you yesterday, remember?"

"I'm still here, ain't I? You don't get rid of me that easily." He swallowed. "Can you hand me that plastic cup of ice chips? My mouth's wicked dry." Wade picked it up, along with the plastic spoon beside it, and brought some of the chips to Gramps's lips. Another spoonful, and Gramps waved a hand. "I'm good. I'd be even better if they'd turn the lights off in here at night. I'm used to sleepin' in a room that's darker than a pocket."

Wade put the cup down, then took Gramps's wrinkled hand in his. "You gave us all a scare."

Gramps sighed. "We all gotta go sometime, right?"

"Sure, but not you. Not yet. You got *years* left in you." He hoped.

"There are days when I'm more than ready to slip my wind, and others when I'm happy to say 'whoa there, let's negotiate.'"

Wade had to smile. "Grandma used to say that too. Whenever I scared her, or made her jump, she'd yell at me, 'Wade Christopher Pearson, I am *not* ready to slip my wind just yet.'" He'd thought it was a charming way to speak of dying.

Gramps's eyes glistened. "Who'd you think *I* got it from?" Wade handed him a Kleenex from a box on the locker, and Gramps wiped away his tears. The nurse came back in and went over to the computer. Gramps gestured to her. "This here is Clare. She's from away, but we won't hold that against her." He cackled again.

Clare rolled her eyes. "I knew the moment you woke up this morning, you were going to be a handful." She peered at the monitor. "Looking good here, Lionel." She typed, the keys clacking in the quiet of the room. "I'll be right back."

When she was gone, Gramps snorted. "I remember when it would have been Mr. Pearson. I think I preferred that. Don't feel right, having a young little thing like her call me by my first name." He sighed heavily. "Sign of the times, I guess." He frowned. "Where was I?"

Wade chuckled. "Negotiating with God for more years."

"Ayuh, that was it. Nope, I'm not done yet. Few things I want to see come to pass before I go."

Wade was intrigued. "Such as?"

"Your mom, for one thing. 'Bout time she found herself a guy."

Wade hadn't expected that. "Dad's only being gone—"

"Seven years. I know. And maybe she's still grievin'. Lord knows, not a day goes by when I don't think about your grandmother. Not that I'm lookin' to replace her, you understand. Even if I *would* be quite a catch." He did his best to preen.

Wade had to smile. "Oh, you are that, and then some. Even in a hospital gown."

Gramps rolled his eyes. "Don't remind me. These things sure ain't the latest fashion, and they gape something awful at the back." He frowned. "Your mom could have decades left—I hope. T'aint right to spend all that time alone. She needs to go to dances, socials, stuff like that. Hell, even the local business owners' shindig has gotta have *some* potential for romance." He paused. "And then there's you."

"Me?"

Before he could ask what Gramps meant by that, Clare returned. She replaced his cup of ice chips with a plastic cup and a straw. "Don't go drinking it all at once." She set it down on the bedside table.

"Yes, ma'am."

"Now, if your grandson can move back a bit, we'll get you into your chair."

Gramps gave her an amused stare. "'We'? Pretty sure I can get into a chair under my own steam."

Clare narrowed her eyes. "I don't doubt it for a second, but I'm going to help anyway."

Wade chuckled. "Suck it up, Gramps, and do what she says." He moved his chair back, giving her room, and she waited while Gramps swung his legs out of the bed. She took his arm and helped him to his feet, and soon he was sitting in the recliner. Clare shifted the IV stand a little closer and checked the tubing wasn't getting fouled on the arms of the chair, then grabbed a blanket from the bed and spread it over Gramps's knees.

He sighed, and Clare squeezed his shoulder. "That's better, isn't it? And if you want to sleep, I can lower the back of the chair." Her eyes gleamed. "Anything to keep you out of bed longer."

He waited till she was out of sight before pressing the button on the arm. The footrest of the chair rose, and Gramps sighed. "That's better." He met Wade's gaze. "Now… David is married, got kids… You about ready to settle down?"

It took Wade a second or two to find the words. "Need to have someone to settle down *with* for that to happen." He gestured to the cup. "Do you want some water?"

Gramps fixed him with a pointed stare. "Boy, I see right through you. No, I don't want any water, not just yet. But I get the message. Let's change the subject."

"Fine by me."

Gramps's eyes glittered. "Let's talk about Ben instead."

"What about him?" Wade's pulse quickened just a fraction.

"Nice fella, don't ya think? Kind, considerate, smart…"

"Agreed. I don't hire assholes to work in our stores. And yeah, he's okay."

Gramps raised his almost non-existent eyebrows.

"Judgin' by what *I* see, you think he's more than that."

Wade's heart pounded, and his mouth dried. "Can I have a sip of your water?"

"Be my guest."

Wade sucked on the straw, and the cool water soaked instantly into the dry tissues of his mouth.

"Just the other day, he was busy with customers, chattin' away, laughin' with 'em like he always does." Gramps's gaze was suddenly more alert. "And *you* were busy watchin' him. Like, every time he wasn't lookin' in your direction."

Wade's heartbeat sped up. "Don't know what you mean by that. I was just watching how he interacts with the customers, that's all."

Gramps gave a slow nod. "But you'd rather he was interactin' with *you*. Ain't that right?"

Oh fuck.

Then Clare came back into the room, and Gramps glared at her. "Jeezum crow, you're in an' out of here more times than a guy on his weddin' night!"

She gasped. "Well, that's… graphic."

Gramps softened his voice. "Sorry, Clare. I… I just need to talk to my grandson. Important stuff, and it's difficult when someone—"

She held up her hand. "I'll be back in ten minutes. That okay?"

He beamed. "Thank you, sweetheart."

She gave him a hard stare. "And then you're going to rest. You got that?"

"Yes, ma'am." He waited till she was once more out of sight before returning his attention to Wade. "You think I don't know about you, son? You think I don't know why you've never brought one girl home to meet us?"

No. No. He can't know. Nobody *knows.*

"I've been too busy with my studies and the shops to have time for a—"

"Don't give me that. And it's not as if I'm the only one who noticed. Your dad? He did too. He worried about you a lot."

"He did?" Wade swallowed.

"He knew you were unhappy. He wished you'd open up to him." Gramps's eyes were warm. "But you never got the chance. We were waitin' on you to say something."

"'We'?" Jesus, this was bad.

"Me and your dad. I never brought it up with your mom. I don't know whether he did either."

Wade breathed a little easier. "How did you know? About me, I mean."

Gramps smiled. "Child, I *know* you. I've watched you grow since you were no bigger than a fart in a mitten. So this is all I'm gonna say on the matter. If you like Ben… go for it, with my blessing."

Wade laughed out loud.

The wrinkles on Gramps's brow deepened. "I say something funny?"

"You… you make it sound so simple, but it's not. It's complicated."

"S'not complicated from where *I'm* sittin'. *He* likes guys… *You* like guys… You like *him*… What's complicated about that?"

Wade's heart swelled with love for Gramps. "I know you think it's that easy, but it really isn't. And it's not something I can talk about, not even with you."

"You know it's no skin off my nose if you like boys, right? Heaven knows there are plenty of dubbers out there who take exception to that kinda life, but not me. It's like I told Ben weeks ago. Ain't nothin' wrong with lovin' someone." Gramps clasped Wade's hand in his. "Ever since he started workin' for us, you've had your eye on him." He cocked his head to one side. "Maybe for even longer than that. I'm no fool. I know the two of you got history. Just not sure what kinda history we're talkin' about."

Wade's chest tightened. "The kind I don't want to bring up. The kind of history that means I can *never* tell him how I feel about him."

Gramps stilled. "Then you *do* feel somethin'."

Wade sighed. "Like I said, it's complicated. And that's putting it mildly."

"Well, while you're sittin' there, tellin' me how *complicated* it is, there's something you might wanna think on." Gramps's eyes twinkled. "All those times I caught you watchin' him?" Wade nodded. "Who do you think *he* was watchin' when you weren't lookin'? Not all the time, I grant you, but yes sir, he had his eye on you." He gave a gleeful chuckle. "*Still* think it's complicated?"

He had to be wrong. He was confused. He was seeing things.

Breathing had never been so difficult.

"Can we not talk about this?"

Gramps regarded him with eyes filled with compassion. "Sure. Not gonna make it go away, but…" He squeezed Wade's hand. "Everyone deserves a little happiness, son. Even you."

No, I don't. Not after what I did to him.

The more Wade thought about, the more he thought Gramps was seeing what he wanted to see. Because there was no way on this Earth that Ben could care for him, and thinking he might could only bring one result that Wade could see.

Disappointment.

Chapter Thirteen

It had been two days since he'd set foot in the store, but when Wade walked in there Thursday morning, he felt as though no time had passed at all. He also felt as if he could sleep for a week. One glance in the mirror was enough to tell him the last few days had been a strain.

Not all of it was due to Gramps. In fact, the main cause for his sleepless nights was standing by the cash register, peering at the screen.

Gramps can't be right.

Ben looked up as Wade approached, his eyes widening a little. "I didn't expect to see you."

"Mom's at the hospital with Gramps. She says thank you for the calls, by the way. He's doing well. And you've held the fort long enough."

Ben rolled his eyes. "Jeez. Two whole days. And to quote Gramps, See? The store is still standing." He grinned. "You just couldn't keep away, could you?"

Wade was glad it was a rhetorical question. "I've got some paperwork to do." That grin was a welcome sight, and totally unexpected. It could have been the combination of their late-night conversation, and the shared anxiety over Gramps, but Wade had the feeling Ben had somehow moved on.

Thank God.

"Something that you couldn't have done at home?"

He chuckled. "Not really, seeing as I had to come in for the papers. You okay to take care of things out here if I go in the office for a while?"

"Sure. I made coffee about five minutes ago. Help yourself. Just leave me some for my break." Ben peered at the screen. "Which should be anytime soon."

Wade went into the office and closed the door behind him. Ben seemed the most relaxed Wade had seen him since he started working at the shop. His change of mood couldn't *all* be due to Wade's promise to do better. Unless Gramps *was* right, and there was something else going on—something beyond Wade's comprehension.

His phone rang. When he saw it was Mom, his heart pounded. "Is everything okay? Is Gramps all right?"

"Everything is fine," she assured him. "They're sending him home this afternoon."

Relief swept through him. "Oh that's great news."

"He can't wait to get out of here. I can imagine how difficult he's going to be when they make him sit in a wheelchair to leave the hospital. But I'm calling for another reason."

"Okay."

"I think we should invite Ben to our place for dinner this weekend."

For a moment he was stumped for a response. "Is this some Bring-an- Employee-Home-to-Eat-Day that I know nothing about?" he joked. His pulse raced. *Why? Isn't it torture enough that I have to see him here?*

"He's really stepped up for us. He's gone above and beyond, and we need to do something to show him how much we really appreciate everything he's done. So… Saturday night, he's invited to dinner."

Okay, he could see why she wanted to do this. "So call and invite him."

"No, I thought it would be better coming from you."

"Why?"

"You're the boss. And besides, you said it yourself. He was amazing. If he hadn't been so cool-headed—"

"Okay," he said grudgingly. "I can do that."

"Tell him Clare is driving me nuts," Gramps called out from the background.

Wade laughed. "Sounds like Clare is doing a good job." He said goodbye and disconnected, then poured himself a cup of coffee. He went to the office door and opened it. Ben had just finished serving a customer and was waving goodbye to them.

"You got a sec?"

Ben looked around him. "For the moment. What's up?" He walked over to where Wade stood in the doorway.

"Saturday night. If you don't have plans, Mom would like you to join us for dinner. Gramps comes home today."

"Oh. This was your mom's idea?" Wade nodded, and Ben stroked his jaw. "Well, I suppose I *could* put off my frozen pizza for another night." He smiled. "Tell Mary it's very kind of her, and I'd love to."

"I'll let her know. Anything you don't eat, or you're allergic to?"

"I'm a regular little omnivore. You can put anything in front of me." His eyes sparkled. "Easiest dinner guest ever." Ben cocked his head to one side. "Don't take this the wrong way, but you look like you could do with a break."

Wade arched his eyebrows. "Trying *not* to take that as a comment on my appearance. And I just had two days off."

"That's not what I'm talking about." Ben narrowed his eyes. "What do you do when you're not working?"

Wade gave him a glance of mock bemusement. "What does 'not working' mean?"

"My point exactly. When you're not at this store, you're at one of the others. You know what they say. All work and no play…"

"Are you suggesting I find myself a hobby?"

Ben chuckled. "Nothing like that. But… maybe you need a place where you can go to chill, recharge your batteries… I'm guessing those are almost running on empty by now."

Wade was pretty sure his batteries were about to die on him. "Do you have a place like that?"

"Couple of 'em. Camden Hills Park, up on Mount Battie, Acadia National Park… That last one has a whole heap of trails you can do. Depending on how much energy you want to exert, and if you've got balls."

He blinked. "What does that mean?"

"Do you remember Aaron Allen from Wells? He's a park ranger up at Acadia, and he's always trying to get me to do the Precipice Trail."

"And what's that?"

"Oh, just your basic climb up a jungle gym of iron rungs that lead up a sheer cliff, with hundred-foot plus drop-offs, and rising nearly a thousand feet up the east face of Champlain Mountain, that's all." Ben grinned. "A two-and-a-half-mile round trip, and it takes about two to three hours. So Aaron says."

"That sounds incredible." Wade wasn't joking. It really did.

"Yeah. Maybe one day I'll actually get to do it." A bunch of customers came into the store, and Ben sighed. "No rest for the wicked."

"I'll pour you a cup of coffee, and bring it out."

Ben gave him a grateful smile. "Thank you."

Wade went back into the office and grabbed an empty cup.

He's right, of course. Having a place to chill was exactly what Wade needed. Then he glanced at the sheaf of papers on his desk. *Not right now. There's work to be done.*

Wade filled the cup, and went to the doorway again. Ben was talking with two customers, gesticulating with his hands the way he did, and they were laughing.

He's coming to dinner. Not only that, his remarks about Wade needing a break indicated concern. The thought sent a surge of warmth through him, until he remembered. Their truce was holding, but it was just that—a truce.

I want the one thing I can't have.

It didn't matter what Gramps said. Ben would never—*could* never—have feelings for him, and Wade had no one to blame but himself.

"Thank you for a delicious meal." Ben took the cup of coffee Mary had poured for him. "I can't tell you the last time someone else cooked for me." Everyone had chatted through dinner, including Wade. It had been a little weird at first, seeing him in jeans and a tee, rather than his habitual suit.

It was also a reminder that Wade looked *good,* not that Ben needed one. He was thankful when Wade disappeared into the kitchen with the dishes.

Drooling into coffee was *not* cool.

"I'm glad you liked it." Mary glanced at Gramps, who had dozed off in his armchair, and smiled. "He's been doing that a lot since he came home."

"He *is* okay though?" Gramps looked a damn sight better than the last time Ben had seen him, hooked up to all those machines.

"Yes, he's fine." She chuckled. "He's also less than impressed with the diet recommendations the hospital gave him. It's not as if he has a poor diet to begin with—he looks after himself—but being told not to eat chocolate was apparently a step too far." Mary settled back on the couch. "Do your folks still live in Wells?"

"Yes. I go home for a visit every now and then. My mom has her hands full. I was the oldest, there are four of us kids, and a gap of eight years between me and the last one, my sister Grace. She just graduated from high school. My middle sister still lives at home." He sipped his coffee. "Were you all living in Wells when Wade was at high school?" He couldn't see her doing the commute to the store every day.

"Yes, there was me, my husband Steven, and Wade. David was away at college—there's a gap of six years between him and Wade. Once he graduated, he moved to New York." She bit her lip. "He couldn't get out of Maine fast enough."

Ben had never understood people who felt like that. Then again, he was lucky enough to live in a beautiful part of the state, and maybe some folks weren't that fortunate. "Did you work in the store then?"

"No, Gramps and Judy ran it, along with a handful of staff." She glanced at Gramps again, and lowered her voice. "When Judy died nine years ago, it hit Gramps hard. Steven and I decided he couldn't run the store on his own, not to mention the other stores his dad had set up, so we sold our house in Wells, and moved to Camden to take over the running of the shop." She gestured to the house. "This belongs to Gramps. He couldn't bear to sell it—too many memories here, I guess—so we moved in with him. Wade had graduated by then, and was going to community college."

"Did you always plan for Wade to run the stores?"

"I think that was more a reaction to losing his grandmother. Gramps put the idea in his head, but Wade wanted to run with it. When his studies were finished, he didn't move out. By then of course, we'd lost his dad, so maybe that was why." She gave a sad smile. "Except there's no maybe about it. He's a good boy. He wanted to stay close to me and Gramps."

It was yet another example of a Wade that bore no relation to the boy Ben had known.

"Your place looks nice on the outside," Mary commented. "Not that I could see all that much of it at night."

"It's a big house, and it's all divided up into apartments. Did you see those little windows up in the roof?" When she nodded, he grinned. "One of those is mine. It's not so much an apartment, more of a shoebox. And it comes with a landlady who *really* gets on my—nerves."

She chuckled.

Wade came into the living room, and Gramps woke up as Wade passed his chair. "We not havin' coffee tonight?"

Wade laughed. "Why do you want coffee? It would only keep you awake."

Gramps snorted. "You get your ass over to that table and pour me a cup." When Wade did as instructed, Gramps grumbled about "fool doctors not takin' *that* away from me."

"This place isn't huge," Mary continued. "But then, there are only the three of us." She bit her lip. "Not that there's much space in Wade's bedroom. It's full of boxes. It's *been* full of boxes since we moved here." She gave Wade a pointed stare. "And when he moves out into a place of his own, every last box is going with him."

Wade flushed.

"You're moving out?" Ben asked him.

"I was thinking about it." He glanced at Gramps. "But that was before."

Unfortunately, Gramps caught the look. "Don't you be stickin' around here thinkin' you need to keep an eye on me. I got my own life to lead. Besides, I want you out of here before I start bringin' lady friends home. How am I goin' to impress 'em if they see your shorts dryin' in the bathroom?"

Wade's eyes bulged. "I do *not* hang my shorts up

to dry in the bathroom."

Mary laughed out loud. "'Lady friends'?"

Gramps cackled. "You never know. There may be snow on the roof but there's fire—"

"Please, Gramps, don't," Wade said with a groan.

Mary stared at Gramps, her lips still twitching. "I hate to break it to you, but the snow on your roof has *long* since melted."

It was like visiting Levi and Grammy when Ben was a teenager. The same comfortable sentiments were a slice of his former life, and it felt good.

"Apparently I need a break," Wade declared suddenly. His eyes twinkled. "According to Ben, that is."

Ben gave him a mock glare. "Hey, I think you liked the idea of going up to Acadia." Not for the first time that evening, he marveled at the change in Wade. Maybe it was the fact that Gramps was home, and obviously improving. Whatever the reason, Wade's mood seemed lighter.

Gramps's eyes shone. "I haven't been up there in years. It was one of my favorite spots for takin' my Judy." He cackled. "Back in the day, it was our go-to place when we wanted some alone-time."

Ben couldn't resist. "I was telling Wade about the Precipice Trail."

Gramps nodded. "I've heard of it, but never done it. I think if I'd even suggested it, Judy would have fainted."

Wade chuckled. "She was made of sterner stuff than that. I'll admit, it does sound awesome. Not something I've ever considered doing."

"Then do it," Mary blurted out.

Wade frowned. "Seriously?" Ben gazed at her in

surprise.

"Why not? It would be a new experience." She turned to Ben. "Have *you* ever done it?"

"No, but I have a friend who's been badgering me to try it for ages. He's a park ranger in Acadia." He peered at Wade. "We *could* do it, except you're forever chained to your desk, or on your way to another desk, or doing *something*…"

Then he realized he wanted Wade to say yes.

"That does it," Gramps announced. He pointed his bony finger at Wade. "You're takin' tomorrow off."

Wade blinked. "I am?"

"Ayuh—*both* of ya." Before Ben could say a word, Gramps addressed Mary. "Can you get enough bodies for the store for tomorrow?"

"Sure." Mary reached for her phone. "Cameron and Madison are already coming in, and Abi would love some extra hours. She's saving up for her vacation."

"I can come in too." He scowled when all three of them said "No."

Mary shook her head. "You heard what the doctor said. Rest. Take it easy, for at least a couple of months. That means no work for you."

"I'd only be there as a supervisor," he insisted. "You know, I could sit there lookin' regal and directin' folks around the store."

Ben chuckled. "Persistent, aren't they?" He had the impression both he and Wade had just been steamrollered.

"Are we really doing this?" Wade demanded.

Ben shrugged. "Why not? First time for everything." And now he was really starting to like the idea.

"Just promise me you'll bring him back alive," Gramps said, his eyes locked on Ben.

"I promise."

Wade cleared his throat. "Help me take the coffee things out to the kitchen?"

Ben got the message. Wade wanted to talk. "Sure." He collected the coffee cups and placed them on the tray, then carried it into the kitchen behind Wade. Once they were out of earshot of Mary and Gramps, Wade folded his arms.

"You don't *have* to do this, okay? I know Gramps can be pretty forceful, but you *can* say no. He doesn't get to have everything his own way."

"No, it's okay. I've been meaning to do this for a while." He grinned. "At least now I'll have *you* to call 911 when I fall off the cliff." And if he were honest, there was part of him that liked the idea of being in one of his favorite places—with Wade.

It felt as if God was seriously trying to make up for all the crap Ben had gone through.

We need this. The last few days, Ben had come to accept that holding onto the past would only hurt him. He had to move forward. He thought back to his conversations with Aaron and Dylan.

Maybe they're right, and I should give Wade the benefit of the doubt. He's obviously not the same person I knew.

And that was the trouble.

The Wade he remembered had been physically appealing, but a total dick.

This Wade was ticking more and more of Ben's boxes, and the last thing Ben wanted was to get hung up on a straight guy.

Chapter Fourteen

"Remind me again why we had to leave so early?" Wade asked as they walked along the road that led to the trailhead. "It's only seven-thirty. And there were only two cars in the parking lot."

Ben laughed. "You gotta trust me on this. That lot gets full pretty quickly. Not to mention the cars park all along the road too." He'd phoned Aaron the night before when he'd gotten home, and they'd talked for an hour about the hike. Ben hadn't mentioned the fact that he wouldn't be doing it alone, and he wasn't really sure why.

"This trail is that popular?"

"It will be this weekend. Aaron says it's been closed since March, because there are peregrine falcons nesting up there, but it opens today." Ben glanced at Wade's boots. "Good to see you followed my advice."

"You said to wear something to walk in." Wade rolled his eyes. "I wasn't going to do it in flip-flops."

"You'd be surprised what some people wear." Aaron was always complaining about the dubbers who turned up wearing inappropriate clothing.

Wade looked anything but inappropriate. He wore a pair of shorts and a dark blue tee, and it was all Ben could do not to drool at the sight of the cotton clinging to his wide, firm chest, and the curve of his biceps.

Jesus, you look amazing.

He cleared his throat. "You brought water?"

"And snacks. And sunscreen. And bug spray." Wade gave him a mock glare. "Are you going to be like this the whole trail?"

Ben chuckled. "I'm in a great mood, so don't spoil my buzz." The hike promised to be exciting, and he couldn't wait to experience it. Aaron had sent him a few links to short videos about the trail, to give him an idea what to expect. "There *was* onc thing I didn't ask."

"And what's that?"

"You're okay with heights, right?"

Wade stared at him, his eyebrows raised. "Seeing as you said we're going to climb over one thousand feet, I'd better be." Then he frowned. "*How* long did you say this hike will take?"

"Two to three hours. We could be home by early afternoon." Ben would've preferred it if they weren't, however. He wanted to spend as long as possible in the park.

"But we can take our time, right?"

Ben chuckled. "Sure we can." It seemed Wade was in no hurry to get home either.

Wade pointed to the steps on the other idea of the road, a signpost beside them. "Is that it?"

Ben nodded. "That's the trailhead." A short flight of stone steps disappeared into the forested verge.

"I don't know why you were making this out to be such a difficult trail. That looks easy." When Ben stilled and regarded him incredulously, Wade grinned. "Kidding."

Ben shook his head. "And are you gonna be like *this* the whole trail?"

"Only if you're *really* lucky."

Ben wasn't complaining. Wade away from the store was a revelation. *Maybe he needs this.* A chance to unwind, to breathe… God knew, Gramps's heart attack had been a stressful episode, and knowing he'd come out the other side had been a relief. *But maybe* we *need this too.*

They went up the steps into the forest, and as soon as their feet hit the trail, it started to climb. When they reached a staircase made from boulders, Wade came to a halt.

"We get to stop whenever we want to take a water break, right?"

Ben laughed. "It's not like we're timing this, or I'm gonna be reporting back to Gramps. If you wanna stop, sing out and we'll stop. If you wanna eat something, say so. Breakfast was three hours ago, so we're gonna get the munchies. Well—*I* am."

Wade held up his hands. "Okay. Just checking."

That first staircase was one of a series, and before long they were scrambling over rocks, holding onto iron bars that were set into the stone here and there. The size of some of the boulders blew Ben away—in some cases they were larger than a car.

"How do we know where to go?" Wade asked. "All I see are boulders."

Ben pointed to the splash of blue paint on the rock in front of them. "Follow those." Aaron had mentioned them. But when the blue blaze indicated a path under a boulder, he thought someone was having a joke.

Wade went closer and peered under it. "Looks like we have to squeeze through here." His eyes sparkled. "This is fun."

Ben was glad he wasn't the only one who thought so.

The trail took them under more boulders, over them, around them, the path punctuated by iron rungs with which they hoisted themselves up and over the rocky terrain.

When they got to a flattish part, Wade stopped and grinned. "Hey, this isn't too bad."

Ben laughed. "I hate to break it to ya, but those iron rungs back there? That was kind of a test for hikers." Aaron had told him to think of it as preparation for what was to come.

"Did I pass?"

He chuckled. "Yeah, you passed."

"And is now a good time to say I need some water?"

Ben chuckled. "I think you do. Looks like you need to replenish what you've lost."

Wade glanced at his tee with its dark patches of sweat. He rolled his eyes. "Jeez. Anyone would think it was hot or something. Or, you know, we were doing something strenuous." He peered at Ben's pale yellow tee. "I think you'd better have some too."

Ben had nothing against sweat, especially in Wade's case. Wade smelled good at the best of times—add sweat into the equation, and he was a heavenly assault on Ben's senses.

They took out their bottles of water, and drank greedily. Ben tried not to stare at Wade's throat as he swallowed—the bob of Wade's Adam's apple mesmerized him. He reached into his backpack and pulled out a plastic container. "Want one of these?" He yanked off the lid.

Wade peered into it. "That looks like banana

with—what *is* that in the middle?"

"Peanut butter. My all-time favorite hiking snack. I slice the banana down the center, smear peanut butter all over one side, then sandwich it back together and wrap it up." He held out the box. "Have one. I've got plenty. It's a really healthy snack."

Wade bit his lip. "And there *I* was, thinking you'd bring chips or Cheez-its."

Ben grinned. "The Cheez-its are in the backpack."

He laughed. "Glad to know I hadn't *completely* misjudged you." He took a banana, and the two of them munched in silence, surrounded by trees, and accompanied by birdsong.

Their break over, they continued along the trail until they reached a wooden bridge that spanned the gap between the forest and the start of the cliff face.

Wade stood in the middle of the wooden structure and grinned at Ben. "Hey look, no hands." He waved them at Ben.

"No railing either, so watch your step." From there, they gazed out at the ocean and the Porcupine Islands. On the other side of the bridge began a series of narrow ledges, with rusted iron railings on one side, and the sheer cliff face on the other. They came to a staircase made of cut boulders piled on top of each other, like a child's building blocks. Wade paused at the bottom of it, staring up.

"We must be halfway by now, right?"

Ben laughed. "Good try, but no, not even close. Now get up there."

"Are you going to catch me if I fall?"

He snorted. "If you fall on me, you'll flatten me."

"Then you should go first."

Ben waved a hand. "Just get your ass up those

blocks." Taking up the rear afford him the perfect opportunity to ogle *Wade's* rear.

Damn.

When he reached the top, Wade peered down at him with a happy smile. "That wasn't so bad either."

"I'm glad… you're having a… good time," Ben said as he got to the final rung. When he stood on firm ground once more, he caught sight of a wooden signpost, its base jammed into a pile of rocks. "Okay. Aaron told me about this. We are officially zero-point-four miles into the hike."

"That's all?" Wade appeared horrified. "But you said it's a two-and-a-half mile hike."

"Yes, yes I did. So maybe we should use this moment to consider our options."

Wade blinked. "There are options?"

Ben nodded. "You see, this is make-your-mind-up time. If we go left, we follow the trail to the summit of Champlain Mountain. If you feel it's been too much of a challenge for ya, then we follow the orange and black trail back to the parking lot."

Wade stared at him. "I am *not* going back."

Ben grinned. "Me neither. Though I should add, this is where it gets exciting."

Judging by Wade's smile and the light in his eyes, he was looking forward to it just as much as Ben.

The terrain changed abruptly. Once they were past the signpost, the treetops fell away beneath them. They scrambled up rocky ledges, with the aid of a lot of iron rungs set into the cliff, which appeared as though someone had gotten a little too enthusiastic with a giant staple gun. There were more ledges to walk along, but these were narrow with no railings, only more of those iron rungs set into the rock.

It was a long, long way down.

"Did I ever mention that this is *the* most dangerous trail in Acadia?" Ben said cheerfully when they stopped to drink some water. "Or that hikers have actually *died* here?"

Wade glared at him. "You don't think maybe this is something you might've mentioned before now? You know, like when you brought up the idea?"

"I *didn't* mention it? Wow. I must be slipping." Ben let out a chuckle. "Not a word I should be using up here. Still, luck might be on our side. It hasn't rained, so the rocks aren't slippery."

Yeah, he was having a *lot* of fun.

Once they'd climbed higher, clinging to the rungs that rose up the cliff face like a ladder, the trail went through a forest, always heading up. Wade paused to take a drink.

Ben chuckled. "You doing okay?"

Wade glared at him. "It's that peanut butter. It's made me thirsty."

"*Sure* it has." Then Ben relented. "We can take a break. Lord knows, I'm sweating like a pig too, and the temperature isn't *that* high today, fortunately. Besides, we need to catch our breath for what's coming."

Wade regarded him with wide eyes. "Why? What *is* coming?"

Ben grinned. "The tricky part."

"What the hell do you call the part we just did?" Wade demanded.

"Walk on a little farther, and you'll see what I mean." They continued along the path, finally emerging at a series of iron rungs and cliff walks.

"The reward is the view waiting up there for us."

This was apparently the highlight of the trail, the part of the hike that got the blood pumping and the adrenaline rushing.

Wade stared up at the iron rung ladder. "How come you know so much about this trail if you've never done it before?"

"*I* haven't, but Aaron has, many times. He's been talking about this ever since he started as a park ranger. And last night he made me download a map of the trail, and talked me through every stage of it."

Wade lowered his gaze to look at Ben. "He was taking care of you, just like you're taking care of me."

"You know it." Ben smiled. "Ready for the final bit?"

Wade's eyes shone. "Bring it on."

Within minutes they had climbed hundreds of feet, and it was exhilarating. There were switchbacks, always heading upward. They walked along narrow ledges that ended abruptly, where the only place to go was up a ladder of rungs. The trail hugged the cliff face, and a glance down at the trees below made Ben's heart pound. Finally they reached the top, and the rock plateaued.

"We made it," Ben exclaimed. He couldn't remember ever feeling this *alive*, his heartbeat racing, and adrenaline spiking through him.

Wade's face was flushed, his eyes bright, with a smile that would not quit. "Oh wow. Would you look at that."

They stood at the summit, which was marked by a small round metal plate, and gazed at the panorama. Sunlight sparkled on the Atlantic Ocean, and a breeze ruffled the treetops so far below them. They were the only two people up there, and Ben had the overwhelming sensation of being so very small in the face of all that splendor.

"This is breathtaking." Awe filled Wade's voice. "Tell me we don't have to go down right away."

"We can stay up here as long as we like." Ben knew at some point other hikers would reach the summit, but right then it was just him and Wade, and that felt *right*.

They sat on the rock, opened their backpacks, and took out their snacks and bottles of water. Ben drank deeply, relishing the water's coolness.

"Well? I know you had a fairly good idea of what to expect, but was it everything you thought it would be?"

Ben sighed. "It's so much more." It had to be the most demanding hike he'd ever done. But the rewards… "This is awesome."

"Have to say, there were some scary moments on the way up here." Wade shivered. "You know, times when I looked down and thought, 'Fuck, I shouldn't have done that.'"

Ben laughed. "Did you feel like you were an ant crawling up there?"

"God, yes. Like we were so… insignificant." Wade gestured to the view. "Now I know why you like coming here." His voice softened. "It's a chance to hear nothing but the wind, the birds, your own heart beating, the sound of your own breathing…"

Ben nodded slowly. *He gets it.* "A chance to think, without the clutter of everyday life."

For a moment neither of them spoke, and that was just fine.

"Thank you," Wade said at last.

"For what?"

"For suggesting this. For going along with it when Gramps railroaded us into it. For sharing this with me." Wade peered at him. "This is your special place, isn't it?"

"Down there? In the park?" Ben smiled. "Yes, but it's big enough to share."

"Are we good?" Wade blurted out.

Ben arched his eyebrows. "I'm not sure I understand the question."

"I just feel… I mean, we talked… And I promised I would try." Wade didn't look at him, twisting the bottle in his hands.

Ben got where he was going with this. "I'm not gonna lie. I can never forget the past. After all, that's what shapes us, right? And I have to believe I came through all that to become a stronger person. *But…* I *can* move forward."

He'd thought a lot about their situation. Mary's revelation about Wade's childhood had altered his view a little. Not every bully had something in their past that made them act the way they did—some people were just mean. They got off on hurting others. And Ben would have gone on believing Wade was one of those people, if Mary hadn't shared his history. And so what if that history sucked? It was a *reason* for his behavior, not an excuse.

Wade was so still beside him, his gaze averted.

"When I found out it *was* you I'd be working with, I have to admit, I was dreading it," Ben said in a low voice.

Wade still wouldn't look at him. "I don't blame you for that. Not after how I treated you."

"And you *still* don't wanna shed any light on that?"

The hitch in Wade's breathing told him plenty. "I know it doesn't make any sense, but I *can't*. It's a part of my life I really want to forget. Mostly because I was really shitty to a lot of people. You especially. I know you can never forgive me, but I *am* trying to show you I've changed. I'm trying to make it up to you."

"Can you at least look at me while you're trying?"

Slowly, Wade raised his chin and met Ben's gaze. "This last week, I feel like I've gotten to know you better. I've seen what kind of a man you are. And I don't suppose it comes as any surprise to learn my mom and Gramps adore you."

"They're pretty special people."

"I… I said I owed you an apology, but it didn't sound like much of one, so let me try this again." Amber eyes focused on his. "I am *really* sorry."

He knew what Wade wanted, but it wasn't until that precise moment that he realized he could provide it. Ben took a deep breath. "I'm never going to understand why you treated me the way you did, but with every new day, you show me you're a different kind of man. So… I'll accept the apology."

Wade blinked. "Seriously? You mean that?"

Ben nodded. "There comes a time when holding onto the past does nothing but cause pain. I've had enough of pain."

Wade shuddered out a breath. "Christ, if you only knew how much I needed to hear that."

Silence fell between them, and Ben made no attempt to fill it. Besides, he was all out of words. He opened his bag of Cheez-its and ate, staring at the ocean. *All I had to do to find some peace was climb a mountain.* Except that wasn't quite true.

He'd needed to climb it with Wade.

"Can I have some?"

Ben smiled. "Like grandfather, like grandson." He held out the bag, and Wade helped himself to a handful.

"So what happens now?"

For a second, Ben wasn't sure what Wade was referring to. "Now?"

Wade pointed to the metal summit marker. "We got here. Now what?"

"We go back down the way we came."

He gaped. "Over all those rocks? Climbing up them was one thing—I don't think I can climb *down* them."

Ben laughed his ass off. "If you could see your face. I'm yanking your chain, Wade. This is a one-way route. *Now*, we follow the signs all the way down the mountain. And it's a much easier route. It'll take us back to the parking lot."

Wade surveyed the horizon. "I'm not gonna forget today."

Ben knew he wasn't talking about the hike. "Neither am I."

Chapter Fifteen

Ben lay in bed, his phone on speaker. The day had left him tired but definitely in a happy place.

"So how did it go?" Aaron asked. "You got home in one piece. That's always a bonus."

"It was such a high. I don't think I've come down yet. Puns intended," he added when Aaron groaned. "Now all I want is to do it again."

"Told you," Aaron said gleefully. "Why do you think I've been pushing you to do that hike? I knew you'd love it."

"It was scary. There were times when we thought we'd fall, but when we got up there…"

"Wait. Whoa. Go back a sec. 'We'?"

Fuck. "Okay, I didn't exactly do it alone."

There was a pause. "Gonna tell me who you did it with?"

"I think you already know the answer to that."

Silence, then Aaron's hushed whisper came out of the speaker. "No. Freaking. Way. You took *Wade*? Wow. I didn't expect that."

"It wasn't exactly my idea—well, I told him about it, then Gramps kinda took control—but it worked out well. I think he needed today as much as I did. And once we got to the top, we talked some more."

"Talking is good. And you two have more to talk about than most people." Aaron snickered. "I take it the talking went okay? I mean, he came down the mountain under his own steam, right? You didn't throw him off the top."

Ben laughed. "He made it down okay. And yeah, the talking part was good." He paused. "I told him I accepted his apology, and it wasn't a lie. I guess I'm finally moving on." Ben couldn't deny he felt good about that. They'd taken their time walking down the path from the summit, and by the time they'd reached the parking lot, Ben wasn't ready for the day to be over. Wade had taken him back to Camden, and then he'd gone home to spend time with Gramps.

"So now the two of you are friends? Because this all sounds very friendly."

"Not in the same way *you* guys are my friends, but yeah. I think he could use one of those. I'm not gonna be bringing him to any of our meet-ups though." He couldn't see the others giving Wade a warm reception.

"I'm glad. Not that you wouldn't bring him, I mean—I'm talking about you moving on. Sounds like you're getting your life sorted. A job you love, people you like, a place you love… I couldn't be happier for you. Not everyone gets their shit together."

"Do you think you've got *your* shit together?"

There was a pause before Aaron came back with a response. "I live in Bar Harbor, which I think is my most favorite place in the whole world—not that I've seen much of the world, but based on what I've seen of Maine? Yeah. I do a job I love. Well, *most* days I love it. I get to meet Massholes, this is true. But I also get to meet some great characters. I don't think I could work anywhere else. I think this place has gotten into my *soul*."

"Now all you need is someone to share it with. Someone who loves it just as much as you do. Just don't stop looking for them." Aaron was a good guy. He needed someone as special as he was.

"I could say the same to you. You've got yourself a new friend—now let's find you a boyfriend."

Ben sighed. "I already found him. But don't get your hopes up. It ain't gonna happen."

Aaron's gasp was so loud in the quiet room. "What? Who? You never said."

"Don't get your panties in a twist. He's straight."

Another pause. "We're talking about Wade again, aren't we?"

"Yes, we are. Dylan is the only one I told this to, but… When I was seventeen? I was crushing on someone. Only thing was, he was a bastard. A total asshole, and the *last* person I should have been attracted to, but hey, tell that to my heart. And here we are, years later, and he's even more attractive, and less of an asshole. No matter how many times I tell myself this is going nowhere, I'm still hung up on him."

There was silence for a moment before Aaron spoke. "I don't know what to say. I mean, I'm glad you told me. And I'm sorry. Your dream job doesn't seem quite so idyllic now, if you have to work with someone you want, who will never want you back."

"Yeah, well, them's the breaks." He glanced at the time. "I'd better let you get to bed. You're probably up early in the morning."

"You know it. Sweet dreams."

"At least that's the one place I *can* be with him—in my dreams." They disconnected, and Ben switched his phone to mute. He clicked off the light and lay in the darkness. Only now it wasn't so quiet. *Mrs. Smith is having another party. Yay.* He had half a mind to get out of bed, go downstairs and bang on her door, but right then he was comfortable, he had lube, and there was a gorgeous man waiting for him in the dark.

There was something so illicit about slowly tugging on his dick and imagining it was Wade's hand wrapped around his shaft. Ben rocked his hips, pushing through the funnel of his fingers, eyes closed. He didn't want to see his tiny little apartment—instead, he was out in the open, on the warm rocky bluff that overlooked Sand Beach. The sun felt amazing on his bare chest. There wasn't a soul for miles, except for Wade.

Oh my God, Wade...

Both of them wore jeans, only their flies were open, and Ben had his hand full. He knew any second now there was the likelihood of some hikers stumbling across them, and maybe that accounted for the speed of Wade's hand on Ben's cock.

"Gonna have to work fast." Wade's dark eyes gleamed. "You feel like you're ready to pop."

"Ya think?" Ben groaned as Wade sped up his hand. "Jesus..."

"No, Wade."

Ben rolled his eyes, then glanced down to Wade's crotch. "Whoa. You're big everywhere, ain't ya?"

Wade slowed his hand. "Think you could squeeze that fat dick into your tight little hole?"

A moan fell from Ben's lips. "Aw fuck." He shot hard, his mind already contemplating the delicious stretch. Then he had to stifle a cry as Wade leaned over and sucked on the head of his dick, removing every drop of cum. Ben shivered as Wade flicked the sensitive slit with his tongue.

Ben opened his eyes, shaking, his belly and hand sticky, sweat covering his chest in a thin sheen.

Holy fuck.

Ben told himself Wade wouldn't indulge in dirty

talk.

Wade's cock probably wasn't the size of a small anaconda.

Wade didn't like boys.

Shit, I can dream, right? And speaking of dreams, he wanted to get right back into his.

Ben wanted to see Wade's face when he shot his load.

Ben had an hour to go till his lunch break, but an unexpected attack of the munchies drove him to the office to find his snacks. When he opened the door, he found Wade on the laptop, staring intently at the screen. He'd been there all morning, working on the figures.

"Sorry for disturbing you while you're on your lunch break," Ben murmured as he headed for his backpack.

"Hmm?" Wade glanced up. "Oh, you're fine." Then he went back to whatever was engrossing him. "There's no flow to that," he muttered.

Ben grabbed his bag of Cheez-its.

"Why would you design it like that? Why would *anyone* do it like that? What the hell were they thinking?"

Ben blinked. "You do know it's the first sign of insanity, talking to yourself?"

Wade looked up from the laptop, and gave him an apologetic glance. "I'm sorry."

He chuckled. "Don't apologize. But I *am* intrigued. What on earth are you doing?" He pointed to the laptop. "Can I take a peek at whatever is pissing you off, or is it a secret?"

"No secret." Wade turned the laptop around and Ben gazed at the screen. It appeared to be a home design site.

"O-*kayyy*." Ben helped himself to a mouthful of Cheez-its.

Wade smirked. "Now you want to know what I'm doing on a site like this."

Ben nodded.

"You know Mom said I was looking to move out? Well, I started looking at houses and condos and the like. Trouble is, what *I* was looking at costs an arm and a leg."

Ben swallowed. "What do you want, a mansion? Nine bedrooms, swimming pool, hot tub…"

Wade laughed. "Nothing like that. It's more the *location* that's dictating the price."

"Hang on a sec." Ben stuck his head out of the office door. "Madison? You okay if I take my lunch now?"

"Sure. No problem."

He closed the door, then went over to the fridge they kept in the corner of the office. Ben took out his box of chicken salad, and Wade arched his eyebrows.

"How healthy."

Ben bit his lip. "Man cannot live on Cheez-its alone." He rummaged through his backpack for his fork, then sat in the chair facing Wade. "Okay. Talk to me. Where are you looking that's so expensive?" He stabbed a piece of chicken.

Wade leaned back. "To be honest, I like it around here. I don't want to be too far from Mom and Gramps. And even if I'm overseeing four stores, they're within easy reach of here. But…"

Ben swallowed his chicken. "What's the problem? There must be tons of houses for sale around here."

Wade nodded. "Yes there are. I've seen houses that would be perfect. Where I could look out my window and see the ocean."

"Ahhh." Ben smiled. "*Now* I see the problem. That kind of view comes with a price tag, doesn't it?"

"You said it. We're talking two or three *million* for some of those properties. Mom wants me to use the money my dad left me to buy a house, but it's going be nowhere near *that* much. So I got to thinking. What if I could get *exactly* what I wanted, where I wanted it, for the right price?"

Ben pointed at the laptop with his fork. "Wanna explain the home design sites?"

"When I was in high school, I took drafting. I often troll these sites. Been doing it for years."

Ben chuckled. "Yeah. Telling them they haven't built it right. Or you could have done it better."

Wade laughed. "I know it sounds crazy. Somebody my age even *thinking* about having a home custom-built. It's not like I've lived in a lot of other places—we're talking two—and have much to compare it with. Going down this route is something an older person would do."

Ben stared at him. "Says who? Finn Anderson—he went to high school with us—went on to become a carpenter. He builds houses up and down the coast. Right now he's building a hotel in Kennebunkport.

He's our age, and he dreams of building his own house."

Wade closed the laptop. "I'll keep looking for a house. I might have to compromise on the location, but I'll find something. It's not like I'm in a hurry to move out, right?"

Ben speared another piece of chicken. "I know what you mean about prices. You should've seen me trying to find a place to live in Camden. That's why I ended up living in a shoebox apartment."

"Is it really that small?"

Ben snorted. "So small, I have to step outside it to change my mind." He chewed his food, trying to ignore the glimmer of an idea that had just come to him. *That's crazy.* But it wouldn't go away.

Wade got up from his chair. "I'm done for today. Well, here at least." He picked up his laptop and stowed it in its bag.

"Another store to visit, another piece of the empire to build."

Wade laughed. "I wouldn't call four stores an empire." He slipped his arms into his jacket. "By the way… I really loved that hike. Do you think…?"

When nothing else was forthcoming, Ben gave him an inquiring glance. "Go on. Finish the sentence." Wade's hesitation was almost cute.

"Could we do something like that again?"

Ben had nailed it in that conversation with Aaron. *He really does need a friend.* "Sure. How about next time, we do the Ocean Path? It'll take just as long, but it's on the flat, with a route that hugs the coastline."

He smiled. "I like the sound of that. Let's do it."

Ben chuckled. "What—no directive from Gramps this time to get you to do it?" Wade laughed. "And how about this time *I* get us there?"

"On your motorcycle?"

Ben grinned. "Come on. Live a little." Wade gave an exaggerated swallow, and Ben burst out laughing. "Okay, I promise not to go *too* fast."

"It's a deal. Let's pick a day when neither of us is working, and then we'll make plans."

Ben *really* liked the sound of that.

"And now I'll leave you to finish your lunch in peace. See you tomorrow."

Once Wade had gone, Ben pulled out his phone.

I wonder…

Wade clung to the seat, his fingers digging into the padding. "Want to tell me where we're going?" he yelled as they rode along Route 1. All Ben had said the previous night in his call was that he wanted to take Wade for a ride before work the following day. Intrigued, Wade had said yes. When Ben had appeared at the end of the driveway, gotten off the motorcycle, and removed a second helmet from the box at the back, he was even more intrigued, especially when Ben wouldn't tell him their destination, merely promising to have him home in plenty of time before Ben would need to go to the shop.

They headed north out of Camden, the sun was

rising over the Atlantic, and the sky was a stunning mix of colors—red, orange and gold. It was his first time on a motorcycle, and he got the impression Ben was taking it easy on him.

"We're almost there," Ben hollered back.

"Fine, but almost where?" They were about ten minutes from Camden, and there wasn't much to see, apart from trees to their left, and the ocean to their right. They passed a few houses here and there, and a health center.

Then Ben slowed and indicated a right turn. He pulled off Route 1 and onto a narrow dirt road. When he came to a dead stop and switched off the engine, Wade gazed at their surroundings.

What the hell?

"This is it." Ben got off.

Wade clambered off the bike and removed his helmet. "Yes, but what are we doing here?"

Ben took off his helmet and ran his fingers through his hair. "Welcome to Lincolnville."

Wade smiled. "There's not a whole lot to see in Lincolnville."

Ben beckoned with his finger. "Come this way." He led Wade along the rough road.

"This mysterious act is driving me crazy," Wade remarked. There was nothing to see but trees, and ahead of them was the glint of morning sunlight on the ocean.

"All will be revealed, I promise."

He snorted. "As long as *we're* not revealing anything."

"The other day when we were talking, you got me thinking."

"Uh-oh. Should I be worried?" What filled him

with elation was not the ride along the coast, but the way Ben was interacting with him.

I never thought we could have this. Since their hike, there was an ease to their relationship. *Except we don't have a relationship.*

What he had was a *friend*, and that was fine by Wade. It was the closest he'd get to what he really wanted, but that was a pipe dream, and he knew it.

I'll settle for a friend.

Ben laughed. "Patience." They walked along the road until at last they faced the ocean. "How's that for a view?"

"Pretty damn amazing." Wade could stare at it for hours. There was something about the ocean that pulled him. He loved all its moods: the calm *and* the storm.

"Imagine stepping out onto your front porch and seeing that. Or opening your bedroom window and hearing the sound of the waves."

Wade chuckled. "Oh, *I* get it now. You've brought me out here to torture me."

Ben turned to face him. "On the contrary. I've brought you here to give you hope."

Wade had no clue what to make of that statement.

Ben pointed to where he'd left the bike. "There's a sign back there. Not sure if you noticed it. This land is for sale."

Wade scanned their surroundings. "I don't see any boundaries. How much of it are we talking about?"

"A little more than two acres."

Wade huffed. "I can just imagine what the asking price is for the lot."

Ben's eyes gleamed. "How does sixty-nine thousand grab you?"

Wade gaped at him. "Seriously?"

Ben nodded. "That's the asking price for the lot. 2.08 acres to be precise. Now, I have no idea how much it costs to build a house, but I'm pretty sure it wouldn't require millions to build something big enough for your needs. Those houses you were looking at on that site… They weren't huge. We're talking cute little Cape Cod cottages." Ben folded his arms. "So here's my idea. I'm not saying buy *this* lot, but change your thinking. Go with your gut. Start looking at *land* for sale, rather than houses. When you find a lot you're happy with, I know someone who will build your house for you. Probably. And if he's busy, he'll know someone else who can."

It took a moment for his words to sink in. "You're serious."

Ben nodded. "And you love the idea."

Wade grinned. "Fuck yeah. That's definitely worth considering." He glanced around at the empty land. A little way off he could see houses, but nothing too close. Two acres sounded like a lot. *But that view….*

"How long does it take to build a house?"

Ben's eyes twinkled. "How long is a piece of string? I don't know the answer, but I know a man who does." He put his helmet back on. "And now I've messed with your head, it's back to reality. I have work, remember?"

Wade stared at him. "You expect me to concentrate on work after dropping this in my lap?

He wanted to get onto his laptop and find the perfect house plan.

Chapter Sixteen

Ben, Mary, and Wade stood in the middle of the store, surveying the available space. Late Saturday afternoon was usually a quiet time, and Cameron and Madison were dealing with what few customers they had.

Mary shook her head. "I still think it's too soon to be considering holiday stock," she said. "We're still in August. And although I love the idea of those tree decorations you were talking about, tell me one thing." She flung out her arm. "Where would you put the display?"

Ben chuckled. "I know where this is coming from." He gave Wade a pointed stare. "You were looking at those online ads for that Christmas store near Niagara Falls, weren't you? I saw ya."

"I still say there's a market to be tapped there." Wade folded his arms. "At least let's think about it. We can order the stock, and do a launch in September, if you prefer to wait a while."

"What kind of stock were you thinking about?" Mary inquired. She moved around the store, nudging here and rearranging there. Ben loved that about her, how she was always searching for ways to make the store look better.

"I've got a catalog. We can take a look at it this evening when we get home."

Mary sighed. "You're determined, I'll say that for

you. And you *are* the general manager. Fine. We'll discuss it. And you *know* Gramps will want to get involved too."

Ben laughed. "That'll be a fun conversation." He liked Gramps's no-nonsense approach to the store.

Mary turned around to smile at him. "Then why don't you come with us, and that way, you get to be a part of it."

He frowned. "If you're going to be talking about the shop, I—"

"Mom's right," Wade interrupted. "You work here every day. Your input is important."

Ben opened his mouth to disagree, and Mary cleared her throat. "Plus, Gramps called to say he's got clam chowder and oyster crackers for us."

Oh my God. "Hey, no fair." He usually grabbed a bowl of soup when he got home, because of the hour, so clam chowder was definitely fighting dirty.

Except I'm not working late tonight. Cameron and Madison were going to close the shop. Ben was already drooling at the thought of the chowder.

Wade chuckled. "I think that's a yes."

"Besides, Gramps was asking about you only this morning," Mary added. "I think he misses your chats."

"I miss them too." Ben knew Gramps had to take things easy, but he hoped they hadn't seen the last of him at the store. "Okay. Clam chowder, crackers, and Christmas. Sounds like a great evening."

Who was he kidding? It sounded awesome. The last time Ben had spoken with his mom, he'd joked that he'd been 'adopted' by the Pearsons. She had no clue what had gone on in high school or the part Wade had played in it—Ben had taken great pains to hide his ordeals and adversities.

It was better that way.

Ben carried the empty bowls out to the kitchen where Wade was loading the dishwasher. "That was amazing. Does Gramps make it often?"

Wade chuckled. "Why do you ask?"

Ben rolled his eyes. "Duh. Because I wanna be here the next time he does it, of course. Mary said she'd like chamomile tea, and Gramps said he wants his new usual, whatever that means."

Wade smiled. "Mom is trying to get him out of the habit of drinking coffee in the evening. He now has this special tea that helps him sleep. At least, that's what it says on the box." He grabbed cups from the drainer. "Want to try it?"

Ben snorted. "Not something I have a problem with. My head hits the pillow and I'm out like a light." Well, *usually* he was. The past week, his mind had been on other pursuits apart from sleeping.

The reason for that was busy making tea.

Mary came into the kitchen. "By the way…" She smirked. "You might have a problem getting into bed tonight."

Wade stilled. "I haven't been in there. What have you done?" No sooner had the three of them walked through the front door at six o'clock, than Gramps declared supper was ready and to 'get your asses to the table.' And once they'd finished, out had come the catalog, and Wade had gotten a lively debate going at the table.

Mary had nailed it. Gramps had a lot to say on the subject.

She bit her lip. "Nothing, really."

"Mom."

Ben smothered a chuckle. He was so used to seeing Mary and Wade interact as manager and employee, that at times he forgot they had a whole other relationship. He supposed Wade took after his dad—Mary wasn't much bigger than Ben—and seeing the tall hunk trying to stare down his diminutive mother was adorable.

And he is *a hunk.*

"Gramps and I got to talking, that's all, and we decided it was time for a clean out. So this morning before I left for work, I went up into the attic, and I took every box marked *Wade* and put it in your bedroom." She gave him a hard stare. "Took me *ages*."

"Mom!" Wade glared at her. "You didn't think there were already *enough* boxes in there? You had to add more?"

She beamed. "Now you have no excuse." And with that, she left the kitchen, calling out, "I'll have my tea in the living room, thank you."

Ben gave Wade as innocent a gaze as he could manage. "Is there a problem?"

Wade scowled. "Just my mom being a—" He lowered his voice. "PITA, that's all. She knows I hate doing that shit."

"What shit would that be?" As if he didn't have a fairly good idea.

"Throwing stuff out. You never know when something's going to come in handy."

Ben took a step back, his mouth open. "Oh my God," he said in a tone of mock horror.

"What?"

"You're a *hoarder*."

Wade chuckled. "And your point is?"

Ben shook his head. "No, no, no. You have to learn to be ruthless. Brutal, even. You should see my apartment. Minimalist doesn't even come close. When I first left home, I got rid of so much stuff."

Wade poured boiling water into the cups. "I'm happy for you. But that's not me, okay?"

Ben grinned. "I bet I could look at all your crap—I mean, stuff—and decide instantly whether it's a keeper, Goodwill, or the dumpster."

Wade looked him in the eye. "I accept."

"Huh?"

"I'm hiring your services. You're going to help me sort out my cra—stuff." His eyes twinkled.

"You're serious."

"Serious about what?" Mary poked her head around the kitchen door. "Gramps sent me to see what's taking so long with the tea. He said at this rate, he'll fall asleep before he has time to drink it."

"Ben is going to help me sort through my boxes," Wade declared. "Apparently, he's an expert at it."

Wade's teasing tone and amused expression sealed the deal. "Fine. I will."

Mary let out a smothered gasp. "I think you should take a look at the scale of the problem before you let Wade railroad you into helping him. I really wasn't exaggerating about how much there is."

"Show me." Ben was *not* going to let Wade win

this one. He locked gazes with him. "You think I'm gonna back out, don't ya?"

"If you're wise, you will," Mary murmured. "Step this way."

He followed her out of the kitchen and along the hallway, Wade behind them. She paused at one of the doors. "Brace yourself." Mary pushed it open.

Ben peered inside. "Holy sh—"

Mary laughed. "Believe me, I expected you to come out with far worse. But seeing as you're here, take a look. *I'll* deal with the tea. That way, we might actually get some in the remaining few hours before bedtime tonight."

Ben stepped into the room. "There's a bed in here somewhere, right?" he joked. There were boxes piled against the wall, at the end of the bed, under the desk, under the window… He turned to Wade and gaped at him. "I take it back. You're not a hoarder. You're a *mega*-hoarder." Then he scanned the room once more. "And I bet most of this can be thrown out."

"We'll see. Why don't you pick a box, and cast your expert eye over it?" Wade grinned.

"You're on." Ben grabbed the nearest box, set it on the bed, then sat next to it. He pried open the flaps and peered inside. "Oh dear *Lord*."

"What? What have you found?"

Ben carefully removed the lump of fired modeling clay. "What is this supposed to be?"

Wade bit his lip. "It's a crocodile. I made it in kindergarten."

Ben tried not to laugh. "It's the weirdest-shaped crocodile I've ever seen." He placed it on the bed and gazed at it dispassionately. "Okay. Dumpster."

"What?"

Ben gaped at him. "Oh, come *on*. If it was a magnificent artistic masterpiece, I'd say yes, in a heartbeat, but it doesn't even *look* like a crocodile. Hell, I had to ask what it was." He reached into the box again, and this time pulled out a block of plaster. "And this?" He set it down on the comforter.

"That's a plaster print of my palm."

Ben arched his eyebrows. "And you were *how old* when you made this?"

"Five." A note of belligerence had crept into Wade's voice. "Mom made me keep it."

Ben folded his arms. "And when Mary goes—eventually—you'll get it, and you'll *still* keep it. Because this is what you do." He gestured to the boxes. "As I am now learning." Ben picked up the plaster block and handed it to him. "Dumpster."

"What?"

Ben smirked. "You're saying that a lot tonight. And what are you gonna do with it? Keep it so you can say, 'Gee, hasn't my *hand* gotten bigger since first grade?"

"I've changed my mind," Wade announced. "We're not doing this now. It's late. You should probably go home."

"What—no tea?" Ben was starting to enjoy this. "And it's not late. It's only eight o'clock." He got the message, however. "Okay, so how about we go through *one box*? Hmm? That way we'll have made a start." He glanced around him. "One down, many, *many* more to go."

"Sure. This box."

Ben cackled. "Oh no, you don't. I meant a whole *other* box."

"What else is in this one?"

Ben peered inside. "I'll be honest. I think we could just cut out the middle man and take all of it to the dumpster right now." He picked up the box and thrust it at Wade. "Mark that one with an X. We're done with it." He reached for another.

"Man, you weren't kidding when you said I needed to be brutal." Wade rubbed his bearded jaw. "I'm seeing you in a whole new light."

"Hey, don't mock. You *need* my skills." Ben grinned. "And I need tea. So be off with you, slave."

Wade tugged on that bit of his hair that stuck out at the front. "Yes, sir." He left the room, chuckling.

Ben smiled to himself as he opened the next box. *Man, he needs me.* Not in the way Ben *wanted* Wade to need him, but hey, he'd take what he could get.

The second box was full of… *are those notes from Calculus?* There were text books and more paper in there, and several thin hardcover books that he recognized instantly. Ben pulled one free of the box, unable to stop smiling. *He kept the yearbooks.* Then he chuckled. Wade had kept *everything.* On the front cover was the school photo, all the students in one group, the faculty staff standing at each side. Ben peered at it, trying to remember where he'd been for that final photo. He knew he was close to the front. *Along with all the other short kids.*

Ben had thrown out *his* copy years ago. *Oh man, that photo of me was horrendous.* He leafed through the glossy pages, searching for it. *Maybe it wasn't as bad as I remember.* When he came to the right page, he froze.

What. The. Everlovin'. Fuck*?*

Next to Ben's photo, someone had stuck another. It was Wade, carefully cut around the outline. But what stopped him cold was the crude heart that encapsulated them, drawn in red pen, over and over again.

"Fuck!" A cup bounced on the rug, tea spilling all over it.

Ben jerked his head up, to find Wade staring at him, aghast. Ben held up the yearbook. "You wanna explain this?"

Wade's face was ashen, his lips trembling. He crouched to pick up the cup, his hands shaking.

Ben swallowed. "What kind of sick joke was this?"

"No… no joke." Wade's voice cracked. "I *can* explain, I promise."

"Yeah?" Ben held the book open against his chest. "Look at this. *Look* at it. *You* did this."

Wade nodded.

"Why?"

His chest rose and fell rapidly. "Isn't it obvious?"

Ben blinked. "Seriously? You've got the two of us together in a doodle of a heart, like you had some high school *crush* on me…" When Wade froze, his lips parted, Ben's pulse sped up, and heat flushed though him. "You are fucking *kidding* me. You're *not* gonna feed me some *bullshit* about you bullying me because you were too chicken shit to tell me you *wanted* me?" He got to his feet and dropped the yearbook to the floor, as if touching it burned him. He knew there was a good chance Mary and Gramps had heard every word—it wasn't a big house, and he hadn't bothered to keep his voice down—but right then he was too wound up to give a shit. "You're *not* gonna stand there and feed me some line about how you were crushing on me in high school. Not after all that crap you put me through."

"Wrong tense," Wade croaked.

Ben stared at him. "And what does that mean?"

"I… I *was* crushing on you back then… but… I still am." Those last three words were barely a whisper.

Heat threatened to engulf him. He couldn't think, couldn't *breathe*…

None of it made any fucking *sense*.

Ben needed air. He needed space to think. And he couldn't get either of those while he was staring at Wade.

"I'll be back." He pushed past Wade and headed for the door.

"You… you're leaving?"

Ben whirled around. "Did I stutter? I *said* I'll be back, didn't I? Right now I'm not sure when that will be, exactly. But when I do come back, we are gonna talk." He stilled. "I say we, but *you'll* be the one doing all the talking." And then he was out of there.

He walked into the living room and Gramps stared at him in obvious concern. "Everything okay, son?"

"Not really, no." That was about as much as Ben could manage. He grabbed his jacket from where he'd left it on a chair.

Mary gazed at him with wide eyes. "Ben, maybe you should—"

He held up his hand. "Maybe I should *nothing*. I'm not the one you should be speaking to. I'll be back when I've gotten my head around this." He went to the front door, and then he was outside, shivering and putting on his jacket because the evening air was cool on his bare arms.

Ben got to the end of the driveway and sat on the

low stone wall that ran along the front of the property. He put his head in his hands, shaking.

What the fuck?

Chapter Seventeen

Wade stumbled out of his room, in time to hear the front door close.

Aw fuck.

What were the odds on Ben finding *that*? Not that it mattered anymore. The cat was out of the bag—the box.

"Wade?" Gramps sounded pissed.

He walked into the living room. Gramps had switched off the TV and was staring at him. Mom stood by the window, peering through the curtains.

"He's just sitting there. I'll go—"

"Leave him. And come away from the window." Wade forced as much strength into his voice as he could muster. Mom jerked her head to look at him, her eyes wide.

Gramps narrowed his gaze. "What did you do, boy?"

Fucked everything up, that's what.

His phone buzzed in his pocket, and when he peered at the screen and saw Ben's name, his heartbeat raced. He clicked *Answer*, not daring to speak.

"Changed my mind. I'm not in the right frame of mind to talk about this right now. I'm going home."

"But… you came here in my car. How are you going to—"

"I'll walk."

"Let me take you there?"

"No," Ben fired back at him without a second of hesitation. "I need to walk until I'm not pissed anymore." He snorted. "I might have reached Bar Harbor by the time *that* happens."

"But… we're still going to talk?"

"You got that right. You have a lot of explaining to do." He disconnected.

Wade shivered. He pocketed his phone, went over to the liquor cabinet, poured himself a finger of whiskey, and tossed it back as if it was soda.

When he exploded into a coughing fit, Gramps regarded him dispassionately. "Why, sure. Help yourself to *my* whiskey. As if *that'll* solve anything. Sit your ass down and start talkin'."

Mom turned back to the window, and Wade wiped his lips before calling out, "Don't bother looking. He's gone." The words croaked out of him.

She brought her hand to her chest. "He said he wasn't the one I should be speaking to. What did he mean by that?"

Wade sank onto the couch. "There's something I need to tell you." His pulse raced, and the sound of his heartbeat thrashed in his ears. Pain spread through his chest, and he struggled to breathe. Gramps had been right—the whiskey had solved nothing.

Gramps cocked his head to one side. "This is not about you bein' gay, is it? Because we already talked about this, and if you think this is news to your mom, think again. Ain't no foolin' a mother, son."

Wade whipped his head to gape at her. "You… you knew?"

Mom bit her lip. "Not for certain, until now. But yes, I had an idea. The clues were there, but when you made no move to talk about it…" She sat beside him on the couch. "See? It wasn't as bad as you thought it would be, right?"

"Oh, Mom. If only." He leaned forward, his head in his hands. He couldn't look at either of them. "I need to tell you both about what happened… in high school." When Mom reached for his hand, Wade jerked away from her. "No. You need to hear this first."

"How bad can it be?" she said softly.

"As bad as it gets." He stared at the rug under his feet. "Everything I went through when I was a kid, all that pain and anguish… you'd think it would've taught me something, but no. I fell into the same trap as the dickheads who teased me. I made other kids' lives hell."

Silence fell, broken only by the ticking of Gramps's clock. Finally Mom spoke.

"You… you were a bully? In high school?"

He nodded, unable to meet his mom's gaze. "Picking on others kept the spotlight on them, not me. I only did it to protect myself, to hide. Lord, I was mean. I never once used my fists—I didn't have to. I used my height, my weight, my build, every physical weapon I had, to intimidate them. I jeered and taunted them. Better them than me, right? Because God forbid they saw through me, to what I really was."

"You thought bein' gay made you less of a person?" Gramps's voice was filled with incredulity.

All Wade could do was nod.

"I knew you were insecure, but to turn around and do the exact same thing those dubbers did to you…" Gramps pushed out a heavy sigh. "Disappointed in you, son. Thought you were made of better stuff than that."

"I'm sorry." God, the words seemed so fucking *inadequate.*

"So what criteria did you use to pick on these kids?"

The hard edge to Mom's voice went through him, and he raised his chin to meet flinty eyes. "I—"

"Were they overweight, like you'd been?"

"Some of them. Some were quiet, not into sports…" He'd picked on *anything* he perceived as a weakness.

She nodded. "And maybe some of them were gay?"

His heart pounded. "Some, yeah."

"So why was that? Why go after *them*? You were so insecure about your own sexuality, you saw any sign that someone might be the same way inclined as some kind of *affront*? You made them feel bad about the very thing that plagued you?" She locked gazes with him. "Was there anyone in particular who got more of your attention than most?"

It was as if he'd run into a wall of ice. *She knows about Ben.*

As if to prove she'd read his thoughts, Mom shuddered. "But you didn't break him, did you? Not like *you* were broken, when you were just a little boy. You tried to make him feel that being gay was something to be hidden. That liking boys was *wrong*."

"Mom, I—"

"Ben told me about being bullied in high school. He never said your name, not once, but he told me *why* he was bullied. And hearing you talk… *Now* it all makes sense. That flash of nerves I saw, the day of his interview. I can tell you precisely when it happened." Her eyes blazed. "It was when I mentioned your name. And that boy *still* went in there and faced you. He has more guts than I thought."

Wade swallowed. *He has more guts than I* ever *had.*

"Wait just a minute here." Gramps sat up straight in his chair. "That commotion we heard just now. What was that about? I didn't catch what Ben said, I only know he was pissed."

"He… found something. And he learned how I'd felt about him back then." Another hard swallow. "How I *still* feel about him."

"Damn." Gramps expelled a long breath. "You weren't kiddin' when you said it was complicated."

Mom caught her breath. "You hired him to make amends, didn't you?"

He nodded. "That was my only intention, I swear. I was never going to let him know how I felt. I just wanted to make things right." His chest ached, and his mouth was dry.

For a moment, Mom stared at him in silence, and Wade yearned to take her hand and promise he'd changed beyond recognition from the poor, sad individual he'd been in high school.

She drew in a deep breath. "Okay. Two things I have to say. The first is… you want to show us you've learned from this? Talk to your brother."

He frowned. "I'm not telling David about this. He doesn't need to know."

"Yes, he does. Because right now, your only nephew is suffering, the way *you* suffered, and David's idea of handling the situation is to tell Liam to stop crying and man up. To act more like the other kids. Man up? He's *eight years old,* for Christ's sake."

Wade saw the light. "You think I can help."

She nodded. "Do whatever you need to, to get

David to understand his son, and how to help him."

Wade seized on it. "I can do that." He gazed at her, his heart hammering. "And the second thing?"

She got up from the couch, went into the hallway, and returned with Wade's car keys that he'd left on the small table like he always did. She dropped them into his hand. "You get in that car, you go after that boy, and you *fix* this."

"How? You didn't see his face, Mom."

"And *you* seem to have forgotten what else we discussed," Gramps interjected. "About a certain someone watchin' *you* almost as much as you were watchin' *him*? Well, now he knows how you feel. Let's see what happens next." He coughed. "And you can't see from *here*, sittin' on your butt. Do what your mom tells ya, and go fix this."

Wade curled his fingers around the keys. "You're right."

"You need to do this," Mom stressed. "You and Ben work together. Now, how are you going to do *that*, with something like this hanging over you?"

And that was what got him on his feet. The thought of working in close proximity, with the tension so thick, he'd need a *chainsaw* to cut through it.

Hell no.

"I'll go after him." Wade got to his feet and went in search of his jacket.

"And what if he isn't home?" Gramps called out. "What if he's gone—"

"Then I will drive around Camden until I find him, okay?" He walked back into the living room, in time to see Gramps give a satisfied nod.

"Okay then."

"Good luck." Mom's brow was furrowed.

"I'll fix this, I promise." Then he went out to the car, his heartbeat racing. He didn't have a clue what he was going to say when he caught up with Ben.

This really is a case of playing it by ear.

He hoped to God Ben had calmed down.

Ben sat on the bench, his phone in his hands. He'd sent a text to both Aaron and Dylan, to ascertain who was available to talk. Aaron's reply *pinged* back first.

Sitting down with my feet up and a bowl of chili.

Then Dylan replied. *Watching TV before I go to the hotel. On at eleven.*

Ben called Aaron first. "Can you talk *and* eat chili?"

Aaron laughed. "I don't care what they say about most guys—*this* guy can multitask."

"Hang on a sec. Adding Dylan to this call."

"Okay. In that case, the chili can wait. I'll reheat it. This sounds important."

Ben peered at the screen, clicked on *Add Call.* He dialed Dylan's number, then clicked *Merge Call.*

"Wow. We haven't done this in ages, not since Seb called us all that time while he was watching—"

"Not now, okay?" Ben hadn't intended for that to come as harshly as it did. "Sorry. But I just came from an epic shit show, and I need to talk."

"What's that sound? Are you calling from in the shower or something? I can hear running water," Dylan commented.

He sighed. "I'm sitting in Harbor Park, on a bench, looking at Megunticook Falls, and my head is about to explode."

"What happened?" Aaron's voice was quiet.

"You remember how I wanted to know why Wade had me in his sights? Well, tonight I got my answer, and I'm confused as fuck. There were *so many possibilities* running around my head, but believe me—this was the *last* one I'd ever considered."

"Just tell us, all right?" Dylan demanded.

"So there I was, working alongside him, kicking myself for perving on a straight guy, when I discover not only is he *not* straight, the fucker *likes* me—he liked me back then, while he was treating me like shit."

Crickets.

"Guys? We got a bad connection?"

"When you say he *likes* you… are you saying what I *think* you're saying?" That was Aaron.

"Wade is gay?" Dylan chimed in.

"So what does this change?" Aaron again.

Ben blinked. "Everything?"

"No, hear me out. I get that you're dealing with some very conflicted emotions right now, but—"

"Ya think? Wow. Maybe you're right. Let's do a quick assessment. Elation—yay, he's gay and he likes me. Shock—*fuck*, he's gay and he likes me. Anger—What the fuck? He was gay then, and he picked on *me* for being gay because he couldn't own up to his own desires. And let's not forget confusion, as in… where the *fuck* does that leave us?"

"Before the shit hit the fan… you two were in a good place?" Aaron asked.

"Yes, but—"

"And you *said* he's changed," Dylan added.

"Yes, but—"

"So what's pissing you off is you don't still have all the answers," Aaron concluded.

"Not yet, but I'm gonna. You can trust me on that score."

"It sorta makes sense now," Aaron observed.

"On what planet?" Ben stared at the screen.

"In a kind of twisted, elementary school way. Based on what you told me about him, Wade was obviously overcompensating for his own insecurities. And once you calm down, you'll realize this is *not* the big deal you think it is."

"How do you work that out?"

"Yeah, I wanna hear that part too," Dylan commented.

Aaron sighed. "You'd already worked through so much. You'd be the first to admit he's not the same person. Well, neither are you. You are *so much more* now than that scared teenager. You came through all that, but it's in the past. So now the question is… what is in your future? What do you *want* there to be in your future?" Before Ben could reply, Aaron forged ahead. "Because I know if you asked Dylan, Noah, Seb, any of your closest friends, they'd all say the same thing. They'd want you to be happy, because you fucking *deserve* that."

Ben's throat seized up, and tears pricked the corners of his eyes.

"We already know how you feel about Wade," Dylan said in a low voice. "Well, congratulations. It seems he feels the same way about you. So here's the million-dollar question—are you going to forgive him?"

"Forgive him?"

"This isn't rocket science, Ben. You either tell him to take a hike and you quit your job—because no *way* can you carry on working with him—*or…* you forgive him, and you find out if you two have a future together."

"Just one thing about that," Aaron added. "If you *do* decide to forgive him, you need to consider carefully. It's okay saying *now* 'Yes, I forgive you', but if there's the remotest possibility that five, ten years from now, you're going to throw all this back in his face? That's a hard no. Forgiveness must mean exactly that—*true* forgiveness."

"So I guess the question is, are you gonna hold it against him?" Dylan snickered. "Okay, that sounded *way* dirtier than I intended."

Ben sucked in a deep breath. "You two have given me a lot to think about. So you know what? I'm gonna go home and do just that. Thanks, guys."

"Any time," Dylan said warmly.

"You'd do the same for any of us," Aaron said.

"You know it." He thanked them again, then disconnected the call. Ben got up from the bench, pulled his jacket around him, and headed back into the center of town, his head in a whirl.

Talk about food for thought.

He walked past Mainely Treasures, and stopped to look in the window. Inside, Cameron was sweeping the hardwood floor, and Madison was putting out more tote bags. Ben debated going in, but his head was wrecked, and he wanted to go home. He headed for Elm Street.

A car drove past him on the other side of the street, then did a U-turn and came up beside him. Ben glanced at it, then realized it was Wade's.

Oh God.

Wade lowered the window, and before he could get a word out, Ben leaned in. "How did you know where I'd be?"

"Are you kidding? I went to your apartment, but your landlady said you weren't home. I checked your motorcycle was still there, then I drove into town. I've been driving around in circles, trying to find you." Wade swallowed. "Get in, and I'll take you home."

"I'm fine."

"Ben, please?"

That touch of desperation in Wade's voice was enough to make him reconsider.

Besides, you wanted to talk, right? What better place than his own apartment? Ben's home ground, where he was the one who called the shots.

"Okay," Ben said at last. "As long as you know you're not leaving my place until we've talked."

"That was the whole idea of coming to find you."

Ben got in, Aaron's words still playing in his head.

What is in your future? What do you want there to be in your future?

It wasn't a matter of *what* he wanted, but more a *who*.

Chapter Eighteen

Wade's roiling stomach and tight chest all pointed to one thing.

I'm dreading this.

It had been a while since he'd suffered from them, but the familiar sensations were back with a vengeance.

"My place is on the top floor," Ben said as he led him through the house. He tiptoed past the first door on the left, and before Wade could ask why on earth he was doing that, it opened, and a lady stuck her head out.

"Good evening, Mrs. Smith. Just taking my friend here up to the apartment. No, we won't make any noise. No, we're not having a party. Good night, Mrs. Smith." Ben sped up, and Wade quickened his steps, taking the stairs in long strides. When they reached Ben's door, Ben rolled his eyes. "I swear, she has motion detectors under the carpet in the hallway." He opened the door and pushed it open.

Once inside, Wade gazed at the studio apartment." I see what you mean about it being tiny." He liked the sloping ceiling above the bed and the cute little window with a couch under it.

"Okay, that's enough small talk." When Wade turned to stare at him, Ben arched his eyebrows. "Unless you're looking for a similar place, and frankly, I wouldn't recommend it. You can do better than this." He drew in a deep breath, then looked Wade in the eye. "You're nervous. I can understand that, but I got a newsflash for you—so am I." He went over to the kitchen. "I'm gonna get myself a glass of water. Do you want one?"

"Yes, please." That supposed Wade could swallow. His throat was tight.

Ben gestured to the couch. "Take a seat."

Wade sat, his heart pounding. "I need to tell you some things."

Ben paused as he removed two glasses from the cabinet above the sink. "Okay, first of all, gimme a chance to calm the fuck down, all right? My mind's been spinning at a mile a minute since I left your place." He expelled a breath. "No, that's not right. I *am* calm—*now*—but I need a moment to collect my thoughts." He lifted his eyebrows again. "I mean, you gave me a lot to think about, right?" He turned on the faucet. "Hope this is okay. I ran out of the bottled variety. I was gonna go shopping tomorrow."

"It's fine," Wade assured him. "You… you said first of all."

Ben nodded. "Yeah. My second point is… If it helps, I don't think you're gonna say anything that'll come as a shock. Well, a bigger shock than I've already had tonight." He filled the glasses, then walked over to the couch. After handing one to Wade, he sat at the other end, and Wade's heart was heavy with dismay.

We sat closer than this at the top of Champlain Mountain.

He knew he should say something, but he wasn't sure where to start.

"I think I've put two and two together," Ben said after taking a drink. "Just by adding up stuff you've already told me, plus some things I worked out for myself. But man, you blindsided me tonight."

"I'm sorry." Wade suspected it would be the first apology of many.

Ben scraped his fingers through his unruly hair, and not for the first time Wade ached to smooth it, stroke it. "You know what? My friends nailed it. Before this all came out, we were in a good place."

"And I ruined all that."

"Not sure 'ruined' is the word I'd use. I mean, it can't be wrong that I finally know the truth. Okay, learning it that way wasn't exactly ideal. You could've *told* me, for one thing."

Ben's words sank in. "Wait—you've been talking to your friends about me?"

Ben nodded. "You've been a hot topic of conversation. I needed a sounding board."

Wade's stomach roiled. "I see. I guess I don't need to ask which friends." He knew the crowd Ben had hung around with. One student in particular stuck in his mind. Seb Williams wouldn't have held back on his opinion of Wade.

And I don't want to think about what Ben said to them.

"Only four of them. And they made a lot of sense."

"I bet they gave good advice too." Wade could almost hear their voices.

'Quit your job. You can't work with that asshole.'

'After all the crap he put you through? Is he for fucking real?'

'You told him what you thought of him, right?'

"Actually, they did. Which is why you're sitting on my couch right now, and not on your way home with a flea in your ear."

That gave him pause.

Ben studied him in silence for a moment, and the close scrutiny made Wade squirm. *Please, say something. Give me some hope here. Tell me I haven't lost my only friend.*

"I've been thinking about how you were in high school," Ben said at last. "Damn, that was a good disguise. Totally fooled me. But then again, I should have known. I mean, you see it all the time nowadays. All these politicians, these people who sound off about how the gays are destroying marriage, how they're behind every natural disaster and God knows what else… And then, much later, you discover the person coming out with all this crap? Is in the closet. There's some leaked sex tape, somebody speaks to the press, someone sees them on Grindr, and it *all* comes out."

Wade took a drink, his hand shaking a little. "I couldn't let you see the real me."

Ben widened his eyes. "Why not? Was it just because the real you was gay? Was being gay *so bad*?"

"Oh, come *on*," Wade exclaimed. "Who did I hang around with? I played ball. I was a big guy. Look at the cliques I was part of. Can you imagine even *one* of those guys coming out?"

"So you decided you'd hide in plain sight."

"That's it, exactly." Wade felt sick to his stomach. "I can only apologize again for the way I treated you." He'd apologize for as long as it took to get Ben to believe him—again. *He's right. We were doing so well.*

"Can we talk about the yearbook?"

"That's why I'm here, right?" Wade sighed. "I really had forgotten all about it. When I walked in there, and found you…"

"You wanna know the weird part? If I'd found

my photo covered with a few choice homophobic slurs, I think that would've been less of a shock." Ben shook his head. "This is such a mind fuck."

"I never intended for you to know how I felt." His stomach churned.

"Doesn't matter. It's out now."

"But it should have come out *then*. *I* should have come out. You have no idea how many times since high school I've told myself that if I'd just had the courage to say something, *do* something, my life could have been so different."

Ben sat back, stretching his legs out in front of him. "And supposing you had. Would you have asked me out on a date?"

Christ…

Ben regarded him thoughtfully, as if he was rolling something over and over in his mind. Finally he spoke. "Another newsflash for you. Back then? I'd have said yes."

Wade's world came to a grinding halt. He took a sharp intake of breath, his chest tingling.

Ben nodded. "Yeah, I know it makes no sense. You treated me like shit, and yet you were my first crush. How fucked up is that? So while I might not have known for sure that I was gay, I think if the guy I was crushing on had asked me out, I'd have said yes." He gave a sad smile. "I guess we'll never know for certain, right?"

"But… why me?" He couldn't move, unable to take it all in. *This isn't real.*

Ben blinked. "Have you looked in a mirror lately?"

"But we're not talking now, we're talking about *then*." What Ben described was beyond fucked up—

and more than Wade had ever dared to hope.

"Look at me. I'm short, skinny... But if I think back on all the guys I found attractive? Yeah, they were all big. And I don't mean they were all muscle. We're talking height, build… The kind of guy I'd look at, and imagine him picking me up in his arms."

That was *way* too close to one of Wade's fantasies.

"When he'd hold me, I'd be *surrounded* by him. I could lose myself in him. And at the time, I felt so bad for feeling that way. Because crushing on the guy who obviously couldn't stand me? That is *so* screwed up."

That only renewed Wade's feelings of self-loathing. "You really believed I hated you, didn't you?"

"Like I said, what a disguise." Ben sighed. "When you graduated, I breathed easier. But guess what? You might have been out of sight, but you've never been far from my mind. Don't get me wrong. I didn't think about you all the time, but yeah, there were moments when you'd creep into my head, like a little shadow. And whatever I'd felt for you got swallowed up in painful memories." Wade winced, and Ben sighed. "Sorry, but that's the truth."

"Don't apologize for being honest." A heaviness settled on his chest and limbs. *Christ, what we could've had…* "I wondered about you so often. I never thought I'd see you again."

Ben flung his arm out. "And yet here I am, living in Camden. I guess you don't shop at Hannaford. Either that, or you don't spend much time in town. I've lived here for a while now."

"I was working most of the time in the other stores. I didn't get to Camden that often. And when I *was* here, I didn't go out." First his studies had consumed him, then work.

Ben frowned. "You've spent a lot of time in the Camden shop since *I've* been working there."

Wade swallowed another mouthful of water. "That's because *you* were there." There was a pain at the back of his throat. "I need to be honest about something. When I saw your résumé, it was a shock. I mean, just seeing your name brought everything back—the way I treated you, and the way you made me feel. And then it came to me. I had the chance to put things right."

Ben narrowed his gaze. "Tell me I got the job on my own merits, not because you wanted to make amends."

"You were the best on paper, I promise. But seeing you that day… Let's just say your performance during the interview reaffirmed my decision. And if you don't believe me, ask Mom about the candidates I interviewed before you. She'll be honest with you."

"Okay, okay, I believe you." Ben's eyes twinkled. "I like that about Mary. She doesn't pull any punches."

"And speaking of punches… That's why I had to find you and put this right. Because if I don't, Mom and Gramps will skin me alive." Wade shuddered. "And I am *not* kidding."

"You told them?" Ben caught his breath. "Or did I? I wasn't exactly quiet, was I?"

"I told them everything. *Then* it turns out my eight-year-old nephew is being bullied at school."

"I know. Mary told me."

Aha. "And that right there tells me a lot." His heart thumped, and there was a knot in his belly. "What else did Mom tell you?"

Ben sat so still. "Why—is there more to tell?"

Wade studied his face. "They want me to talk to Liam and my brother. They think I can help, because…" His heart raced, and his stomach was rock hard, but he'd gotten *this* far… "When I was Liam's age, I was bullied. They teased and taunted me because I was this fat kid, and the teachers said and did nothing until Mom went in there, all guns blazing."

Ben nodded. "And now I'm not surprised you took the route you did."

"What do you mean?"

"I read up on bullying," he said with a shrug. "You said it yourself. They bullied you because you were fat. Did you blame yourself?"

"I…" Wade stared at him, cold spreading from his core. "Yes."

"And then you took the one thing they had over you—your weight—and you tried to change that. How do I know? Because the guy who bullied me back when I was a teenager, was *not* fat." Ben looked him in the eye. "Did you know that people who are bullied, are *twice* as likely to go on to bully others? Maybe you thought that by doing that, no one would pick on you."

Wade sagged against the cushions. "Oh my God." He shivered. Never had he felt so *seen.*

"I can see why Mary would want you to do something. If anyone knows what that kid is going through, it's you. And you're in a prime position to let David know what might happen if Liam doesn't get help. He sounds like a great kid—musical, artistic, sensitive—but if he starts to see those things as bad, and tries to change them, he's setting himself up for problems in the future."

Wade drank the rest of his water and set the glass

down on the floor. "I don't want him to go down the same road I did. Years from now, if he's tormenting other kids because *he* was bullied…"

"We're not all that different, you and me." Ben's eyes were kind. "You bullying me had a long-term impact on my life. Well, guess what? It had the same impact on you. And before you get to kicking yourself too much, let me share something else I gleaned from my reading. A lot of high school bullies *continue* to be bullies when they're adults. *You* broke the cycle. You didn't become another typical asshole adult bully. You changed your behavior, and that speaks *volumes* about you as a person."

"Don't," Wade protested.

"Don't what?"

"Speak about me like that. It sounds like… praise, and I don't deserve it."

Ben regarded him with parted lips. "You listen to me. Credit where credit is due, all right? How many times do I have to say it? You are *not* the same person you were then, and that's down to no one but you. So what if I want to tell you how proud I am of you? It's not as if you can stop me."

Wade's throat squeezed shut, and the tightness in his chest worsened. *I don't deserve to have him as a friend.* He made an effort to breathe more normally, and little by little the constriction lessened.

He felt so *numb*. "You know what I won't miss? The hiding. It became a habit. I don't expect you to feel sorry for me after what I did, and I'm not saying this to gain sympathy, but God, I've been so alone." He fought hard to hold back the onset of tears. *I am* not *going to cry*.

"You needed a friend. I could see that much."

"And when we started to get along, I began to feel hopeful. Maybe we *could* be friends. Nothing more. I have no right to expect more than that. I don't *deserve* more than that." He couldn't get his head around it. *He was crushing… on me?* "Wish I'd known how you felt about me back then."

Ben didn't break eye contact. "Do you really think it would have changed anything? If you're being honest…"

"I don't know. How can I answer that?" He expelled a breath. "I still can't believe you felt that way back then." This had to be the weirdest conversation ever, and the most cathartic.

"It feels good to let it all out, doesn't it?"

Wade shuddered. "Christ, yes." He expelled a long breath. "Thank you."

"For what?"

"Listening. Letting me explain." It was as if he could feel the tension seeping from his body, taking with it the ache he'd carried inside him for so long.

"That's everything, isn't it?"

Wade nodded. "No more secrets to tell."

"And I have all the answers *I* wanted." Ben put his empty glass down. "Think you can deal with a final newsflash?"

Wade gaped at him. "If I'm honest, no. I feel wrung out." *Especially if this is the point where you tell me you're quitting.*

"Well, that's too bad, because I'm gonna tell you anyway. So brace yourself."

Wade was hyper aware of every throb of his heart.

"You said you couldn't believe I felt that way about you back then." Ben's eyes glittered. "Wrong tense."

"I don't understand."

Ben smiled. "Then I'll just have to use your own words to get the message across. Now, what was it you said? 'I was crushing on you back then… and I still am.'"

Holy fuck.

Ben shifted closer. "You didn't expect me to feel anything for you, did you? I mean, after what you put me through?"

"No, I did not." Ben as more than a friend was too much to hope for.

Ben gave a slow nod. "Good. Because I hate being predictable." And before Wade could question what the hell that meant, Ben closed the gap between them and brushed his lips against Wade's, a fleeting yet surprisingly intimate gesture. Then he sat back, his eyes watchful.

Wade tuned out the sound of the traffic outside, the electric hum from Ben's fridge, *everything*, except Ben's face. His eyes.

His lips, which were twitching.

"Did I go too fast? Did I scramble your brain?"

The time for hiding was past. "Kind of, seeing as that was my first kiss."

"Your first—" Ben froze. "No way."

"I said I'd been alone, didn't I?"

"Yeah, but… There's been no one?"

"Not a soul." Wade's heartbeat quickened. "How could I love another person when I couldn't even love myself? When I couldn't say the words, even to my own reflection in the mirror?"

"What words?"

Say them. Just say *them.*

Wade closed his eyes, summoning every ounce of

courage he possessed. A gentle hand caressed his cheek.

"Open your eyes, Wade." He did as instructed, and Ben's sweet face was right there. He smiled. "That's better. Let me see those beautiful eyes." Ben traced the line of Wade's beard with his fingertips. "Okay. Those words you can't say? Let's hear 'em."

Wade took a deep breath. "I'm gay."

Ben's smile widened. "Wow. Me too."

Wade laughed, and the release of tension brought with it a lightness that suffused his whole body. "You walked into that store, more gorgeous than ever, and it was like my guts were in a twist and my heart was going to explode."

Ben bit his lip. "I always could make an entrance." His hand was still there, and Wade didn't want him to remove it.

He took a deep breath. "Okay. You can tell me to fuck off, and I'd totally deserve it, but… you said I've changed and… can we do that again, please?"

Chapter Nineteen

Wade caught his breath as Ben moved in, his fingers on Wade's neck, soft as a whisper. Their lips met, and this time it was no fleeting contact but a solid kiss that lit a fire in him, followed by another, and another. Ben's free hand was on Wade's nape, moving higher to cup his head, his tongue seeking entrance.

Then their noses collided, their foreheads bumped, and the spell was broken.

Wade burst into laughter. "Okay, again?"

Ben chuckled. "I've got an idea." He shifted until he straddled Wade's lap, and the feel of Ben's warm body against his set something fluttering in Wade's chest. He shivered, and he ached with the need to touch. "Stay still," Ben commanded.

"Can I touch you?"

Ben nodded, then cupped Wade's face. "That's it. Your mouth is right where I want it." He leaned in and teased Wade's lips with his tongue before exploring him once again.

Wade opened for him with a low moan, moving his hands to Ben's waist, stroking him through the soft cotton of his tee. Ben's soft sigh mingled with his, and Wade stroked his back, struggling to comprehend the enormity of it all.

He was kissing Ben Freaking White, and it was heaven.

Scratch that—it was overload.

He broke the kiss and leaned in, their foreheads touching. "Whoa. I need to breathe."

Ben chuckled. "Wow. I'm good."

Wade laughed. "Yes, you are, but this is just…"

"I get it." Ben pulled back. "You know what? I'm gonna send you home now."

Wade gaped at him. "Seriously?"

Ben cleared his throat. "You have the keys in the morning, mister. And Mary will tan your hide if you're not outside that shop at eight, bright-eyed and bushy-tailed." He moved in slowly, pressing his lips to Wade in a sweet kiss. "This can wait. We got time."

"We've got years to catch up on," Wade complained.

"And we will, only not tonight." Ben placed his hand over Wade's heart. "Lord, it's pounding away in there."

"And that surprises you?" Wade covered Ben's hand with his.

That earned him another kiss. "It's gonna happen, okay? I can promise you that." Ben leaned in closer, and when his lips touched Wade's neck, Wade shivered.

Ben sat back. "Oops, I got another newsflash for you." He grinned. "Sitting like this is giving me *all* kinds of ideas, so you need to go, right now."

Wade laughed. "That's a little difficult when you're pinning me to the couch."

Ben scrambled off him, and helped him to his feet. "Home. Before I change my mind."

"You're right. Besides, I need Mom and Gramps to see I'm still alive."

Ben laughed. "Good point."

Wade didn't want to go. He stood in front of Ben,

his heartbeat still racing. Wade tilted Ben's face up toward his, and bent to kiss him on the lips, a leisurely, tender, *this is a just getting started* kiss.

Ben let out a heavy sigh. "You don't make it easy, do you? I'm trying to be an adult here." Then he looped his arms around Wade's neck and locked their lips in a kiss. When they parted, Ben picked up Wade's jacket, handed it to him, then took his hand and walked him to the door. "You know the way out. Just be careful when you go past Mrs. Smith's door. Remember the motion sensors."

Wade chuckled. "I'll see you at work tomorrow."

Ben nodded. "I'll be there at noon." One last peck on the lips, and Ben ushered him out of the door.

Wade stood at the top of the stairs and grinned.

I bet if I tried, I could float downstairs.

With a heart as light as his, that would be a breeze.

Ben knelt on the couch, watching through the window as Wade headed for his car. When he reached it, Wade turned and gazed up at the house, as if he was searching for Ben. He raised his hand, and Ben waved back. Then he got in and drove away.

Ben flopped onto his back. *Oh my God, why is there*

never anyone around to pinch me when I need it?

His phone buzzed on the table, and Ben darted across the room to grab it.

If you still need to talk, I'm here for you.

Ben could have kissed Dylan right then.

"I guess that means you do," Dylan said as the call connected. "Are you okay?"

"Better than okay." Warmth suffused him, mingled with a tingling sensation that started in his chest and was slowly spreading outward. He sank onto the couch. "I have news."

"Well, don't tease me—tell me."

Ben closed his eyes and replayed the feel of Wade's mouth on his. "Wade kissed a boy… and he liked it."

"Holy fucking shit. You don't mess around, do ya?"

He laughed, unable to stop it from bubbling out of him. "He was driving around Camden, searching for me. So we came back here and talked."

"That *all* you did? Talk? Okay, and kiss. I got that part."

"Yep, and you know what? That was perfect."

"Well, now I've heard that, I can stop worrying and go to work happy." Dylan snickered. "As much as anyone can be happy, facing eight hours on night shift. The things I have to do to stay awake. And it really fucks up my sleep patterns."

"I don't want to hear what you do to stay awake, though I can take a good guess. Thanks for tonight, dude. You and Aaron gave great advice."

"You'd do the same for us. Although, if I ever do need some, I'll make sure not to call you when I'm in the middle of the night shift. Get some sleep, bro.

And sweet dreams." He disconnected.

Ben had a feeling they were going to be the sweetest dreams ever.

Wade walked into the house as quietly as he could. Gramps would be in bed by then, and probably Mom too.

Wade was too buzzed to even *think* about sleeping.

He locked the door and went into the living room to switch off the lamps.

"Still got your balls?"

Wade jumped. "Christ, Gramps, you almost gave *me* a heart attack."

Gramps sat in his armchair, a cup on the table beside him. Mom was nowhere to be seen.

"I sent her to bed. After you left, she called David. I guess she was worryin' about young Liam."

Wade sat on the ottoman. "I will talk to him *and* Liam." Besides, he had something to tell his big brother, not that he was all *that* worried. David wasn't likely to react badly to Wade's revelation, thank God, but Wade knew it was still going to be a shock.

Or will it? His family so far was proving to be more perceptive than Wade had realized.

Gramps' thoughtful gaze settled on him. "So? Did

you put things right with Ben?"

He nodded. "We did a lot of talking."

"Well, don't keep me in suspenders, as your grandmother used to say. What's the deal?"

Wade smiled. "The deal is, I think I have a boyfriend."

Gramps' eyebrows went sky high. "You only 'think'? That doesn't sound promisin'."

He laughed, then hushed at the thought of waking Mom. "Okay, fine. We're an item. Happy now?"

Gramps picked up his cup and sipped his tea. "I will be, when you tell me where you're takin' him for your first date."

First… Wade hadn't even thought about that.

"Take him to Natalie's Restaurant."

Wade blinked. "You think he'd like a high-end French place like that?"

Gramps snorted. "Well, what's *your* idea? House of Pizza? It's your *first date,* for Christ's sake. It's the kinda thing you remember years later."

Wade smiled. "Where did you take my grandmother?"

He grinned. "The restaurant at the Camden Harbour Inn."

Wade blinked. "But isn't that…?" He laughed. "Which is now called Natalie's."

Gramps shrugged. "Hey, it was a good place for me and Judy. Might be the same for you and Ben."

Wade had to admit it was a sweet thought. "Here's a unique idea. Why don't we let Ben decide where he'd like to eat? Or if he even *wants* that kind of a date?" Not that it mattered what Ben chose—Wade would go along with it. *Hell, I climbed Precipice Trail with him—after that, anything else has to be a walk in the park.*

Gramps chuckled. "Go to bed, son. You've had quite a night, and you're openin' the store in the morning, remember? I'll be off to bed myself once I've drunk this concoction." Wade stood and went over to kiss Gramps's wrinkled cheek, and Gramps reached up to lay his hand on Wade's cheek. "I'm happy for ya, boy. Like you wouldn't believe. I already think the world of Ben. All the luck in the world to you both."

"Thank you." Wade kissed the top of Gramps's head. He walked to his bedroom, went inside, and closed the door. Wade leaned against it, his eyes closed, and a smile that would *not* quit.

Holy fuck. After suffering years of regret and remorse, Wade's life had taken a new direction. Someone in authority had apparently decided it was his turn for a little happiness. He wanted to whoop and holler, to let out the elation that filled him.

One thought both sobered and excited him, however. After years of imagining what sex would be like, he was about to discover the truth for himself.

What if I don't live up to his expectations?

Then he reconsidered. Something deep inside told him Ben would make it good for him. Ben would show him the ropes.

Wade *really* liked that idea.

Ben walked into the store and greeted Madison, Cameron, and Abi with a smile. "Happy Sunday."

Abi snorted. "*Busy* Sunday, you mean. You just missed the rush."

"*Someone* got out of bed on the right side this morning," Cameron remarked with a grin. "There must be something in the air. Wade's in a really good mood today too."

That made him smile.

"If you're going into the office, I'd *love* a coffee," Madison pleaded. "Pretty please?" She batted her lashes.

Cameron chuckled. "Those won't work on Ben." His eyes gleamed. "Now, if *I* tried it…" He fluttered his lashes.

Ben let out an exaggerated sigh. "Sorry, dude, you're not my type." Everyone laughed, and he grinned. "I'll make coffee." He headed for the office. When he opened the door, Wade was sitting at the desk, a sheaf of papers spread out in front of him. He glanced at Ben, and his face lit up. He got up from the chair, walked around to where Ben stood, and reached past him to close the door.

"Thank God. I've been going crazy in here, waiting for you to arrive. I couldn't concentrate. It's as if the figures were dancing on the page." He took Ben's face in his hands. "Did I dream last night?"

Ben's heartbeat quickened. "If you did, I think I had the same dream." He smiled. "I am *so* glad this door doesn't have a window. That means I get to kiss the boss without anyone watching." He slid his arms around Wade, his hands on Wade's back. "Now, where's that kiss?"

"Right here," Wade murmured. There were no collisions this time, only the fusions of their lips and Wade's arms enveloping him. All too soon it was over, and Ben gave a hopefully cute pout. Wade laughed. "Is that supposed to make me kiss you again?"

"Hey, that's one of my best weapons," Ben declared. He smiled. "Kiss me again anyway?"

"With pleasure." This time, Ben teased his way between Wade's lips with his tongue, and Wade groaned into the kiss. He released Ben and took a step back.

Ben bit his lip. "That's all I get?"

"For now. I have to work." Wade kissed his forehead. "Did you come in here for a reason, or was it just to disrupt my day with your kisses?"

"I came in to make coffee."

"Then don't let me stop you." Wade went back to his chair.

Ben smiled to himself. *I can see Wade getting a* lot *of interruptions today.*

Wade's afternoon had gone to hell, and it was all Ben's fault.

He'd lost count of how many times Ben had stepped into the office with one excuse or another, and seconds later their lips were locked in a kiss. Not that Wade was complaining about the kisses—it felt as though each kiss was hotter than the previous—he just wasn't getting any work done.

At four o'clock, Wade opened the office door. "Ben? You got a sec?"

Seconds later, Ben was there, all smiles. "Something you wanted, boss?"

Wade beckoned with his finger. "And close the door behind you." No sooner had Ben done so, than Wade took him in his arms. "Do you have any idea what you're doing to me?"

Ben grinned. "It's working, then?" He reached behind him for Wade's hands, then drew them lower until they covered Ben's ass. "You've finished for the day, right? That means you get to touch."

Wade caught his breath, unable to keep his hands from squeezing Ben's firm butt. "You could tempt a saint."

Ben's eyes sparkled. "Damn, I'm good." He rocked his hips, an unhurried, sensual roll that threatened to blow Wade's mind.

"I… I thought you were trying to be an adult?"

Ben grinned. "Changed my mind. Now I wanna be a *dirty* adult." He ran his finger down Wade's neck to his open shirt. "I finish at nine."

"I know. I wrote the schedule, remember?" Ben chuckled at that. "So… I'll be here when the shop closes to take you home."

Ben's face glowed. "Aw, that's sweet. I do have a question though." He gave another slow roll of his hips, and Wade groaned.

"You keep doing that, and you can ask whatever the hell you want."

"Would Mary object if you didn't go home

tonight?"

Oh fuck.

Wade forced himself to remain calm. "Would your landlady object if you had an overnight guest?"

Ben widened his eyes. "After all the shit she pulls? Like I give a fuck." He teased the tip of his finger under Wade's shirt. "I just want you to myself tonight." Wade shivered, and Ben withdrew his hand. "Am I moving too fast?"

Yes? No?

"You need to remember—"

Ben stopped his words with a kiss. He looked Wade in the eye. "I haven't forgotten. I won't rush you. As long as you're sure you still want this?"

Wade stared at him. "You're kidding, right?"

"Then I'll see you at nine. Now get out of here." His eyes twinkled. "Some of us have work to do."

"Something I'd like you to think about while I'm gone." Wade let go of Ben with extreme reluctance. "Where you'd like to go for our date."

Ben stilled. "We're going on a date?"

Wade arched his eyebrows. "You don't want to?"

"To quote you—you're kidding, right? Of *course* I wanna go on a date with you. Did you have anything in mind?"

"Not really." Except that was a lie, and he'd promised, no more secrets. "Okay, maybe keep one word in mind when you go over the possibilities."

"And what word is that?" Ben grinned. "Cheap? Local?"

Wade leaned in and kissed him on the mouth, a fleeting brush of lips, reminiscent of their first kiss. "I was thinking more along the lines of… romantic," he murmured. Then he straightened. "See you at nine."

Wade got out of there, his heart pounding, his pulse rapid.

I think I just laid my cards on the table.

Chapter Twenty

Ben locked the door behind them. "Now you know what I meant about Mrs. Smith." Before they'd reached the front door, the sound of loud music greeted them. Thankfully, she was too busy with her party guests to be interested in Ben.

Wade lowered his bag to the floor, then stood in the middle of the apartment, his hands stuffed into the pockets of his jeans, which had the effect of stretching the denim tight across his crotch.

Oh my God, he's nervous.

Ben toed off his shoes and walked toward him slowly. "Wanna know what I thought when you came out of that office, the day of my interview?"

Wade bit his lip. "I think you're going to tell me, whether I want to know or not."

He smiled. "I said to myself, 'Now *there* is a vision of hotness.' One look at you in that suit, and my fingers itched to touch you." Ben placed his hands on Wade's chest. "I wanted to slide my hands under your shirt, and explore."

Wade swallowed. "I'm all yours. Explore all you want."

Ben's pulse quickened. "And the only reason I didn't dissolve into a puddle of lust was because it was you." He shivered. "I was *this close* to turning around and walking out of there. And now that we've worked through all that?" He smiled. "I am *so fucking happy* I stayed."

Wade closed his eyes briefly. "So am I." Then he opened them, and tilted his head to one side. "Seeing as we're being honest… Want to know what I thought when I saw you?" His eyes gleamed. "'He didn't get any taller, thank God.'"

"Excuse me?" Ben wasn't sure what to make of that.

"You told me you like big guys. Well… Apparently, I like small guys."

Ben gave a slow smile. "This gets better."

"But… can we be serious for a minute?"

Wade's earnest tone and flushed cheeks stopped Ben in his tracks. "Of course."

"This *is* what you want?"

Ben bit back a smile. "I have been fantasizing about this since I was seventeen. I've finally got you where I want you."

Wade shook his head. "I wasn't talking about that… although damn, you're good for my ego. I meant… you really *do* forgive me?"

Ben placed his hand on Wade's chest, over his heart. "A good friend told me that if I said 'I forgive you,' I had to mean it. That if there was the *slightest possibility* that at some point in the future, I'd bring up our past and throw it back at you, then I should walk away." He brought his free hand up to Wade's cheek. "This is me not walking away. This is me saying, 'I forgive you.' Not just now, but for always."

Wade's chest hitched, and his hand shook as he covered Ben's. "So where do we go from here?"

Ben placed his head against Wade's broad chest, aware of his rapidly beating heartbeat. "Well… *I* was thinking, the bed." He tilted his head to gaze at Wade, his pulse quickening. "If you still want me."

Wade cleared his throat, but the words still came out husky. "For a smart man, you say some dumb things." He swallowed. "But you have to understand…I … I—"

Ben covered Wade's lips with his fingers. "I know. You're nervous. So I'm gonna tell you something to ease those nerves." He cupped Wade's nape and pulled him down until his mouth was barely an inch from Ben's. "You can't screw this up," Ben whispered before kissing him, a soft brushing of lips.

Wade let out a groan. "Yes, I *can*. I keep thinking this is all going to be over in seconds."

Ben took his hand and led him toward the bed. "Which is where *I* come in." He stopped at the foot of it. "You gonna let me take charge here?"

Come on, Wade, trust me.

Wade struggled to breathe. "Yes," he whispered, squeezing the word out.

Ben smiled. "Wise decision." He pointed to the floor. "Shoes, off." Wade complied. Then Ben pushed at his chest, and he fell backward onto the bed. "Scoot up there, and put your head on the pillows."

Wade shuffled higher up the bed, his heart pounding. Ben climbed onto it and crawled toward him, his eyes so dark and so big. "I feel like I'm being stalked," Wade joked.

Ben chuckled as he stretched out beside Wade. "Does that make you my prey?" Then he stroked his thumb over Wade's beard. "Kiss me again?"

Wade didn't hesitate. He tugged Ben closer, cupped his head with both hands and took his mouth in a heated kiss, Ben's hands on his chest, brushing over his nipples through the cotton of his tee.

"Fuck." He shivered. "I feel it all the way down to my balls when you do that." Then Ben moved his hand lower, and Wade rolled his hips up to meet it, groaning when all he got was Ben's fingertips grazing the outline of his erection.

Ben smiled. "I want to see."

Wade's fingers trembled as he popped the button free and lowered the zipper. His hard-on swelled against his briefs, bulging through the open fly of his pants, and Ben turned his face toward Wade's with a grin. "How did I know you'd be a big boy? Of course, it stands to reason. You're big all over. You having a tiny dick would just be plain wrong." He traced the curve of Wade's shaft with one finger. "I had this dream one night." He smirked. "Well, it was more of a fantasy. I dreamed you had a cock like an anaconda."

Despite his heart palpitations, Wade managed a light laugh. "It's not *that* big." Then he gasped as Ben shifted position to press his face into Wade's crotch.

That had to be the sexiest thing ever. Ben rubbed his nose along the cotton-encased shaft, then pushed it against his sac, nudging his balls before covering Wade's erection with his open mouth. Warmth surged around his covered dick, propelling him closer to the edge.

"Show time," Ben whispered, grasping the waistband of Wade's briefs and easing it lower to free his cock that sprang up, so very heavy and thick. "Jesus." He eased the wad of cotton under Wade's balls.

And then Wade's heart stuttered as Ben took him in his mouth, his head bobbing. Wade was thankful to be lying down, because his legs would surely have given way. That first electric touch of Ben's tongue on the head of his cock was nothing like he'd imagined—it was *so* much better. Wet heat surrounded his shaft, and each time Ben gave it a hard suck, Wade shuddered. There was something so hot about a fully dressed Ben sucking him off.

Ben paused and worked the slick shaft with his hand, his gaze on Wade's face. "You have a beautiful dick." Then he reclaimed it, his head sinking lower until his nose met Wade's pubes. Wade stared at him in concern when Ben pulled free, his face red, tears in his eyes, but before he could tell him to stop, Ben took him again with a groan. Wade felt that sound through every inch of his cock and right into his balls.

It felt too good.

"I think I'm gonna come," Wade gasped, pushing deeper into Ben's throat.

Ben freed his dick with a splutter. "Oh no, you're not." He gripped Wade's shaft, his fingers tight around its girth. "Breathe, breathe. Relax."

Wade forced himself to do as instructed, shuddering out a couple of long exhalations. Ben didn't move his hand but kept his gaze focused on Wade. "There ya go. It's not time yet. Hold it."

"Not sure how much longer I can do that." He was already hanging on by a thread.

Ben kept a tight grip on his cock, and leaned over to kiss him. "You're gonna stay hard long enough for me to ride this. You got that?" Another kiss, only this time with a little more heat.

"I got it." Wade took a couple of deep breaths. "But I think I'd be a lot harder if I was looking at you naked."

Ben grinned. "Good point. Take off the rest of your clothes." He let go of Wade's dick and knelt on the bed, popping the button on his pants, and tugging his shirt free of them. Ben locked gazes with Wade as he slowly undid the buttons before slipping his arms free and tossing the garment aside.

Wade forgot about undressing, lost in the mesmerizing, sensual strip tease before him. "Fuck, look at you." Ben was smooth all over. His lean body was toned, the reddish-bronze of his nipples standing out against the creamy skin of his chest. Then Ben shoved his pants down to his knees, along with his briefs, and Wade got a first glimpse of the hardness he'd only felt thus far. Ben's dick wasn't long, and it was slim, a pretty, firm pink shaft rising from the fuzz of his pubes like a fleshy exclamation point.

Just *looking* at it made Wade's mouth water.

Ben attempted to remove his socks and pants, overbalanced, and fell onto his side, laughing. "That's what I get for trying to be sexy."

Wade caught his breath. "Are you kidding? You're sexy as fuck."

Ben knelt beside him, bending over to kiss him, and Wade lost himself in it. Then he swallowed as Ben straightened, taking Wade's hand by the wrist and bringing it to his cock. "Play with yours, too," Ben instructed.

Wade tried to stroke his own cock, but the feel of his fingers curled around someone else's dick for the first time was too much of a distraction. It was warm and silky-soft, the skin tight and shiny over the head. His fingertips encountered stickiness at the slit, and his breathing hitched.

"What do you expect?" Ben's chest heaved. His lips parted. "Taste it."

Wade brought his fingers to his lips and licked the clear fluid. It was slightly salty.

"Keep stroking your cock, I said."

Wade chuckled. "Yes sir. I forgot. You're in charge."

"You'd better believe it." Then Ben lay on the bed once more, spooning against Wade's side. "Put your arm around me. Hold onto the headboard if you need to." Ben kissed him, his hand once more wrapped around Wade's shaft, tugging gently. When he skated too close to the edge again, Ben stopped, squeezing his dick, waiting for him to take a step back from the precipice. When the moment passed, Ben started again.

Wade lost track of time as they lay there kissing, while Ben played with his dick, pausing now and then when he got too close. "I just wanna come so badly," Wade groaned, pushing his cock through the funnel of Ben's hand.

"Patience," Ben said to him in a gentle voice. "Just wait, okay? I'm teaching you how to hold it, to breathe deep." He pulled on Wade's shaft. "Such a nice, hard cock."

Wade let out a wry chuckle. "How am I supposed to respond to compliments like that?"

Ben rubbed his thumb under the head, and Wade

bit back a whimper. "Just say thank you."

He swallowed. "Thank you. And don't stop."

They kissed, and Ben looked him in the eye. "How do you feel?"

"Pretty fucking amazing."

"Think you're ready for my hole?"

Wade almost shot his load right then. "Christ, can you not say things like that? Not when I'm this close."

Ben chuckled. He reached over to the nightstand, opened the drawer, and took out a bottle of lube and a couple of condoms. He squinted at the wrapper. "Thank God. They're in date." When Wade stared at him, Ben flushed. "It's been a while, okay?" He tore the wrapper. "Next time we'll take longer preparing my ass." Ben gave Wade's cock another squeeze. "Right now I'm in too big a hurry to feel this inside me." He unrolled the latex down Wade's shaft, then applied a generous amount of lube to the head. Wade smeared it along his length, and Ben got onto his hands and knees in front of him, legs spread wide, his ass tilted high. "Come on, baby. Now." He reached back to rub slick fingers through his crack.

Wade scootched up behind him, his dick pointing toward Ben's hole as if it knew *exactly* where it was going. He stroked a finger over it, watching it contract.

"Ever fingered your own ass?" Ben twisted to gaze at him over his shoulder.

"Once or twice. Do *you* like it?"

"Love it." Ben's eyes focused on his. "Do it. But slowly, okay?"

Wade penetrated Ben's hole with the tip of his finger. "God, it's so warm." The *heat* of him… "Does that feel good?"

"Fuck, yeah. It'll feel even better if you go deeper.

Come on, I wanna feel it."

Wade sank his finger into Ben's body. "It's so tight."

Ben snorted. "It won't be tight for long, not with that *python* you got there. That's gonna open me right up." He met Wade's gaze. "Please."

Wade couldn't ignore the entreaty in Ben's voice. He guided his cock into position, and carefully pushed against the tight, slick pucker.

Ben lowered his head to rest it on his forearms. "Stay still. I'm gonna back up, okay?" And then he moved, and Wade gasped as he watched his shaft slide into Ben's body.

"Holy fuck," he choked out. The sensation was exquisite. His skin tingled and his dick throbbed.

"Grab my hips," Ben ground out. Wade did as he was told, and Ben rocked back and forth, taking more of Wade's cock each time, until Wade's dick was buried up to the hilt in Ben's ass. "Oh, fuck." Ben continued to rock, only now he was moving faster, slamming against Wade's body with a *slap*, while Wade dug his fingers into Ben's hips, jerking him back hard, forcing him onto Wade's shaft, Ben's ass cheeks rippling with every jolt. And now Wade was meeting him, hips bucking, lunging forward, thrusting deep into him.

Then Ben pulled away. "Wanna see your face when you come." He flipped onto his back and grabbed his knees, drawing them to his chest and rolling his ass up off the bed. Wade shuffled closer, aimed, and drove his dick into the glistening dark, slick hole. He fell forward, his arms taking his weight, his shaft sliding fluidly in and out of Ben's body. Fuck, the *sight* of him: Ben's flushed face and reddened chest, his open mouth and wide eyes, and his hand on his cock, jerking it with little grace but a speed that spoke of urgent need, all combined to send Wade tumbling over the edge, and he cried out as he came, pulsing cum into the latex, his body shaking with every jolt of the orgasm he'd strove to hold off.

Ben wrapped his arms around Wade and clung to him, kissing his forehead, his cheeks, his lips, both their bodies slick with sweat. Wade shivered as the last tremors ebbed away, leaving him hollowed out and sated, his dick still inside Ben. He eased out of him, then bent over to get his first taste of Ben's dick. He filled his mouth, flicking the head with his tongue. Ben arched up off the bed, and seconds later Wade's lips and face received a warm anointing.

Ben kissed him, licking every trace of cum, and smiling as he tried to remove drops from Wade's beard. "Leave it," Wade instructed. "I'll take a shower." He kissed Ben, a leisurely, thorough exploration, feeding each other soft sighs of pleasure. Then he flopped back, one leg bent, his chest still damp. "Wow."

Ben rolled onto his side, tracing a line from Wade's collarbones to his pubes.

"Good wow?"

Wade chuckled. "Exhausted wow. Mind-blown wow."

"See? I said you couldn't screw it up."

He rolled over to face Ben. "I'm not so sure. I think I need to try that again."

Ben's eyes sparkled. "Oh yeah?" He glanced toward the nightstand. "Well, we have plenty of condoms." He cocked his head to one side. "Do you think it'll take you a while to get the hang of it?"

Wade grinned. "Possibly. In fact, it could take us all night."

Chapter Twenty-One

"Now I know what an addict goes through," Ben murmured between kisses. Wade had walked into the store fifteen minutes ago, and Ben had been bouncing from foot to foot while he waited for Wade to go through the pleasantries of greeting Cameron and Zach, running the report, and checking the stock levels. Once all that was completed, he'd gotten Wade into the office on some pretext, closed the door, and launched himself into Wade's arms.

"I know what you mean." Wade lifted him and set him down on the edge of the desk.

Ben wrapped his legs around him. "Gotcha," he said with a grin. "You wanna be set free? Pay the ransom."

"How much are we talking?" Wade leaned in and kissed his neck, and Ben shivered.

"Just keep doing what you're doing. I'll let you know when you've done enough." Ben tilted his head to give Wade more access. "*Jesus*. You kiss me there, and I swear, it scrambles my circuits. It's only been three hours since you left my place, but it feels longer." Then he froze. "Wait a sec. I thought you were going to the Rockport store today."

"I was. Changed my mind." Wade gave him a mock glare. "Hey. You stopped kissing me, and I can't have paid enough yet to get my legs back."

"Have I told you how much I love the way you kiss?" Ben locked his arms around Wade's neck and tugged him down into a long, lingering kiss.

"You might have mentioned it a few times," Wade whispered against his lips when they finally stopped. "But please, tell me again. Let me know I'm on the right track."

Ben pulled back and looked him in the eye. "Can I tell you again how much I loved last night?"

Wade smiled. "So I didn't suck?" Then they burst out laughing. "Okay, don't answer that."

"Aw, but I want to," Ben said with a little whine in his voice. He brought his lips to Wade's ear and whispered, "You sucked, I shot…"

Wade coughed. "You are a dirty man." When Ben leaned back, chuckling, Wade shook his head. "You amaze me."

"I do?" Ben preened, then frowned. "In a good way?"

He laughed. "I know exactly how much sleep we got last night—or should I say how little—and yet here you are, full of beans, whereas *I* need toothpicks to prop up my eyelids."

Ben cupped his cheek. "No regrets?"

Wade swallowed. "Only one. That I didn't have the courage to—" Ben stopped his words with a kiss, and Wade sighed into it. When they parted, he brought his forehead to Ben's. "Sorry. I know we said it's all in the past, but…"

Ben cupped the back of his head with both hands. "Baby, it's okay." He tilted his head back and stared into those mesmerizing amber eyes. "Kiss me," he whispered. Wade's lips found his, and Ben lost himself in the sweetness of the embrace, the scent that had permeated his bed that morning, the *feel* of him…

The door opened. "Hey, Gramps is here—oh my God."

Ben jerked his head to peek around Wade. Cameron froze to the spot, his eyes wide. Ben released Wade's legs, and Wade stepped back. Ben bit his lips. "Oops." Wade flushed.

Cameron grinned. "O-*kay*. That explains a lot."

Wade blinked. "Excuse me?"

"Well, I just meant… there was just something about the way you two were around each other… like, a lot of… tension." Cameron's eyes glittered. "At least now I know what *kind* of tension." Then he pushed the door shut. "Actually, now might be a good time to mention… when you're doing the roster, if you want to put me down for more evenings, that's fine by me. I don't mind working those, and I can get some reading done when it's quiet. You know, just in case you want to free up some of your evenings." He waggled his eyebrows. "You know, if you have something else you'd rather be doing."

Then the door opened, and Gramps stuck his head around it. "Am I interruptin' something?" He glanced at Ben still sitting on the desk.

Wade coughed, and took another step back. "Cameron, we'll talk about this later."

"Sure thing, boss." Cameron grinned. "I'll leave you to it."

Gramps stood aside for him to walk out of the office, then regarded them with arched eyebrows. "Tell me he didn't catch you with your pants down." Both Ben and Wade gaped, and he snorted. "I was your age once." Then he smiled. "It does my heart good to see you smile though."

Wade cleared his throat. "What are you doing here? You're supposed to be home, resting."

"Restin'? Gettin' bored to tears is more like it. There's only so much TV a body can stand, you know? And I'm not here to work, I promise. I just want to be here, talk to the customers, make people coffee…"

Wade's frown melted away. "As long as you don't overdo it."

Gramps beamed. "You just made my day. Now, should I leave so you two can go back to your 'meeting'?" His eyes twinkled. "Looks like you could do with some more coffee, Wade. I'll have some too if you're makin' it." Before they could utter a word, he left them alone and closed the door.

Wade sighed. "There's not enough coffee in all of Maine to wake me." Then he smiled. "But I don't regret one minute of last night—or this morning."

Ben hardly heard him. He was too busy mulling something over. "Can we be serious for a sec?"

"Should I be worried here?"

"You said you changed your mind about going to Rockport." Ben fixed him with a pointed stare. "That was because of me, wasn't it?"

Wade closed the gap between them and put his hands on Ben's shoulders. "You got me. I just wanted to see you."

Ben sighed. "I know that feeling, but you can't let this interfere with how you run the stores. Don't go changing your schedule, okay? If you have to be elsewhere, then that's fine. We *will* find time to be together, without resorting to jumping on each other's bones every five minutes." When Wade's breathing hitched, Ben rolled his eyes. "I mean, look at us. We need to be professional at work. Gramps might've been joking with that pants down remark, but we both know neither of us would do anything like that." He widened his eyes in mock horror. "Unless you're harboring some deep-down desire to have your wicked way with me on the office desk."

Wade chuckled. "I prefer a bed myself."

He laughed. "Me too. Although…" Ben ran his fingers lightly down Wade's back, loving the full-body shiver that resulted. "Ever thought about open air pursuits?"

Wade snorted. "Why do I get the feeling you're not talking about hiking? Now, get your cute butt off my desk, and make me some coffee, please?"

"I can do that." Ben cupped his nape. "In return for one more kiss."

Wade smiled. "Why do I also get the feeling that where you're concerned, there's no such thing as one more kiss?" His lips met Ben's, and Ben made it last as long as he could.

Then he gave a heavy sigh. "I'll be good. I'll keep my hands off you during work hours." He shuffled off the desk.

Wade caught his arm. "Can I stay again tonight?"

Warmth surged through him. "You can stay every night. And my day just got a whole lot better."

He could put up with fewer days of working alongside Wade, if it meant he got to spend his nights with him.

Gotta have balance, right?

Ben paused at the door and gazed at Wade as he opened a folder and removed some papers, placing them on the desk in front of him.

Fuck it.

He walked over to Wade's chair and stood beside it. Wade glanced up at him with an inquiring gaze. "I thought you were making coffee."

"I am. At least, I will—after one more kiss."

Wade leaned back, his eyes darkening. "I'm not going to stop you." His voice was husky.

Ben cupped Wade's bearded jawline and moved in, his tongue grazing Wade's lips. Wade stroked Ben's neck, making him tremble, and suddenly he wanted to be anywhere but the office, preferably naked. His fingers ached to touch the firm flesh that lay hidden below Wade's suit.

"We should stop this," Ben murmured, shivering as Wade kissed his neck.

"Mm-hmm."

"No, I mean it. Anyone could walk in."

"Mm-hmm."

"Wade, I'm being serio—"

"So where's this coffee—Jeezum crow! You two are worse than those damn Bonobo monkeys!"

Ben had never moved across a room so fast.

Wade glanced up from the laptop as Ben entered the office. "Has it quietened down out there?" It seemed as if at least three buses of tourists had descended on Camden during the last couple of hours.

An exaggeration perhaps, but there had been a lot of people browsing in the shop.

Ben laughed. "It's gone so quiet, some tumbleweed just rolled right on through the store and out the back door." He pushed the door shut.

Wade arched his eyebrows. "I think I need to go buy some lip balm."

He chuckled. "Your lips are safe—for the moment, anyway. I need to talk to you." Ben held up his phone. "I just got a text from Aaron." He peered at the screen. "'Hey. Keep the last weekend this month free. BBQ at my place Saturday. You can stay here—two guest rooms, two couches, and tents in the back yard are available. Bring Wade.'" He pocketed his phone.

Christ.

Wade opened a folder and pulled up the work schedule. "I'll take a look, but I'm pretty sure I can cover you for that weekend." When Ben made no response, he raised his chin. Ben was leaning on the desk, regarding him with a thoughtful expression. "Well, *I* can't go. I'll be too busy."

"Babe." The word was uttered softly.

"I *can't*." He was having heart palpitations just *thinking* about it, and breathing had gotten difficult.

"Yes, you can." Ben came around the desk, and took Wade's hands in his. "Listen to me. You can do this. It's not as if some of them don't already know about us. *Two* do, definitely. One might have a pretty good idea. And as for the others, they'll deal with it, as soon as they see us together." He squeezed Wade's hands. "You gotta face this demon. You *need* to."

"I remember these guys from high school. I can already see the look of horror on their faces when I turn up with you." His stomach churned.

"But you don't know that for sure. And give them a little credit, okay?" Ben kissed him, a light touch of the lips, but with an intimacy Wade hadn't thought possible until a few days before. "If I walk in there, holding your hand—" Wade stared at him, and Ben's smile reached his eyes. "Did I not warn you about that part? You okay with that?"

Tears pricked his eyes. "More than you can possibly know."

Ben lifted Wade's hand to his lips and kissed it. "If *I* forgive you, what right have they got *not* to?" Then he leaned over and kissed Wade on the lips. Ben chuckled. "Yeah, I'd think seriously about lip balm if I were you."

Wade had to fight the urge to tug Ben into his lap, wrap his arms around him, and kiss him until his lips were swollen.

Then Ben straightened. "Sorry. You were working and I interrupted you." He smirked. "And then there's the whole being-professional-at-work thing." His eyes twinkled. "At least Gramps isn't about to walk in on us. He just left."

"God knows what he's going to say to me when I go home."

Ben guffawed. "He said enough while he was here. Or did you miss that comment about keeping a bucket of cold water handy?"

"Let me show you what I was looking at this morning." Wade pulled up the site.

Ben peered at the screen. "Houses. Gee, what a surprise. Didn't expect that." He rolled his eyes.

"Be serious for a moment." Wade clicked on one of the properties. "What do you think about this place?"

Ben looked closely. "Hey, I know that place. It's on Elm Street. I pass it every day when I walk to work." He gave Wade an incredulous stare. "Okay, one—you don't need four baths. Two—it's on Elm Street. Do you have any idea how much traffic goes along there? And three—it's a condo. Now, I have nothing against condos, but I was under the impression you were looking for a house."

"Okay." Wade moved the cursor on the screen, then clicked on another property. "What about this one?"

Ben stared at it. "Okay, it's cute. Tiny, but cute."

Another click. "And this one?"

Ben straightened. "Wait—you're just gonna move on? You're not gonna argue?"

"If you don't like it, then yes, I move on to another." When Ben stilled, Wade sighed. "Okay. I'm asking for your opinion because it's important. Because if things work out, I won't be living there alone—will I?" There was the million-dollar question. Wade knew it was a hell of a presumption, but better to know now.

Ben drew in a sharp breath. "Whoa. That sounds kinda—"

"Serious?" When Ben nodded, Wade wiped his brow. "Phew. Good. I hoped it would. I'm not saying we do this tomorrow, or next week, or even next month. I'm not going to pin a date to it. I'm just putting it out there as a… possibility." He took Ben's hand. "You said it yourself this morning—we'll find time to be together. To my mind, this makes sense, even if we started out as just roommates. I'd go to work—wherever that happened to be—and come home to you. And it's not as if you *like* living where you are, right? With that woman watching you all the time?" His heart hammered. "Look, I know it's fast, but—"

"I love the idea," Ben burst out. "And yeah, I wanna think about it. *Talk* about it some more. So… You're coming over tonight, right? We can talk about it then."

Wade bit back a smile. "Is that *all* we're going to do? Talk?"

Ben grinned. "Why, Mr. Pearson. Are you suggesting I have an ulterior motive?"

Wade rolled his eyes. "Duh."

"Oh good. Glad we got that sorted out." Ben kissed the tip of Wade's nose, an absurdly sweet gesture that made him grin like an idiot. "And now I'll let you get back to work." He headed for the door, pausing before he opened it. "So… what do I tell Aaron?"

Wade took a deep breath. "Tell him you'll be there. We'll *both* be there."

Ben's face glowed. "*So* fucking proud of you," he said softly. Then he was gone.

Wade leaned back in the chair.

God, I hope he's right about this.

Chapter Twenty-Two

Ben buzzed to let Wade in, then went out to the top of the stairs to wait for him. He caught the murmur of voices. *Damn her.* Maybe it was time to find alternative accommodation. As soon as Wade came into view, Ben knew she'd said something: he was scowling.

Ben grabbed Wade's hand and tugged him through the door, then locked it. "Whatever the old battle-axe said, it can wait. This is more important." He glanced at the bag in Wade's hand, took it from him, and dropped it to the floor. Then he threw his arms around Wade's neck, jumped, and nimbly wrapped his legs around him. Wade's hands were there, supporting him as Ben kissed him, but then Wade turned, and Ben's back hit the door, pinned against it by Wade's body.

Wade stilled. "Why do you taste of tomatoes?"

Ben laughed. "That would be my supper. I haven't finished my soup." He arched his eyebrows. "You got something against tomatoes?"

"No."

"Good. Then go back to doing what you were doing."

Wade chuckled, and Ben's lips were once more claimed in a lingering kiss. He sighed into it. "Now *that's* what I've been waiting for." He grinned. "You can put me down now."

"Do I have to?"

Ben gave him a mock glare. "My soup is getting cold." Wade laughed and set him down. "Shoes." Wade duly removed them. "So what did she say?"

"Oh, she made some smartass comment about how this was the third time in as many days that she'd seen me here. Then she said something like, 'At this rate, I'll have to start charging you rent.'"

Ben guffawed. "Oh man. How come I never knew you could do that?"

Wade frowned. "Do what?"

"You are a *great* mimic. It could've been her."

"Oh, come on. She's easy to mimic. All you've got to do is whine. You know, I thought you were exaggerating when you said what she was like. I take that thought back." Wade pointed to the bowl of soup on the floor beside the couch. "Finish it."

Ben sat and picked it up. "I meant to ask you something today," he said after a couple of mouthfuls. "Have you thought any more about my idea? About buying land instead of a house?"

Wade smiled as he sat beside Ben. "I've thought about it a lot."

"Then let me give you some *more* food for thought." Ben grabbed his phone from the floor and scrolled. "I made some notes this evening, when it got quiet." He peered at the screen. "Okay. On average, it can cost between a hundred and seventy-eight thousand and four hundred and eighteen thousand to build your own house. Of course, four hundred and eighteen thousand would be for a high-end property. A contractor's expenses can vary, depending on where you live. Plus, there's the cost of the land." He put his phone down. "Those houses you showed me today.

There wasn't *one* of them that was going for less than half a million, and that includes the teeny tiny one." Another mouthful of soup.

Wade stretched out his long legs, crossed at the ankles. "When I left the store today, I drove up to Lincolnville."

Ben grinned. "You *do* like my idea."

"Will you stop preening? I just wanted another look, that's all."

"And?"

He gave a wistful smile. "I could *so* see myself living there."

Ben finished the soup and set the bowl down. "Okay. Then let me call Finn." He held up his hands. "Just to get him to meet with you."

"To meet with *us*," Wade corrected.

That sent warmth flooding through him. "Before you do anything hasty, like buying the lot—you haven't, have you?"

Wade gave a sheepish smile. "I *might* have made a phone call, to see whether it's still for sale."

Ben laughed. "Fine. Let Finn take a look at the land, so he can give you his expert opinion." He picked up his phone again.

"You're going to call him now?"

Ben rolled his eyes. "I need to find out when he's free, and then *you* need to find a time when *we* can both go and see it. And all I'm doing right now is sending a text." His thumbs flew over the screen.

When do you have some time to look at a plot of land and discuss building a house?

Seconds later, Finn's reply *pinged* back. *Who is buying land? And where?*

Ben sent him the link from the site. A couple of

minutes later, Finn replied. *Earliest I can do is this Wednesday morning. Building inspector coming so we have to wait till we get the all-clear before proceeding on the hotel. I can meet you there at ten. That okay?*

Ben grinned and relayed the message.

Sighing, Wade removed his phone from his pocket. "You're not going to let me rest until I do this, are you?"

"Nope."

Wade glanced at the screen. "Okay. I can rearrange things so we can see him Wednesday."

Ben let out a gleeful noise and typed fast. "Okay. That's *one* thing taken care of."

"There's more?"

Ben opened his eyes wide. "You asked me to think about where I'd like to go for our first date, remember? Well, I have a suggestion, providing you don't mind if it's not local."

"How far away is *not local*? I mean, it *is* in Maine, right?"

Ben laughed. "It's about a ninety-minute-ish drive from here, in Portland."

"Portland is okay. Where did you have in mind?" Ben handed him his phone, and Wade blinked. "DuckFat?"

Ben let out a gasp of mock horror. "You haven't eaten there? Oh my God. Their Belgian fries are to *die* for."

"Fried in duck fat, I presume."

"Duh. With garlic mayo. Their poutine is the *best*. And if salads are your thing, there's this awesome one with smoked duck breast, blue cheese, cranberries, chopped duck egg, and sprinkled with duck fat breadcrumbs."

Wade gaped at him. "How can you eat like that, and be the size you are?"

He chuckled. "I don't eat there *all* the time. But every chance I get, I take it. Mind you, it gets wicked busy. People line up around the block to get a table."

"Sounds like we'd be lucky to get one."

"We-ell… yeah, possibly—unless *one* of us *happens* to know someone who works there."

Wade burst out laughing. "Reserve us a table." Then he stilled. "Wait. I asked you to keep a word in mind. Does DuckFat live up to that?"

Ben smiled. "It's gonna be just us, staring at each other across a candlelit table. That says *romantic* to me." Wade's hand trembled as he took hold of Ben's and brought it to his lips to kiss his fingers. Ben furiously blinked away the tears that pricked his eyes.

Since when did I become such a sap? Except he already knew the answer to that. He wasn't being sentimental—he was giving his heart permission to be *happy*.

"Reserve us a table."

"Yay." Ben composed a quick text to Shaun. *This Friday night, table reservation for two? Whenever you can fit me in?*

Shaun's reply came a minute later. *I've got one table at 8.00. Any good?*

Ben let out a whoop. "We got one." *Yes. You rock.* He put down his phone with a contented sigh. "Okay, that's all set." He glanced at Wade. "Did your mom or Gramps make any comments about you staying over again?"

"Mom didn't say anything, but she had this sappy smile. Gramps said, 'Ayuh. Get it out of your system, so you can get your mind on your job.'"

"Oops. We'd better be on our best behavior from now on." Ben shifted across the couch until he was in Wade's lap. "Are we all done talking?" He put his arms around Wade's neck and did a slow, sensual hip roll.

Wade cleared his throat. "Not quite."

Ben stilled immediately at the sight of his furrowed brow. "Something wrong?"

"I called David this evening, before I left the house."

"Oh wow. I was going to ask if you'd talked yet. How did it go?"

Wade sighed. "Better than I thought it would. Well, the coming out part was okay." He sucked in a quick breath. "I'm waiting for the time when I tell someone I'm gay, and they're surprised, because *so far…*"

"Was the rest of the conversation not okay?" Wade's mood seemed a little darker than it had been that afternoon, and he held himself stiffly.

"I was blunt with him. He told me at first that how he raised his son was none of my damn business. So I told him exactly why it *was* my business, and the risks he was running if he continued with his attitude. Then Mom came in, and demanded I hand over the phone."

Ben's chest tightened. "Oh God. That doesn't sound like it ended well."

"Actually, *then* it got better. Turns out, Debra's mom is coming to New York to visit, to spend time with her and Lucy, so David suggested he and Liam visit Uncle Wade, and Gramps, and Grandmom Mary, as he calls her." Wade smiled. "So it's good that our date is Friday, because they'll be here the following morning. I told Mom that David and Liam could have my room, and that I'd stay with you."

Ben bit his lip. "What a noble gesture. Offering up your room like that…" He grinned. "Bet it didn't fool Mary either."

"Not for a second." They laughed. "So I was thinking…. If I can arrange it so neither of us is working next Sunday, maybe you and I could take Liam out for the day."

Ben nodded eagerly. "We could go to Sand Beach up in Acadia. And then we could go for a walk along Ocean Path. Liam could manage that."

Wade gazed at him with warm eyes. "See, that's why you're amazing. The idea of spending a day with my nephew doesn't faze you in the slightest. You don't grumble about not getting me to yourself."

Ben smiled. "You forget. *You're* spending the following weekend with me and my friends. Give-and-take, sweetheart." He slid his hand along Wade's thigh. "Now, if you're ready to give, I am *most definitely* ready to take."

"Well, I don't suppose you're all that much into giving," Wade commented with a smile.

Ben became *so* still. "Wanna run that by me again?"

Wade got the impression he'd finally lived up to

his own expectations and screwed up. "I mean…" His heartbeat climbed into a higher gear, and his breathing quickened.

"Oh, *I* get it." Ben arched his eyebrows. "A guy my size could only be a bottom, right?" He bit his lip. "You know what they say about assumptions, don't ya?"

"I guess I just made one." And was regretting it with every breath.

Ben nodded. He reached for his phone, his thumbs a blur over the keys. Before Wade could ask what he was doing, Ben turned the phone to face him.

There were guys fucking on the screen, and they weren't being quiet about it.

"This is porn."

Ben rolled his eyes. "Duh. But with a difference. On *this* site, all the little twinky guys are fucking the big hunky guys." He swiped, then held up the phone again. "See him? The big Daddy with the tattoos? Looks like a total top, right? Well, he *loves* taking a dick." He tossed the phone onto the seat cushion.

"I'm sorry. I shouldn't have said that."

"I'd understand it if I'd said I only bottom." Ben's eyes gleamed. "But I don't."

Wade's heart thumped. "Don't *understand*?"

There was a glint in Ben's eyes. "Don't only bottom." He smiled. "Your lesson for today. Size and/or appearance is *not* an indication of preference." That twinkle was still there. "So this is what you do. If you want to experience *all* the options available… you *say* something." He cocked his head to one side. "I'm open for discussion. Something you wanna say? Or… try?"

Wade swallowed.

Ben cupped Wade's head in both hands, and gazed into his eyes. "Okay, listen to me. One. I am *not* gonna judge you, all right? Two. It's okay to talk about this. Three. No one is saying you *have* to bottom. And four." He stroked Wade's beard with gentle fingers. "I just want to give you the option." His eyes were warm. "I can't give you what you need if I don't know what that is."

"And what if *I* don't know what I need?" Wade burst out. "This is all so… new."

Ben leaned in and kissed him on the lips, and that had to be the best response. Then he climbed off Wade's lap, stood in front of him, and held out his hand. "Then why don't we play this by ear, and see where it takes us?"

Wade could do that. He grasped Ben's hand, and Ben made a big show of hauling him to his feet, straining comically. Wade laughed, seeing the move for what it was—an attempt at humor to lighten the mood. Ben led him to the bed, then pointed to it.

"Face down, sweetheart, ass toward me. Legs spread."

Wade chuckled as he lay down. "I take it back. You're bossy enough to be a top."

Ben cackled. "Nah, I'm just plain bossy." He got onto the bed behind Wade, and knelt between his legs. "Fuck, do you know how *amazing* your ass looks in these jeans? I could stare at it all day."

"Then wearing a suit to work is a good idea. Wouldn't want to give Gramps something else to complain about." Wade caught his breath when Ben reached under him, popped the button on his jeans, and lowered the zipper. He raised his hips to help Ben remove them. "We could've both just taken all our clothes off," he grumbled.

"Hush. I'm in charge here."

Wade chuckled. "You say that a lot, you know."

"Will you hush? I'm busy here, ogling your ass." And with that, he eased Wade's briefs down over his hips with infinite care, then removed them completely, Wade doing his best to help him without falling over. "Would you look at that?" Ben said in an awed whisper.

"Not without mirrors." Wade didn't know how to react to such effusive praise. Then he gasped as Ben pulled his ass cheeks apart, and a warm tongue licked a path over his hole. "Oh fuck." He grabbed hold of the comforter and tilted his ass higher.

"Oh, you like that, huh?"

The sensation shot straight to Wade's cock. "Understatement of the century." He groaned as Ben pushed at his pucker with the tip of his tongue. "Fuck, that feels…"

Ben broke off and reached down to stroke Wade's dick. "Yeah, you like it." Then he was back, licking and sucking, and Wade shuddered from head to toe.

"You keep doing that, and this is going to be over real quick."

"Not yet. You've got a job to do first. On your back, babe."

Wade flipped over, and Ben slowly removed his own clothing, taking his time. "*Now* I get it. You're a tease."

Ben laughed. "You can take off your top now."

Wade's arms got tangled in his tee, he was trying to take it off so damn fast. Ben helped him, freeing his arms, and tossed the tee aside. Then he straddled

Wade's chest, his cock pointing straight at Wade's mouth. Ben grabbed the headboard and gazed down at him. "Get me nice and hard."

Wade gave a wry chuckle. "It's doing very well without my help." Ben's shaft was a stiff pink arrow. He took Ben into his mouth, going as deep as he dared, and Ben moaned, his hips rolling. He held onto the bed frame and rocked back and forth, never giving more than Wade could take. Wade grabbed Ben's ass and squeezed the firm globes, pushing him a little deeper. Ben picked up speed and rocked a bit faster, until finally he pulled free of Wade's mouth, his face and neck flushed.

"Think you're ready?" He knelt once more between Wade's spread thighs, only now he gripped Wade's ankles and lifted his legs.

"I feel like the wishbone of a chicken. I bet I look like one too," Wade observed.

Ben grinned. "From where I'm standing—kneeling—the view is just perfect. Grab your knees."

Wade complied, unable to stifle a groan as Ben shuffled forward, slid his hard dick over Wade's balls, through the crease where groin met thigh, and over Wade's own stiff shaft. Ben wrapped his hand around both cocks and moved it up and down, squeezing them together—a tantalizingly slow act that felt incredible.

Ben stared at his hand. "Fuck, I can barely get my fingers around them."

There was something missing from the equation, and Wade realized what it was. "Kiss me?"

Ben didn't hesitate. He let go of their shafts, leaned forward, and their lips met in a heated kiss as he slid his dick over Wade's in a sensual rocking motion. Wade enveloped him in his arms and held him through kiss after kiss.

Ben pulled back and looked him in the eye. "Still want to try?" Wade nodded, his throat tight, and Ben kissed his forehead. "I'll go slow. If you want to stop, tell me. Okay?"

"Okay," he croaked.

Ben sat up and stretched toward the nightstand drawer. He dropped the lube and a condom onto the comforter, then slicked up a couple of fingers. "Gonna finish what my tongue started."

Wade caught his breath as Ben cautiously penetrated him with a single finger. "Fuck, I feel that."

Ben's eyes sparkled. "If you didn't, I'd be worried." He stroked it in and out of Wade. "Breathe. Relax."

Wade couldn't help smiling. "I've got déjà vu here." Had it only been twenty-four hours before that Ben had said those same words?

Ben nodded, his gaze fixed on Wade's face as he added another finger, except now he wrapped a slick palm around Wade's dick, tugging on it, synchronizing his hands, until Wade was almost at breaking point. Ben withdrew his fingers and picked up the condom. "You want it?"

Wade took a deep breath. "Give it to me." When Ben lifted his eyebrows, he added, "Please."

Ben bit his lip. "Remember. I'll take it nice and easy." He gloved up, squeezed lube onto his slim, hard shaft, and rubbed its head over Wade's hole in a teasing motion.

Wade nodded. "In me, please."

With one hand on Wade's cock, Ben pressed the head of his dick to Wade's hole and ever so gently, *pushed.*

Oh God. It was as if nothing else existed but Ben's hand on his shaft, Ben's cock in his ass. Ben moved as slow as molasses in winter, teasing his hole again as he pulled out almost to the point of complete withdrawal, only to slide back into him.

"No rush," Ben whispered, rocking forward, his hand warm on Wade's dick. "You choose the pace." He stared intently at him. "Does it feel good?"

"Starting to," Wade admitted. That initial burn was fading with every stroke of Ben's shaft inside him. It wasn't long before he wanted more. "Pick up the pace a little?"

Ben gave a nod, his hips rolling a little faster. Wade couldn't take his eyes off the sight of that lean torso, the faintest hint of definition in his abs. Ben brushed his hair out of his eyes, and the gesture made Wade smile.

"You're too far away," he complained.

Ben hooked his arms under Wade's knees and leaned over to kiss him, rolling Wade's ass up off the comforter. Except now his hips were pumping as he thrust deep into Wade's body, his upper body still as they kissed, tiny grunts escaping Ben's lips with each plunge of his shaft.

Wade moaned into the kiss. "Can't make it last," he gasped, his hand on his cock, tugging at it. Every cell and fiber of him was screaming for him to let go.

"Then don't try." Ben's eyes were locked on his. "Come. Then we can do this all over again, as many times as you like."

The thought of making love into the night was all it took to propel Wade into his orgasm, and warmth creamed his fingers. Wade couldn't keep quiet, feeding

Ben sounds that made no sense, forced out of him with every thrust of Ben's dick. And through it all, Ben kissed him, their lips and tongues colliding in a heated exchange, Wade's hand on Ben's neck, holding him close.

Then Ben drove deep into him and stiffened, a low cry forced from his lips. Wade's heart soared at the feel of Ben's cock throbbing inside him, and he pulled Ben deeper into a kiss, wrapping his legs around him, Ben's dick in him up to the hilt. They clung to each other, their sweat mingling as they lay pressed together, almost fused into one. Ben rubbed his face over Wade's beard, a sweet gesture that spoke of intimacy.

At last, Ben raised his chin. "It's no good. I gotta pull out."

Wade tensed himself for the moment of loss, and when it came, it was so acute, like a wave that hit him with full force. Ben dealt with the condom, and returned to lie beside him. For a while, neither of them spoke, and Wade's heartbeat eased down into its more usual rhythm.

"So have I made a bottom out of you?"

Wade laughed. "If I'm honest, I enjoyed both positions."

Ben let out a contented little sigh. "I can live with that." He paused. "How long are David and Liam staying?"

"A week." Wade gave a soft chuckle. "I think we'd better go shopping. Because if every night is like this, we'll need more supplies."

Ben rolled onto his side. "There *is* an alternative."

Wade stilled. "Oh?"

Ben brushed a fingertip over Wade's nipple, and

Wade learned for the first time that sex made them unusually sensitive. "We're going to Portland for dinner on Friday, right?" Wade nodded. "Well… we could go earlier than intended. There's a place I visit regularly. It's where I go to get tested." Ben's gaze met him. "So, I was *thinking…*"

Wade saw where he was going, and his heart rate climbed again. "Yes," he blurted out. "Let's do it."

Ben's eyes widened. "You mean that?"

He nodded. "I want that."

"Me too." Ben snuggled closer and rested his head on Wade's chest, his arm draped over Wade's belly.

No words, only the peace that Wade had wanted for so long.

Chapter Twenty-Three

Wade spotted the truck parked ahead in the dirt road as they turned off Route 1. His stomach had been churning all morning, ever since he'd left the house. "You didn't tell Finn, did you? That I'm the one buying the land?"

"No, but he's not stupid. He'll have figured it out."

Wade pulled up behind the truck and switched off the engine. *Not sure I'm ready for this.* In front of them, a door opened, and Finn got out. Wade gaped at him. "Whoa. He's worked out a *lot* since high school."

Ben laughed. "No, he hasn't. It's called physical work. He has to carry huge wooden beams and hunks of… whatever around." He patted Wade's thigh. "And he might think the same about you." He sighed. "I think everyone got bigger, except me."

"I wouldn't complain about that, not after the other night." Ben's size and flexibility made for some interesting positions. Then he froze. "He's walking this way."

"Well, duh. He's here to see us." Ben unfastened his seatbelt, and Wade grabbed his hand. Ben gave him a compassionate glance. "It'll be *fine*, babe." Then he opened the door and called out to Finn in a cheerful voice as he got out of the car. "Hey."

There was nothing to do except follow him.

Wade's fingers fumbled as he popped his seatbelt

free. He opened the door and climbed out, his stomach churning. "Long time, Finn." He walked around to the front where they stood.

There was no mistaking Finn's reaction. He froze, his mouth fell open, and he stared at Wade with a dazed look.

Then Ben reached for Wade's hand and squeezed it. "You remember Wade, right?"

Finn jerked his head to stare at their linked hands, then up to their faces. He arched his eyebrows. "I guess you really *have* moved on since we spoke last." His lips twitched. "Something you wanna tell me?"

"You're not gonna give me a hard time about this, are you?" Ben asked.

Finn sighed. "You're an adult—most of the time, at any rate. Let's assume for the moment you know what you're doing." His gaze flickered to Wade, his eyes cool. "I guess this is where we shake, and I say, 'Hi, Wade, good to see you.'" The words came out kind of stilted.

Wade's throat seized. "I guess. Especially since the Wade *you* remember doesn't exist anymore."

Finn blinked. "Okay, I hear ya." He extended a hand. Wade released Ben's, and shook it. Finn coughed. "Right. So. About this lot. Want to know what I think?"

"That's why we're here." Wade's heartbeat climbed down a notch or two, and he breathed easier.

Finn smiled. "Well…. If *I* had sixty-nine thousand dollars to spare, you'd have a fight on your hands for it. I'd snap it up and build my own place here. It's beautiful."

"It is, isn't it?" Wade reached for Ben's hand again, and squeezed it.

Finn appeared momentarily distracted by the sight, then jerked his head up to Wade. "What did you have in mind?" Finn asked.

"Nothing too big. Three bedrooms at the most. A fireplace. Maybe something like a Cape Cod."

"Gotcha." Finn went back to his truck and returned with a folder. "I brought these along. Just some house designs I figured might interest you. Of course, I wasn't too sure who I'd be consulting at that point. *Someone* didn't mention any names." He gave Ben a hard stare.

Ben bit his lip. "Surprise!"

They all laughed, and with it the tension dissipated a little more. Wade leafed through the designs, and his heart stopped when he reached the last page. "Oh my God. That's it." The artist's rendition of a Cape Cod grabbed him instantly. It was perfect: the central front door stood at the top of some steps, with two shuttered windows on either side, and the front and side were covered in cedar shakes. There were three dormer windows set into the sloping roof, giving it a thoroughly charming appearance.

Ben leaned in to take a look. "Two thousand one hundred and ninety-nine square feet, not bad. Three beds, three-and-a-half baths. Open floor plan—I like that." He beamed. "And a fireplace." Ben's face glowed. "That is *so* pretty."

Finn pointed to the design. "This door leads from your dining room out into the backyard, so I'd maybe build it with the rear facing the ocean."

Wade couldn't take his eyes off it. "If you can build this, you've got yourself a client."

Finn laughed. "Slow down. You don't even have

the land yet."

Wade got out his phone. "I can soon change that." He paused and turned to Ben. "You like it?"

"No," Ben said solemnly. Then he grinned. "I fucking *love* it."

"Then that's going to be our house." Before Wade could get another word out, Ben claimed his lips in an exuberant kiss, and Wade forgot about Finn and kissed him as if his life depended on it.

Finn coughed again. "Er, guys?" They broke the kiss and turned to look at him. Finn's eyes sparkled. "Just reminding you there's someone else here."

Ben laughed, and it was such a happy sound, it sent Wade's spirits soaring.

Finn took a deep breath. "I think there's something I need to do again." He held out his hand to Wade.

Puzzled, Wade took it. "Didn't you do it right the first time?"

Finn smiled. "Hi, Wade. Thank you for making my friend Ben happier than I've ever seen him."

Wade gripped his hand and shook it, his throat tight. "Thank *you*."

According to what Ben had told him, that was three friends down—four to go.

Then he realized he'd just done something huge. It wasn't just his house anymore—it was *theirs*. And *that* was one awe-inspiring commitment.

They needed to talk.

The entrance to DuckFat sat beneath a burnt orange and brown striped awning, surrounded by black fabric walls with clear panels set into them. On either side, large windows afforded views of the diners inside, and from what Ben could see, it was packed. Tables stood outside, and all but one were occupied. Patio heaters had been provided as insurance against any drop in temperature.

"What do you think?" he asked Wade as they drew closer.

Wade chuckled. "It looks like it's a popular place. That's good."

Ben rolled his eyes. "Would I bring us on our *first date t*o a place that *wasn't* good?" Then he fell silent as Shaun walked out, dressed in black, a notepad in hand, and went over to a table.

"Don't I know him?"

Ben nodded. "Shaun Clarke from high school." At that moment, Shaun turned his head, and his smile froze. In fact, all of him froze for a second, and he was caught open-mouthed, his eyes wide. He hastily scribbled on his pad, then came over to where they stood. "Good evening."

Ben gave him a quick hug. "Hey. We're not too early, are we? It's not quite time."

Shaun blinked. His gaze flickered from Ben to

Wade and back to Ben again. Another blink. He cleared his throat. "It's ready. Step this way." He led them to a table in the farthest corner from the street. As Ben and Wade took their seats facing each other, Shaun leaned in and whispered, "Dude. You could've warned me. If I'd come out with what I was thinking, they'd have fired me on the spot." He glanced at Wade and gave a curt nod. "Wade. Been a while."

Ben took one look at the diners around them, and grabbed Shaun's arm. "Hey. We don't have a candle on our table."

Shaun frowned. "Why would you want a candle?"

Ben arched his eyebrows. "Well, if *you* took someone on a date, wouldn't *you* want it to be romantic?"

Shaun's jaw dropped again, but he recovered faster this time. "I'm asleep, right? This is a dream." Ben gave him a good pinch above the elbow, and Shaun winced. "Ouch."

Ben locked gazes with him. "Are we okay here?" he asked in a low voice.

Shaun sighed. "We're okay. Confused as hell, but okay. Lemme get the menus." He headed back indoors.

Wade leaned forward. "I'm starting to think Aaron's BBQ is not such a good idea."

Ben could understand that reaction. "Is it worth an evening of possible discomfort, weird glances, and muttered comments, if it means we get this out in the open so they can all learn how the land lies, and then we can just get on with living?" He took a breath and reached across the table for Wade's hand.

Wade pushed out a sigh. "I suppose." Then Shaun returned with the menus, and Wade went to pull his hand back, but Ben was having none of it. He held on tight.

Shaun glanced at their laced fingers and shivered. "Okay. It's official. I'm in the *Twilight Zone*. Might as well go with it." He put down the menus and held out his hand to Wade. "Hi. You might not remember me from high school. I'm Shaun."

"But I know you remember *my* name," Wade replied softly. He let go of Ben's hand and took Shaun's, shaking it. "Good to see you again. Ben talks a lot about his friends."

"Hmm. Whereas lately, he's been keeping quiet about *some* things." He gave Ben a brief stare. "I'll be back with your water and to take your order. Today's soup is tomato, and the specials are on the board behind the counter." Then he left them to it.

Ben bit his lip. "That went well."

Wade picked up a menu. "I know what he means about the *Twilight Zone*." When Ben gave him an inquiring glance, Wade gave a nervous smile. "First date with a guy. Whoa."

"Did you ever date anyone in high school?" Ben couldn't recall seeing any girls hanging around Wade. *And the amount of time I spent looking at him? I'd have noticed.*

"No, but I did a lot of bluffing. It kept the other guys from guessing the truth." Wade coughed. "Can we talk about something you just said?"

Shaun appeared with their glasses of water. "Do you need more time?"

Ben smiled. "That'd be great, thanks." He waited until they were alone again. "Sure. Is something wrong?" Because if Wade wasn't going to relax, Ben was going to call it a night. *Maybe coming here wasn't such a bright idea.*

"You mentioned us getting on with living."

Ben frowned. "Okay."

"And the other day, when we were talking with Finn… I said it was going to be *our* house."

Ben grinned. "Yeah. I got that part."

Wade gave a brisk nod. "So I guess what I want to know is… are we moving too fast?" Before Ben could get a word in, Wade continued. "For God's sake, we just got tested so we can ditch the—" He leaned forward and whispered, "Condoms. That sounds an awful lot like… commitment."

To Ben's mind, it sounded *exactly* like commitment.

He went quiet for a moment, taking Wade's hand in his and rubbing it gently. "This is how *I* see it," he said at last. "Given our history, and the way we found out how we felt about each other… This could've only gone one of two ways. We crashed and burned, *or…* we moved on and tried to make a go of this. Now, after all we've been through? What's the worst that could happen to us, compared to that? We've already conquered *so much*. Why take our time?" He squeezed Wade's hand. "We know we want to be together, right?"

"Yes, but—"

"But nothing." Ben inclined his head toward the door where Shaun had gone back inside. "I'm making sure my closest friends know *exactly* how important you are to me. I'm helping you to build your—*our*—new home. I'm doing something I have *never* done for any guy—well, I will, once the tests results come back." He gave Wade a hard stare. "Do I have to spell it out? Because when you add up all those things, it sounds a helluva lot like I'm in love with you."

Wade's breathing hitched. "In love—"

"And no, this *isn't* fast. We're only playing catch-up to get to where we *should* have been if only things had been different in high school." He looked Wade in the eye. "You chose your path, and that set us back eight years." Another squeeze of his hand. "All forgiven, I promise. So now let's get to where we *should* be—stupid in love."

Wade's face tightened. "Back then, I wasn't stupid in love—I was just stupid."

"And now?" Ben's stomach was tense. *Tell me how you really feel.* Because he felt as if he'd just laid open his *soul.*

"Now?" Wade smiled. "Now, I'm wishing we were alone, so I could take you in my arms, kiss you, and tell you I am head over heels in love with you."

Ben's throat seized. "I think you managed just fine right here."

A choked sound burst their bubble, and Ben jerked his head to find Shaun standing there, eyebrows lifted, eyes wide, his mouth slack. Shaun cleared his throat. "I think I'll give you guys a minute longer." Then he paused. "And I'll be back with the biggest candle I can find." He scurried away.

Ben burst out laughing. "Well, there's another one who'll have our backs at the BBQ—if he's there." He picked up the menu. "Wanna choose something now?"

He didn't care what he ate—he was on a date with a man who loved him.

Wade buried his face in Ben's hair, breathing him in, Ben's arms around his neck as he moved in and out of Ben's body, Ben's legs tight around his waist. "Can't wait to get our results," he murmured.

Ben rocked with him, his breathing shallow. "Me too."

Wade kissed his neck as he thrust deep. "Nothing between us."

Ben's beautiful eyes widened. "Nothing."

"Will you feel it?" Wade picked up the pace, hips pumping. "When I shoot deep inside you…?"

"Don't. You're gonna make me come." Ben's breathing grew erratic, his fingers digging into Wade's shoulders, his chest slick against Wade's.

"Do it. But let me know when you're almost there." Wade quickened the pace, sliding into Ben's ass in short, fast thrusts. They kissed, Ben moaning into it, both of them in constant motion.

"Gonna… gonna…."

Wade's dick bottomed out, and he looked into Ben's eyes. "I love you."

"Jesus." Ben trembled as he shot hard, warmth spreading between their bodies. He clung to Wade, tremors wracking him, and Wade kissed him through the jolts and shocks. Then he began a slow rocking motion, in and out, gathering speed, his heart pounding as he neared orgasm. And when it came, Wade shuddered through every pulse of his cock.

Ben stroked his cheek, his beard, his neck. "Love you too."

They lay beneath the single sheet, kissing and touching, until Wade finally came back down to earth, his softened dick slipping from Ben as Wade rolled him.

Ben lay on him, the perspiration on his forehead gleaming in the lamplight. "Your timing…"

Wade laughed. He enfolded Ben in his arms. "And once we've cleaned up, we really should get some sleep. We've got a busy day tomorrow. You've got work, and I've got David and Liam arriving."

"As long as you don't plan on going home to sleep, it's all good." Ben kissed the tip of his nose.

If Wade had his way, he'd sleep in Ben's arms every night for the rest of his life.

Ben walked out of the ocean, shaking the water from his hair. He smiled to himself as he recalled Wade's response to his suggestion of a swim. He'd said he liked to find his dick and balls without the aid of a microscope.

Sand Beach was heaving. It seemed as if the whole of Maine had descended on it—by the time they'd arrived at eight that morning, there were already people setting up for a day of sun worship. Wade had picked a spot by the trees, Ben's beach umbrella providing welcome shade from the midday sun.

And speaking of midday… It was time for lunch. Mary had filled a cooler bag with sandwiches, fruit, water, and snacks.

Ben crossed the sand to where Wade and Liam sat beneath the umbrella, facing each other. Ben liked Liam. He was a cute little boy, with a shock of dark brown hair and warm brown eyes. Liam had greeted him so shyly when Ben climbed into the front seat beside Wade, but as the morning had worn on, he'd relaxed. The first time Ben leaned across and kissed Wade on the cheek, Liam had blinked, but said nothing.

Ben wasn't about to hide.

Wade and Liam appeared deep in conversation, and as Ben drew closer, their words came to him on the warm breeze.

"Dad says I should fight back," Liam said, absently scooping a plastic shovel full of sand into the castle-shaped red bucket in front of him. The sand construction hadn't progressed much while Ben had been for a swim. "He says I need to stand up for myself."

Ben froze, unwilling to disturb the conversation.

"Does it feel like it's your fault those kids pick on you?" Wade asked.

Liam jerked his head up, his eyes widening. "Yeah. They call me names because I want to paint instead of playing ball with them. And when I was showing Mrs. Landon what I can play on the piano… later, when she wasn't around, they… they were mean. So maybe if I *didn't* play piano, or paint… maybe they'd leave me alone."

Wade placed his hand on Liam's shoulder. "But those things are what make you Liam. And you're not on your own. Lots of kids get bullied, but it's not their fault—it's the *bullies* who are behaving badly, not you."

"But why, Uncle Wade?" Liam stared at him. "Why are they like that?"

Wade was quiet for a moment, and Ben's heart went out to him. "Bullies need a victim—someone who is… different in some way. Picking on them makes a bully feel important, like they're in control." He paused. "And sometimes, they bully other kids because that was the way *they* were treated." Another pause. "I'm going to tell you something now, and it's very important, okay?"

Liam nodded, his eyes huge. "Okay."

"When I was your age, I was bullied too." Liam's mouth fell open, and Wade nodded. "I looked different. That was why they picked on me. And I still remember how it used to make me feel."

Oh, Wade.

Liam swallowed. "I hate it. I go into the classroom and I feel sick, because I know they'll start on me. Some mornings I don't want to get out of bed, but Dad says if I don't, then…" Another swallow. "He says I need to tough it out."

"We'll talk later about what your Dad says. What you need to know is… I went the wrong way."

"What do you mean?"

Oh shit. Ben held his breath.

"When I was older than you are now, I did something very bad. I… I picked on other kids."

Ben's heart was so full of love right then. *Does Wade have any idea how much courage it takes to admit to being a horrible person?* Especially to a little kid who was being bullied—a little kid who clearly looked up to his uncle.

Liam gaped at him. "But… why would you do that when you know how it felt?"

"I was ashamed of feeling the way I did. I thought that by picking on others, they wouldn't pick on me, and that was the wrong thing. I made a lot of kids very unhappy. Like I said, kids pick on others for lots of reasons. I had my reasons too, but none of them made what I did right. I didn't learn from what had happened to me. Because you're right. I knew how it felt to be bullied, and I still did it. Although now I know better, I will be sorry about that for the rest of my life."

Tears pricked the corners of Ben's eyes. Liam fell silent for a moment, and Ben held his breath once more.

"Did you say sorry to those kids later?"

"So far, I've only had the chance to say sorry to one of them. I met him again a few months ago."

"Was he okay about it?"

Wade turned his head at that moment, as if he was looking for Ben, and froze.

Ben mouthed *I love you.*

Wade shuddered out a breath, and turned back to

Liam. "Well, why don't you ask him yourself?" He beckoned to Ben, who stumbled over the sand to join them under the umbrella.

Liam stared at him, and Ben smiled. "Uncle Wade said sorry, and I told him I forgave him. But what he said to you was right. Don't you change yourself because of those kids. You do that, and it won't be you anymore." He cocked his head to one side. "It makes you feel angry, doesn't it, when they pick on you? Sometimes, so angry that it hurts."

Liam caught his breath. "Yes."

Ben nodded. "We can talk about that too. The important thing to know is you're *okay*. There is *nothing wrong* with you. And you have people who will listen to you and be there for you."

"Like Uncle Wade is here for you?"

Ben smiled. "Smart kid." He leaned into Wade and kissed him, not caring who saw. Then he opened the cooler bag, removed three bottles of water, and handed them around. "I don't know about you two, but I'm hungry. There's plenty to eat in here."

Wade opened his bottle. "How much of that did you hear?" he murmured.

Ben reached over and stroked his cheek. "Enough."

"Are you and Uncle Wade gonna get married?"

Wade almost choked on his water.

Ben chuckled. "Why? You think we should?"

Liam gave a shrug. "Why not? You kiss all the time like my mom and dad do, and *they're* married."

He grinned at Wade. "Gotta love a kid's logic." Ben peered at Liam. "So you think it's okay for men to get married?" He was still astounded by Liam's casual acceptance.

"Why not? My best friend Kazy has two dads. And Denny has two moms."

Ben ruffled Liam's hair. "Stick with Kazy and Denny, kid. They sound like they're just the kind of friends you need." He met Wade's gaze. "Because we all need good friends, right?"

Ben wished he could take away Wade's concerns about Aaron's little shindig, but then again, Wade didn't know Ben's friends the way he did.

It's gonna be all right, babe. Ben just knew it.

Chapter Twenty-Four

"Turn left into that parking lot."

Wade did as instructed, scanning the lot for a space. "There's one." He drove into it and switched off the engine. "Want to tell me why we're parking here?"

Ben snorted. "Because one, this is Bar Harbor, and two, it's August. That means parking space is gonna be limited. Aaron's house isn't far from here. This is the closest we can get to it."

Wade popped the trunk, they got out, and he walked around to the rear of the car, conscious of the empty feeling in the pit of his stomach. "Another thing," he said as he lifted their luggage from the trunk. "If Aaron's house has two guest rooms and two couches, why did we bring your tent?"

Ben arched his eyebrows. "You're asking that *now*? You didn't say a word about it when you picked me up."

"That's because my mind was… occupied." He'd been too busy thinking about the event that lay ahead of him. Despite Ben's assurances, there was a quiver in his stomach that wouldn't quit.

"Hey." Ben's voice softened.

"It's okay, you don't have to tell me again that it'll be all right." *Because my brain apparently doesn't believe you.* "So… why the camping gear?"

Ben's eyes glittered. "Because there could possibly

be ten guys in that house tonight. Aaron *might* share his bed, but if it were me, *I* wouldn't. That leaves all the guest accommodation to be divided between nine of us. If Finn brings Joel—which is probable—they're gonna want a bed to themselves. And we'd be *more* likely to be alone in Aaron's backyard. Hence the tent."

"Finn might have the same idea."

Ben erupted into laughter. "Fuck no. Finn and *camping*? No, we're safe. Besides…" He leaned in, and his voice dropped to a seductive whisper. "Don't you *like* the idea of making love under the stars in Aaron's private, high-fenced back yard?"

Wade chuckled. "You've clearly given this a lot of thought." He thrust the drawstring bag into Ben's hands. "*You* can carry the camping gear." He gazed at their surroundings. "Which way do we go?"

Ben pointed to an exit. "Out onto Main Street, and right. Wayman Lane is four or five streets down." They left the parking lot, and Ben took Wade's hand in his. Warmth flooded him at the intimate gesture.

"I know you keep telling me not to be nervous, but it's hard." They strolled at a steady pace. Ben hated it when Wade walked briskly. He usually complained his legs were half the length of Wade's.

Ben squeezed his hand. "You're just gonna have to trust me. It'll be okay."

The streets were full of people meandering along, many in hiking clothes. "Is it always this busy here?" Wade wasn't familiar with Bar Harbor. That visit to Precipice Trail with Ben had been the first time he'd visited.

"Yup. It gets a bit quieter once September settles in." Ben stopped at a corner. "This is Aaron's street."

He pointed to a town house on the left, its exterior walls covered in cream cedar shakes, with buff-colored tiles on the roof over the front porch, and a patch containing flower beds in the center of the yard. Steps lined with white railings led up to two front doors, a pair of octagonal windows between them.

Ben headed for the house on the right.

"This is nice," Wade observed. Laughter came from the rear, and he stiffened. "Maybe it would have been better to get here earlier."

"This is the best way," Ben assured him. "They should all be here by now. Get it all over with in one go, like ripping off a Band-Aid."

"That analogy does *not* help." They climbed the steps to the front door, but before Ben could use the doorbell, it opened, and a vaguely familiar tall man with reddish-brown hair and matching beard stood there, wearing a pair of dark blue shorts and a black tee.

"Hey, you got here," he said with a smile. He gave Wade a nod, his blue eyes cool. "Glad you decided to join us. I don't suppose you remember me from high school. Aaron Allen."

"Not really," Wade admitted.

"That's okay. You'll know us all a lot better before the weekend is out." He gave Ben a tight hug, and when he released him, Aaron studied Ben for a second. "Well, *you* look happier than the last time I saw you."

"I blame him," Ben replied without hesitation, digging his elbow into Wade's side.

Wade could live with that kind of blame.

Aaron stepped aside to let them enter. "Leave your stuff by the door." He glanced at their things and grinned. "I see. The backyard is all yours then." His eyes gleamed. "I'll make sure everyone else stays in the house."

Wade's cheeks grew hot at the implication.

"Is everyone coming?" Ben asked as Aaron led them into the kitchen and toward the rear of the house.

"Miraculously, yes. Well, Seb said yes, but he'll be late." He paused at the back door. "Have you heard from him lately?"

"Not a word, not since Grammy's party."

If there was one of Ben's friends Wade wasn't anxious to reconnect with, it was Seb Williams. Something of his anxiety must have shown, because Aaron didn't open the door.

"Wade." Aaron's eyes were kind. "It'll be okay."

"You sound just like Ben." Then Aaron's words sank in, and Wade's throat tightened. "With everything that went on in high school… you can still find it in you to make me feel welcome?"

Aaron patted his arm. "One look at Ben tells me everything I need to know about you." He grinned. "That, and a couple of late-night phone calls." Then he opened the door, Ben took Wade's hand, and led him out into the sunlit backyard. The smell of grilling meat filled the air, music came from somewhere, and Wade was momentarily blinded by the bright light.

"Jeezum crow!" A stunned voice cut through Adele's vocals.

Oh God.

"Hey, Wade." A familiar figure got up from a patio chair and walked toward him.

He grasped Finn's hand with relief and shook it. "Hi."

Finn beckoned to the man he'd been seated next to. "This is Joel, my partner."

Joel turned out to be an older guy, with salt-and-pepper hair, blue eyes, and a great smile. "He only says that because he thinks it sounds weird to call someone my age his boyfriend." He shook Wade's hand. "You're the guy who's buying the land. Finn was telling me all about it."

"Yeah," Ben interjected before Wade could respond. "He's gonna build us a beautiful house."

"'Us'?" It was the same stunned voice from a moment ago. A dark-haired bearded guy came toward them, aiming a mock glare at Ben. "Something you want to tell us, Ben?"

"Aw, Levi, they just got here. There'll be plenty of time for that. And the only thing getting *grilled* out here today is the meat, okay?" The speaker came over to them, hand outstretched. "Hi, Wade. Don't suppose you remember me. Dylan Martin."

"You do look familiar," Wade mused. They all did. As Wade took in their faces, he could see remnants of the boys they'd been eight years ago.

Shaun appeared at his side, his eyes twinkling. "You look like you could use a drink."

Wade gave him a grateful look. "*Fuck* yes." The words fell from his lips before he had time to rein them in.

A moment later, laughter erupted, and Ben chuckled. "Yeah, they have that effect on me too sometimes."

"And don't worry. We don't bite," Dylan assured him. His lips twitched. "Well, I'm not too sure about Seb, but we won't go there." More laughter followed that.

"There are drinks in the kitchen, and snacks. The meat is almost done," Aaron told them. "And there are enough chairs out here for everyone." He gazed at the guy with the dark beard. "Safe space, okay?"

"It's okay, I've got the message. You don't have to worry about me. I've got over the shocks now—although it would've been nice to be in the loop." Blue-gray eyes sparkled. "I'm not sure which was the biggest—Wade Pearson walking in here, or the fact that Ben was holding his hand." He offered his. "Levi Brown, and since you've caught up with everyone else, that tall drink of water over by the fence is Noah Smith."

Wade gave Noah a nod. "I think I could use that drink now."

Ben chuckled and tugged him toward the house. "Me too."

Once they were inside, Wade expelled a long breath. "Okay. Maybe the lions' den wasn't as scary as I imagined it would be." Six down—one to go.

Ben locked his arms around Wade's neck, and their lips met in a lingering, gentle kiss. "I'm right here. And you've got this." Ben's voice brimmed with confidence.

For the first time, Wade allowed himself to consider the possibility Ben knew what he was talking about.

Ben leaned in close to whisper, "Back in a sec. Gotta take a leak."

Wade had to fight hard to quash his first instinct—he figured yelling You're going to leave me *alone* with them? wouldn't have been the right thing to do in the circumstances. Instead, he pasted on what he hoped was an assured smile. "Bring us some snacks on your way back?"

"I can do that." Ben got up from his chair. He fired a glance at the others, his lips twitching. "Be nice?" Then he walked into the house.

It was as if someone had trained a spotlight on Wade, and everyone was looking in his direction.

Oh fuck.

Levi cleared his throat. "So, Wade—"

Aaron cut him off. "Safe space, remember?"

"You knew all about this, didn't you, Aaron?" Noah folded his arms. "*Now* I know what you meant about there being a surprise for us." Then his eyes widened. "Just how many of you knew about Ben's little secret?" Dylan chuckled.

Wade's heart felt as if it were about to explode.

"And will you relax?" Levi speared Aaron with a mock glare. "All I was *going* to say was…" He locked gazes with Wade. "Sorry about the cussing when you came through that door. You have to understand, it really was a shock. I mean, after everything that happened, you're the *last* person I expected to see holding Ben's hand."

"Hey, dude, I hear ya," Shaun remarked. "But… you didn't see them on their date." His eyes shone. "Wish I had someone look at *me* the way those two were gazing at each other. Talk about loved-up."

Wade gave him a grateful glance.

"I know this feels like the Spanish Inquisition—"

Finn aimed a hard stare at Levi. "Ya think? Wonder why *that* is?"

Levi hushed him with a wave of his hand. "Will you let me finish? I was *just* going to say… It might *feel* that way, but it isn't. We're not going to hold your past… behavior against you, because Ben clearly doesn't. And let's face it, if *he* doesn't, we have no right to."

"You're watching out for Ben. I get that." At last Wade found his voice. "I wouldn't expect anything less. You love him. Well… so do I."

There was a moment of stunned silence.

"Now *that's* what I call a mic drop," Levi said with obvious approval. He raised his bottle. "Glad you could make it tonight, Wade." The others raised theirs, murmuring in agreement, and Wade's throat tightened.

Holy fuck. Ben had been right all along.

"You'll have to wait a while for your membership card," Dylan joked. Then he raised his bottle once more. "Welcome to the family."

"Thanks." Wade lifted his chin. "You don't have to worry. I'm not going to hurt him. I couldn't. I… I've waited too long for this."

Then they fell silent again as the door opened and Ben stepped out onto the patio, grinning. "Hey, I found Cheez-its." He clutched two giant bags.

After all the emotion of the previous few minutes—*has he only been gone a couple of minutes?*—Wade couldn't hold in his chuckle. "Wow, it's as though Aaron *knows* you."

Finn guffawed. "You've worked it out. Batman and Robin, Dorothy and Toto, Tom and Jerry, Snoopy and Woodstock—Ben and Cheez-its." Laughter rippled across the backyard.

"Yeah, yeah." Ben gave them the finger, and rejoined Wade. "Did I miss anything?"

There was something a little *too* innocent in that question.

"You knew, didn't you?" Wade gaped. "You did."

Ben blinked. "Knew what?" He held out the bag. "Cheez-its?" He grinned. "Come on, you *know* you want to."

A new boldness seized him. "I'll take a kiss instead."

Ben's eyes widened, and Wade took that for a yes. He reached over, cupped Ben's head, and gently pulled him close until their lips were almost touching.

"Love you," Wade murmured, before taking Ben's mouth in a lingering kiss.

Ben's happy sigh sent his spirits soaring.

Dylan broke the spell. "Fuck, Shaun nailed it. I want someone to look at *me* like that."

"Never mind *looking*—I want someone who can *kiss* like that," Aaron fired back.

Wade let their comments flow over his head. He was too busy being stupid in love.

It was eight-thirty, and the sun had set over an hour before. Aaron had switched on strings of lights that he'd hung from the top of the fence and over the back porch, and a cast iron fire pit sat on the patio, all the guys seated around it, drinking beers and talking.

Ben glanced at Wade, who was chatting with Finn. They'd been doing it most of the late afternoon, discussing house design. Joel had commented that their boyfriends appeared to be more interested in each other than him and Ben.

Ben didn't mind in the slightest.

There was still no sign of Seb, which had prompted a discussion. It seemed no one had seen him all summer, except for a couple of Face Time calls with Levi.

"He *is* okay, isn't he?" Ben inquired. "I mean, he didn't fall overboard or something, and get eaten by lobsters."

Raucous laughter broke out.

"He's fine," Levi assured him. "Well, he was the last time we spoke. And it sounds like I'm the only one he's been talking to." He sighed. "He's had a lot going on these past couple of months."

"Call of nature," Noah said, getting to his feet. "Anyone want anything from the house?" He got a chorus of *no's,* and headed inside.

Ben watched him go. "Is he all right?" Noah had been quiet all afternoon, and it wasn't like him.

"He hardly said a word all the way up here," Levi said, staring at the back door. "I was hoping being with everyone would lift his mood, but…" He huffed. "I don't have a clue what's going on."

"Then *say* something. Or if *you* don't want to, I'm sure one of the others will." Ben straightened. "*I'll* ask him when he gets back from the bathroom." He couldn't rid himself of the feeling that something was wrong.

Wade looked across at him. *You okay?* he mouthed. Ben nodded. Then Noah returned, carrying a bottle of beer. He sat back down and rolled it between his hands, staring into the fire.

"Hey, Noah?" Ben leaned forward. "You can tell me to fuck off, or it's none of my beeswax, but… is everything okay?"

Noah's breathing hitched, and he stared at Ben. Then his shoulders sagged. "I should've known I couldn't hide anything from you guys."

Ben's heart sank. "Then there *is* something wrong."

"Not *wrong*, exactly, just… complicated."

"Save that for Facebook, and *talk* to us," Finn said earnestly. There was a chorus of 'yeah' from the others.

Noah took a drink from his bottle. "You are never gonna believe what my mom said to me a couple days ago. I was up in the garage roof, adding a new section—"

"Playing with your trains," Finn, Dylan, and Aaron said at the same time.

Noah rolled his eyes, then continued. "My mom came up. She'd made me a sandwich. Only, she didn't leave. She kinda... hovered. So I asked if there was something she wanted." He took another drink. "She said, 'Is there anything you want to tell me and your dad?' I'm like, 'such as what?' 'Oh, I don't know. Maybe you had something you wanted to share, but you felt nervous about it.'" Noah took a deep breath. "I had no idea what she was talking about. Then *eventually* she said, 'It's just that… well, we've noticed… you don't have a girlfriend. So we were *wondering*… Because if you don't because you're not into girls, we just want you to know it's okay with us." Noah's eyes widened. "I was like, WTF? They think I'm *gay*?"

Aaron chuckled. "Well, dude, look at who you hang out with. I totally understand why they'd think that."

"But I'm *not gay*," Noah stressed.

"Did you tell her that?" Finn asked.

"Yes, but that just made things worse. 'Well… you're twenty-six now. Don't you think it's time you found yourself a girlfriend? Maybe think about settling down?'"

"What did you tell her?" That came from Dylan.

"What *could* I say? 'Sorry, Mom, but I'm not into girls either'?"

Crickets.

Ben cleared his throat. "Something you wanna tell us, dude?"

Noah shuddered out a breath. "Okay. I've been meaning to say something for a while now. I almost did at Teresa's wedding, but I chickened out." Another sharp intake of breath. "What I said just now wasn't quite right. It's not that I don't like girls—I just don't want to go to bed with any of them. But I couldn't say that to my mom."

"And you don't want to fuck boys either," Dylan commented.

"Yes. I mean, no. See, *this* is what I mean about complicated. And I'm making a total mess of this." He gazed at them, his chin high, his brow furrowed. "Do you all think I'm weird?"

Ben gaped at him. "Are you kidding? We *love* you, you doof." He launched out of his chair, went over to Noah, and threw his arms around him in an awkward hug. "Whatever this is? It's *totally* okay."

"Dude, it really *is* okay. There's a word for people like you," Dylan told him. "Celibate."

Noah gave him a patient smile. "No—asexual."

"I'm sorry," Joel interjected. "I don't know much about the LGBTQ spectrum. But if you met the right person and fell in love, would that make a difference or change anything?"

Noah breathed deeply. "It doesn't work like that. There isn't someone out there who could 'cure' me," he air-quoted.

Joel's face fell. "I've offended you. I'm sorry."

Noah gave him a half smile. "No offense taken. And just because I'm ace doesn't mean I'm gonna be lonely, all right?" He flung out his arm. "There are ace people out there who are married, have babies, are romantically attracted to people…"

"But what about—?"

Noah held up his hand. "I've got a better idea. How about I talk and you listen? School is In, and it's Asexuality 101. Here are all the things it *isn't*. It *isn't* celibacy or abstinence. It *isn't* a lifestyle choice. It *isn't* some kind of social comment. I haven't *lost* something—it's just a different experience of sexuality. What it boils down to? And this is the part I *know* you're all *dying* to ask, so let's get it out in the open. Yes, I have sex, okay? I enjoy it. I jerk off the same way you do. The only difference is… the person I'm with? I'm not sexually attracted to them. And you know what? If there's stuff you still want to know after all that? I've got the perfect site for you. I'll send you the link." He was trembling.

Seconds later, they surrounded him, and Noah was on the receiving end of many hugs. He wiped his eyes. "You guys…"

"Nothing's changed, man," Shaun assured him.

"What he said," Aaron added.

Levi squeezed his shoulder. "We've got you."

Noah held up his hands. "Okay, can everyone just sit down now? Because being the center of all this attention is freaking me out."

That earned some chuckles. One by one they went back to their seats.

Ben grabbed Noah's hand and squeezed it. "Hey, you and Wade have something in common."

Noah frowned. "What's that?"

Ben smiled. "You both just came out."

Noah stared at him, then started laughing. "I guess we did at that." He took a couple of deep breaths. "Man, that was scary as fuck."

"Bet you're glad you did it though," Ben commented.

Noah nodded. "I should have done it a long time ago." He looked at the faces lit by the fire's glow. "Thanks, guys."

"We've got your back," Levi said in a low voice.

"You know it," Shaun added.

"And Seb missed it," Dylan remarked.

Noah shook his head. "I'm not going through all that again. Do you know how many times I've rehearsed this in my head? It took everything I had to come out with all that."

"Don't worry. We'll bring him up to speed," Ben assured him. He glanced at Wade. "I should've mentioned—when we all get together, it's never dull."

Wade bit back a smile. "No shit."

"Just wait and see." Aaron's eyes sparkled. "I have a feeling we'll be seeing you at more of these get-togethers."

Ben said nothing. He'd already had the same feeling.

Aaron had added more wood to the fire pit as the night closed in, bringing with it a chill in the air. There was still no sign of Seb.

Is it mean of me to hope he'll be a no-show?

Noah seemed more relaxed, and Wade couldn't help but notice how the guys went out of their way to reassure him. A squeeze of the shoulder here, a warm glance there…

They really are a tight group.

It made his heart ache to think he could have been one of them. Then Ben caught his eye and mouthed *Love you*, and Wade pushed aside such painful thoughts.

The past was gone. Only the future mattered, and Wade would do everything within his power to ensure Ben never regretted his decision.

"What are you thinking?" Ben came over and sat beside him.

"When you walked into the shop that first day, I

had an agenda. I was going to make it up to you for the way I treated you. I was going to prove to you that I'd changed."

"And you did all that." Ben rested his head against Wade's shoulder.

"So now I have a new agenda." Wade kissed Ben's head. "I'm going to make you happy."

"You're already doing that too," Ben murmured.

Joel pulled his chair closer to them. "I saw the photos Finn took of your plot." Joel peered at Wade. "It *is* your plot now, isn't it?"

"I set the wheels in motion last week." Wade hadn't wasted any time.

"It's beautiful. Those views…" He gave a wistful smile. "That's my dream."

"What is?"

"Oh, to have a home where I can look out at the ocean. Maybe open a window and hear the waves." He leaned into Finn. "And get this guy here to build it for us. One of the things I discovered about Finn? He has the same dream."

Wade's heartbeat quickened. "Well… why not make it a reality?"

"What do you mean?"

"Yes, what *do* you mean?" Ben demanded.

Wade had been rolling this over in his mind, the whole time he'd been talking with Finn. He took Ben's hand. "How would you feel about having Finn and Joel for neighbors?"

Ben gaped at him. "Excuse me?"

Joel beckoned to Finn. "I think you need to hear this. Get over here."

Wade waited until Finn had joined them before continuing. "It's a two-acre lot. What if Joel and I bought the lot between us, then divided it in two? One acre is plenty big enough for a house, right? With a high fence between them, maybe a hedge…" Wade grinned. "I promise we wouldn't be forever popping over for a chat." Then he glanced at Ben. "Who am I kidding? You and Finn will be forever in and out of each other's houses." Wade stilled. "That's if you like the idea." His chest tightened. "I should have spoken to you first before I opened my mouth—"

Ben stopped his words with his hand. "Stop digging that hole. I fucking *love* the idea."

"Me too." Finn's face glowed.

"Are you serious?" Joel demanded. "*Can* we do it?"

"I don't see why not. When I spoke to the developer, the first thing he said was if two acres was more than I wanted, the plot could be severed in two, but that there would be additional costs if that took place." Wade smiled. "I like the idea. Makes me feel good to know we'll have good neighbors. And you don't need to build a place right away. Do it whenever you feel ready."

Finn stared at Joel. "You're gonna say yes, right?"

Joel laughed. "You don't think we should discuss it?"

"Sure, we can discuss it all you like—then sign on the dotted line." Finn beamed. "I am gonna build us the most beautiful house you ever saw."

"If you're in it, it'll be beautiful," Joel said in a low voice.

Ben said nothing but squeezed Wade's hand, his eyes reflecting the firelight.

Wade hadn't thought it possible to be this happy.

Aaron stepped out of the back door. "Okay, guys?

Seb just texted. He's on his way. In fact, he'll be here within minutes." He chuckled. "Oh, and can I remind you we won't be staying out here *too* late. After all, you're all sitting in Ben and Wade's bedroom for the night."

Finn's eyes gleamed. "Hey, guys? Keep your phones away from the windows. Videoing Ben *dance* is one thing—we don't want any sex tapes *accidentally* finding their way online, do we?"

Ben gasped, and Wade burst out laughing. "God, they certainly know how to yank *your* chain, don't they?"

"We've had plenty of practice," Aaron told him with a grin. He inclined his head toward the fence. "I hear a car. That must be him. Open the side gate for him, Dylan. You're closest."

Dylan did as instructed. He peered through the gap. "Yup, it's Seb's car." He headed for the kitchen. "I'll get him a beer. He needs to catch us all up."

Ben took Wade's hand in his. "Don't worry. He'll be like the others."

Before Wade could reply, Seb came through the gate. "Tell me you guys haven't eaten all the food. I'm starving." Then he rolled his eyes. "Fuck." Seb went back to the gate and called out, "Grab the beers, babe. They're in the trunk. Which means they'll probably go off like rockets when we open 'em." Then he returned his attention to the group, and came to a dead stop. "Why are y'all staring at me like that?"

Ben smirked. "'Babe'? And who is 'babe'?"

Seb sighed. "That… would be my boyfriend."

For a moment there was silence, broken by a chorus of raised voices, as synchronized as if they'd rehearsed it.

"What the *fuck*?"

The End

Coming next in the Maine Men series!

Seb's Summer (Maine Men Book Three)

Steamy summer nights with a hot older man aren't the smooth sailing Seb expects.

A mysterious older guy

Seb Williams has one plan for the hot, sultry nights of his summer vacation - to get laid. What isn't on the agenda? Running his uncle's fishing business. Seb has no choice but to help his family. So it's goodbye, Ogunquit's gay bars and hook-ups.
And it's hello, Cape Porpoise, a quaint, quiet fishing harbor. A small town that promises to be boring AF until he meets Marcus Gilbert. His summer prospects start to look promising. Silver fox – hell yeah. Hot bod? Check. Slow sultry gaze? Oh *yes*!

Only one problem. Marcus Gilbert plays hard to get.

A hot distraction

Cape Porpoise is exactly how Marcus remembers it from long-past childhood, and just what he needs. A sabbatical to get his life back on track, and work on his book. Peaceful surroundings. The calm of the ocean.

Perfect – until Marcus's boat is well and truly rocked by a hot, younger guy.

Marcus can't ignore the lure of Seb's lean frame and gorgeous eyes. One night can't hurt, right?

Except one night leads to another, and another.

It's just a summer fling - until it isn't, and the pair are suddenly in uncharted waters.

Because now, Marcus's past threatens to tear apart their future.

Maine-isms

(Yeah, there are a few of them)

right out straight: Extremely busy.

cunnin' : Cute, adorable

finest kind: Used variously, as a general indication of approval; also used ironically; "That was an awesome dinner; finest kind."

numb: stupid

wicked: Synonym for 'very,' to a high degree, extremely, exceedingly

Massholes: People from Massachusetts.

Ayuh: Yes, affirmative

spleeny: Feeling nervous or anxious about something

darker than a pocket: no light

slip one's wind: to die

from away: A slightly pejorative term for someone who is not originally from Maine.

a fart in a mitten: tiny

dubbers: stupid people (singular: dub)

Jeezum crow!: Holy cow!

About the author

K.C. Wells lives on an island off the south coast of the UK, surrounded by natural beauty. She writes about men who love men, and can't even contemplate a life that doesn't include writing.

The rainbow rose tattoo on her back with the words 'Love is Love' and 'Love Wins' is her way of hoisting a flag. She plans to be writing about men in love - be it sweet or slow, hot or kinky - for a long while to come.

Other titles

Available titles

Learning to Love
Michael & Sean
Evan & Daniel
Josh & Chris
Final Exam

Sensual Bonds
A Bond of Three
A Bond of Truth

Merrychurch Mysteries
Truth Will Out
Roots of Evil
A Novel Murder

Love, Unexpected
Debt
Burden

Dreamspun Desires
The Senator's Secret
Out of the Shadows
My Fair Brady
Under The Covers

Lions & Tigers & Bears
A Growl, a Roar, and a Purr

Love Lessons Learned

First
Waiting for You
Step by Step
Bromantically Yours
BFF

Collars & Cuffs
An Unlocked Heart
Trusting Thomas
Someone to Keep Me (K.C. Wells & Parker Williams)
A Dance with Domination
Damian's Discipline (K.C. Wells & Parker Williams)
Make Me Soar
Dom of Ages (K.C. Wells & Parker Williams)
Endings and Beginnings (K.C. Wells & Parker Williams)

Secrets – with Parker Williams
Before You Break
An Unlocked Mind
Threepeat
On the Same Page

Personal
Making it Personal
Personal Changes
More than Personal
Personal Secrets
Strictly Personal
Personal Challenges

Personal – The Complete Series

Confetti, Cake & Confessions

Connections
Saving Jason
A Christmas Promise
The Law of Miracles
My Christmas Spirit
A Guy for Christmas

Island Tales
Waiting for a Prince
September's Tide
Submitting to the Darkness

A Material World
Lace
Satin
Silk
Denim

Southern Boys
Truth & Betrayal
Pride & Protection
Desire & Denial

Maine Men
Finn's Fantasy

Kel's Keeper
Here For You
Sexting The Boss
Gay on a Train
Sunshine & Shadows
Watch and Learn

My Best Friend's Brother
Bears in the Woods
Double or Nothing
Back from the Edge
Switching it up
Out for You
State of Mind

Anthologies

Fifty Gays of Shade
Winning Will's Heart

Come, Play
Watch and Learn

Writing as Tantalus
Damon & Pete: Playing with Fire

Titles also available in French, German, Italian, and Spanish.

Printed in Great Britain
by Amazon

63025750R00180